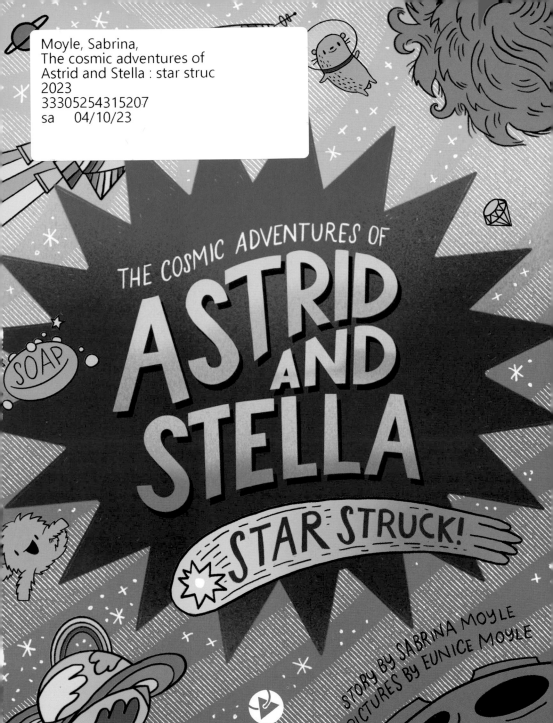

THE COSMIC ADVENTURES OF
ASTRID AND STELLA

STAR STRUCK!

STORY BY SABRINA MOYLE
PICTURES BY EUNICE MOYLE

AMULET BOOKS · NEW YORK

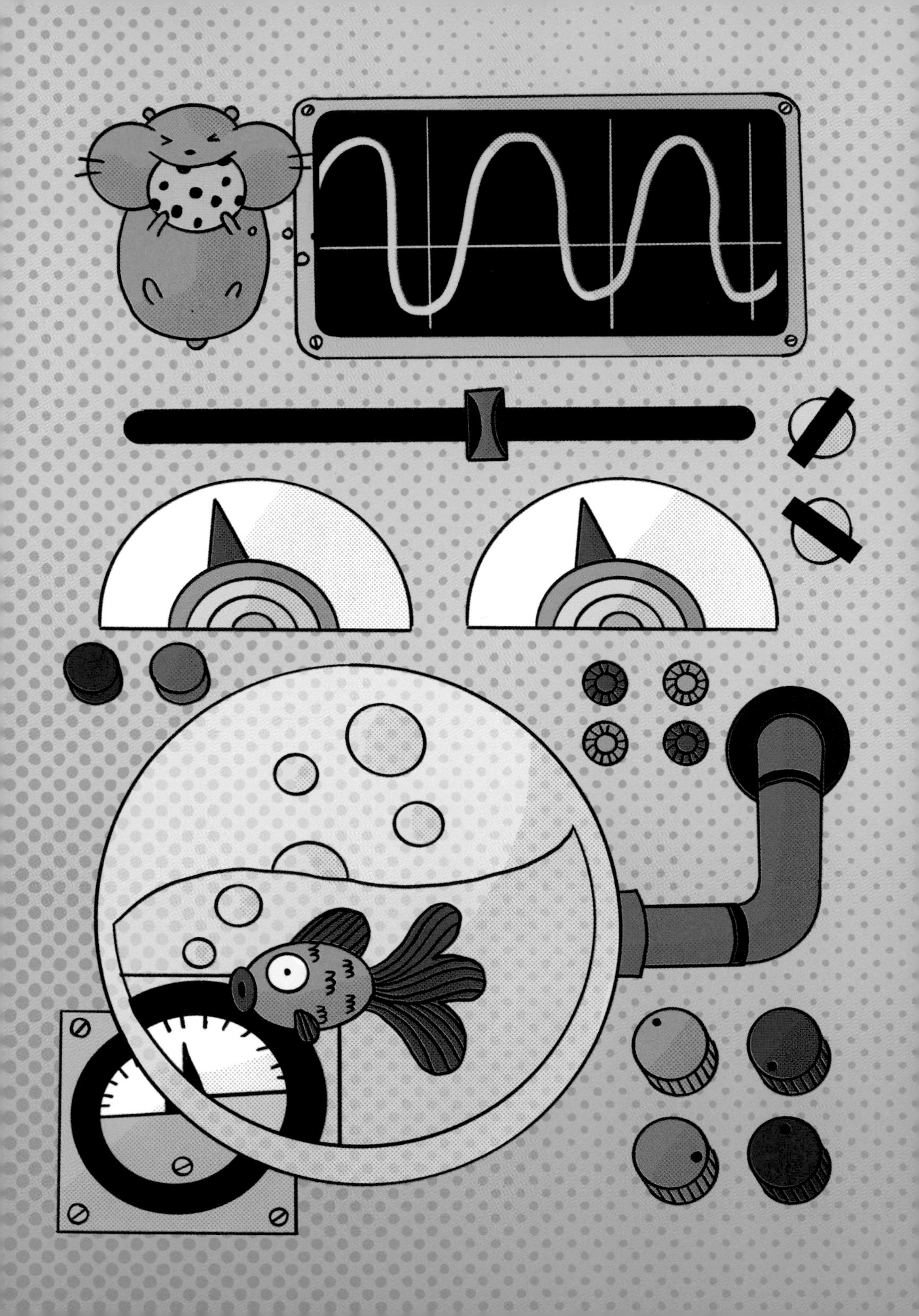

CONTENTS

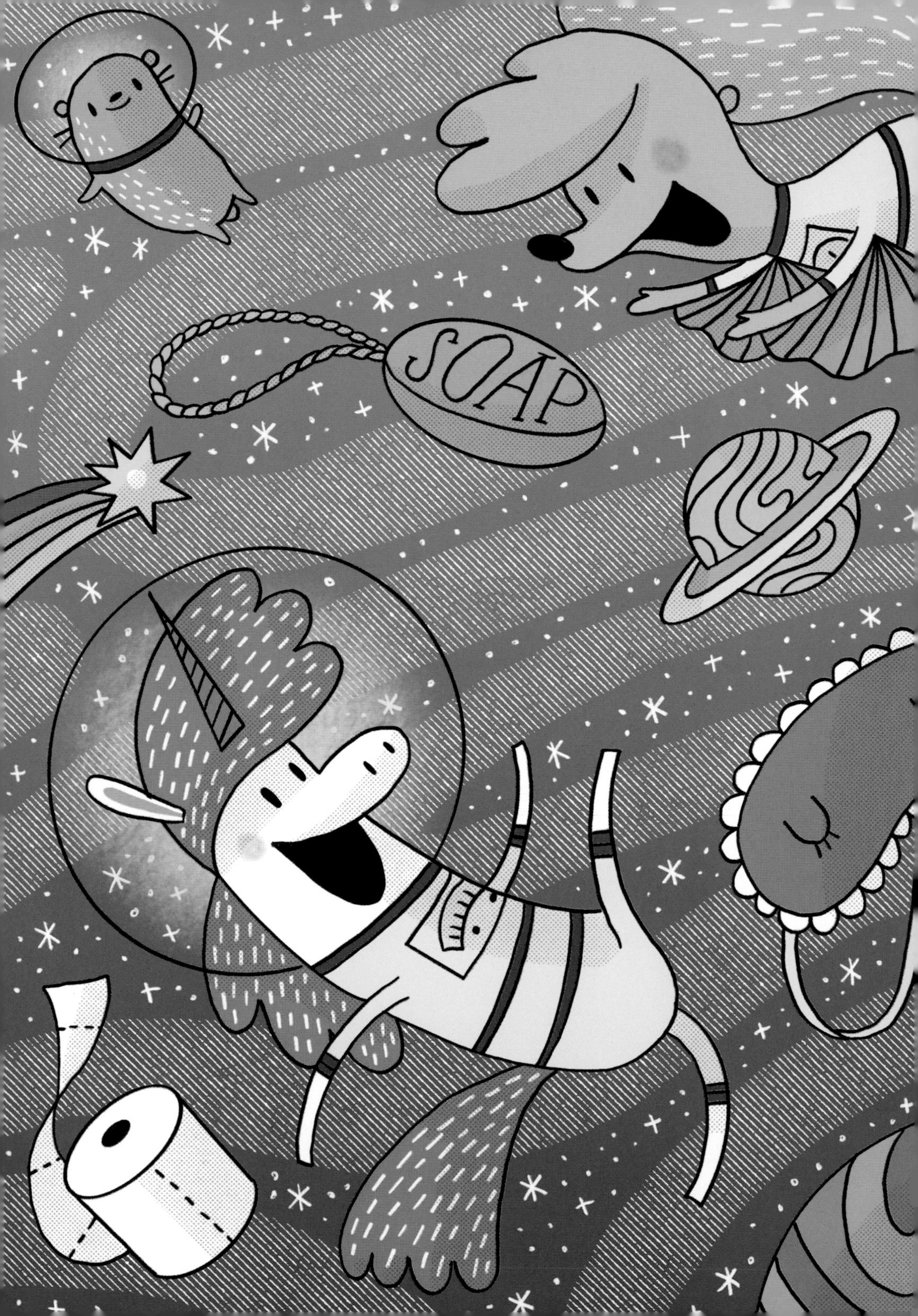
SOAP

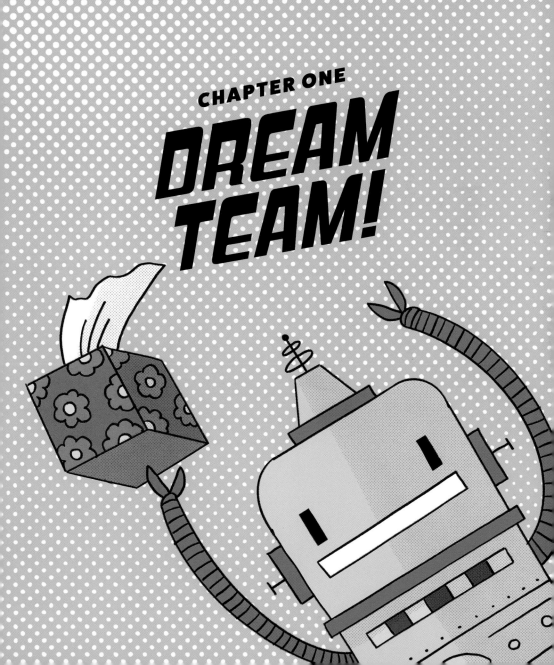

CHAPTER ONE

DREAM TEAM!

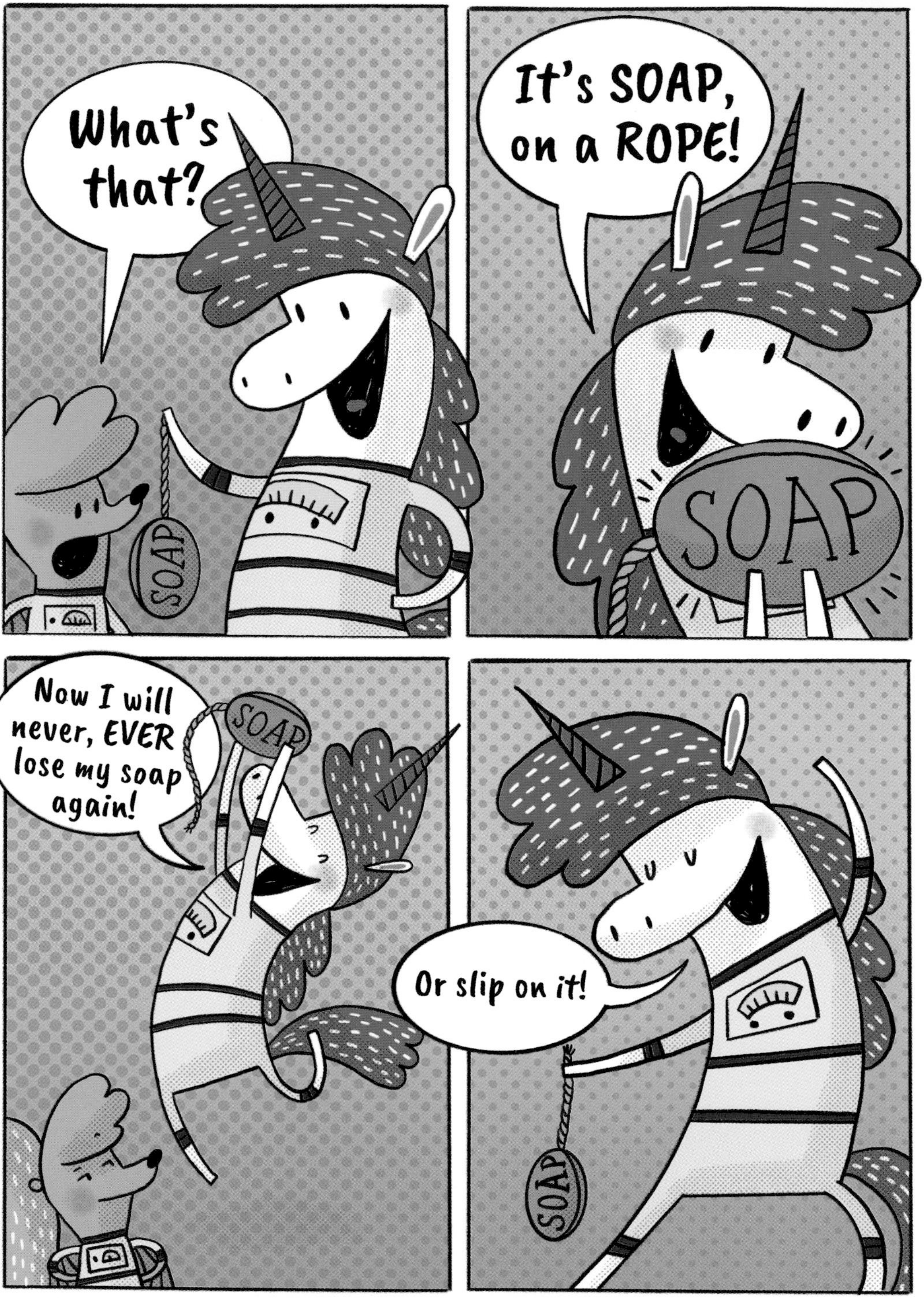
What's that?
SOAP
It's SOAP, on a ROPE!
SOAP
Now I will never, EVER lose my soap again!
SOAP
Or slip on it!
SOAP

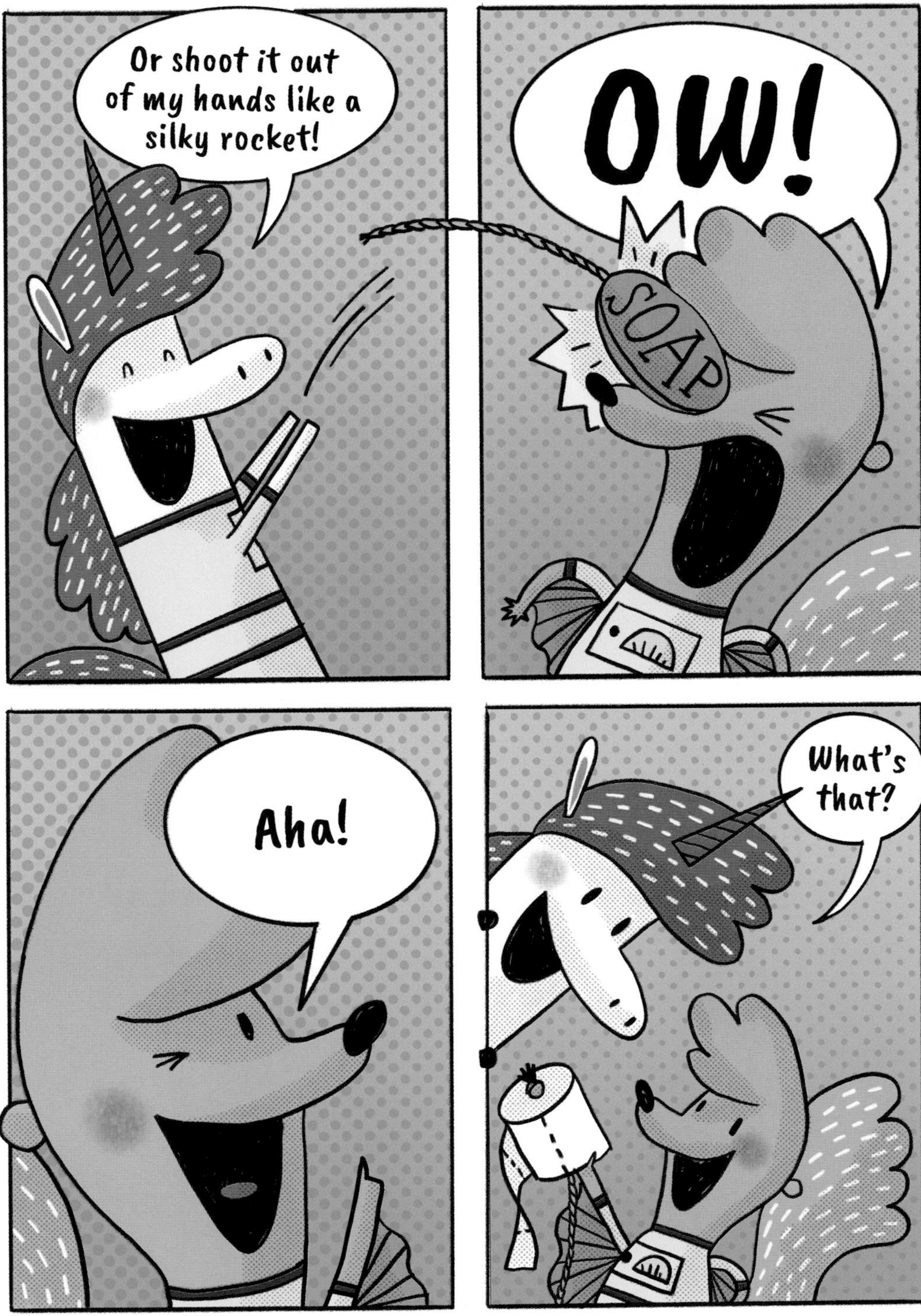
Or shoot it out of my hands like a silky rocket!
OW!
SOAP
Aha!
What's that?

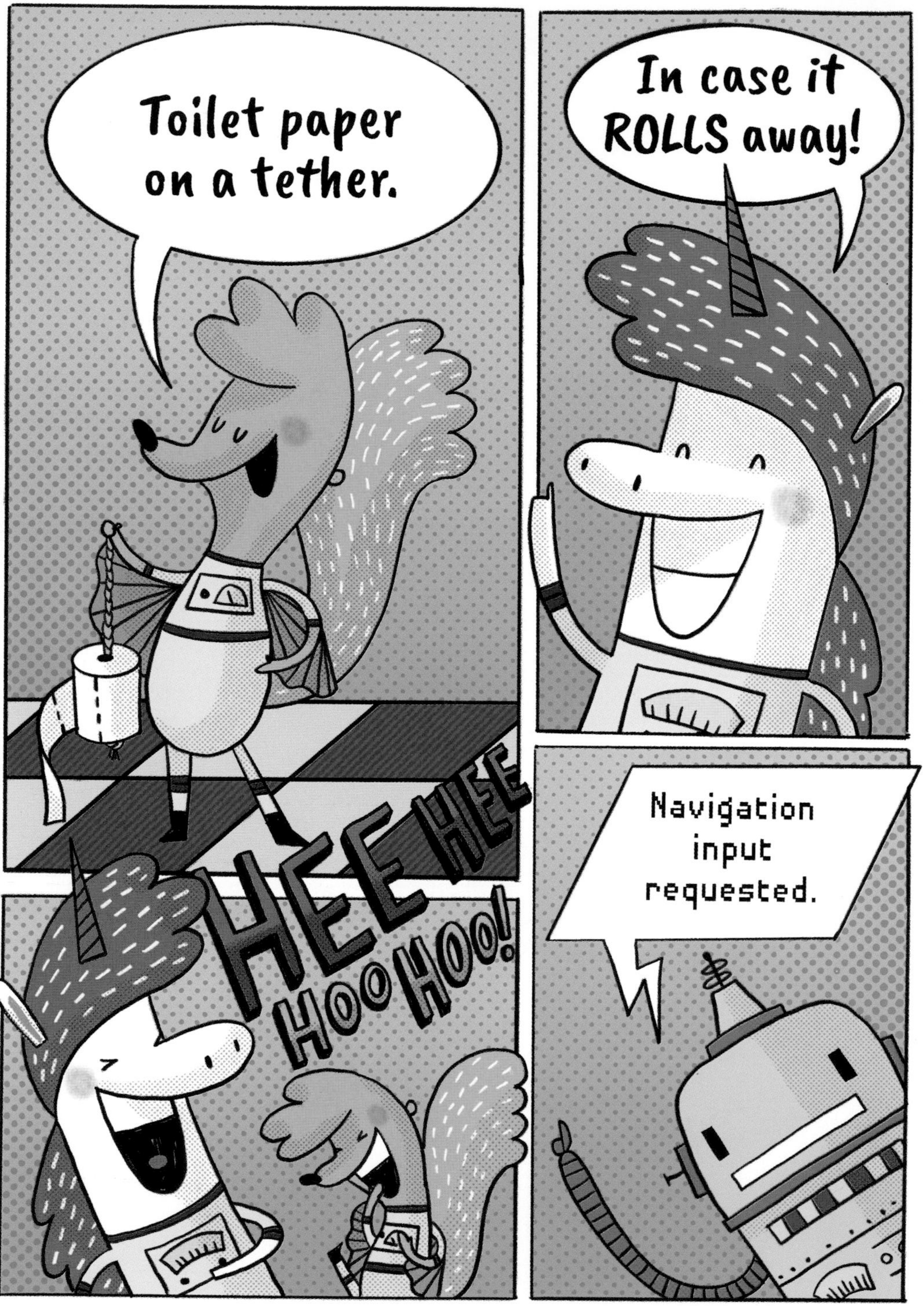
Toilet paper on a tether.
In case it ROLLS away!
HEE HEE HEE
HOO HOO!
Navigation input requested.

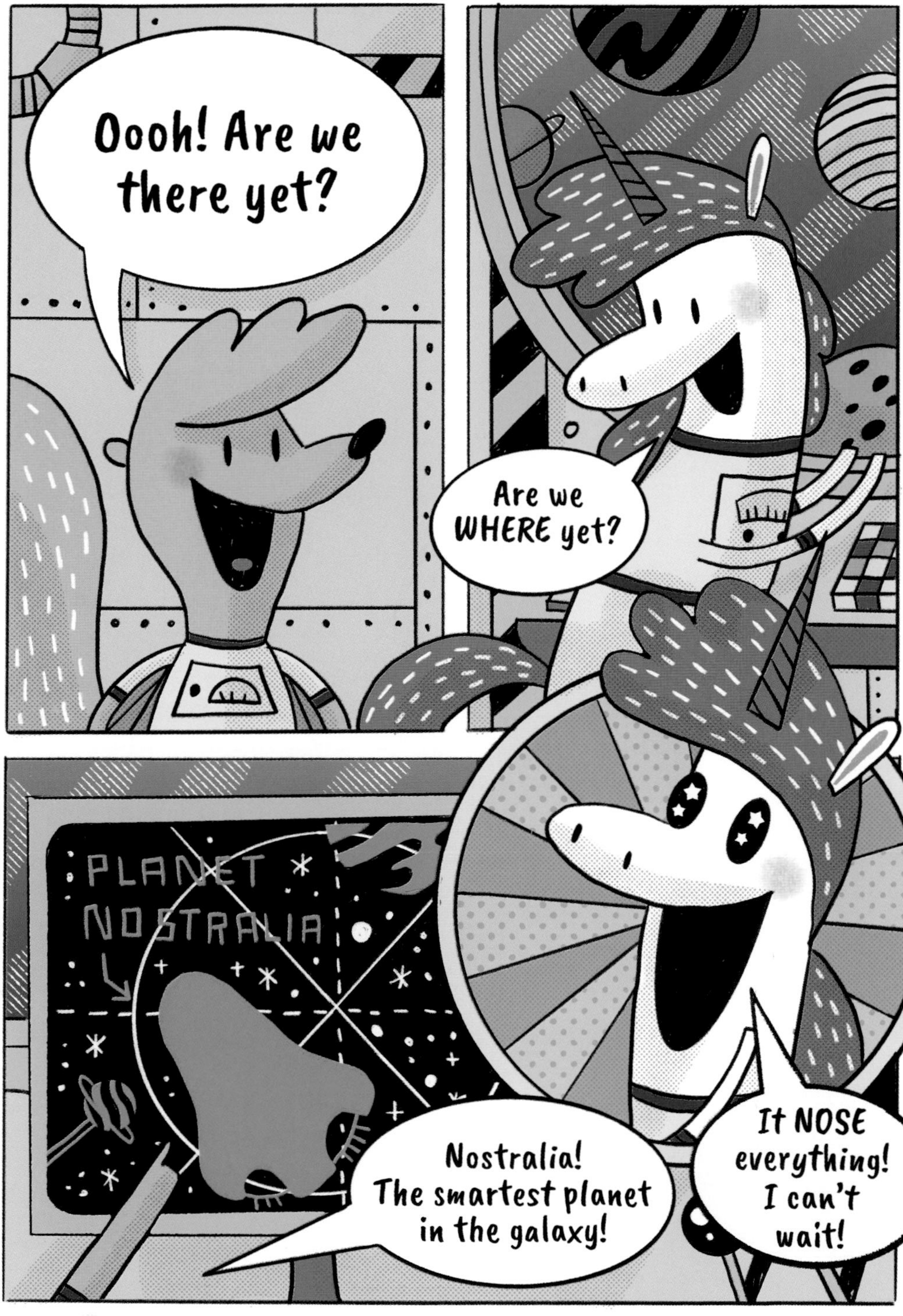

Oooh! Are we there yet?
Are we WHERE yet?
PLANET NOSTRALIA
Nostralia! The smartest planet in the galaxy!
It NOSE everything! I can't wait!

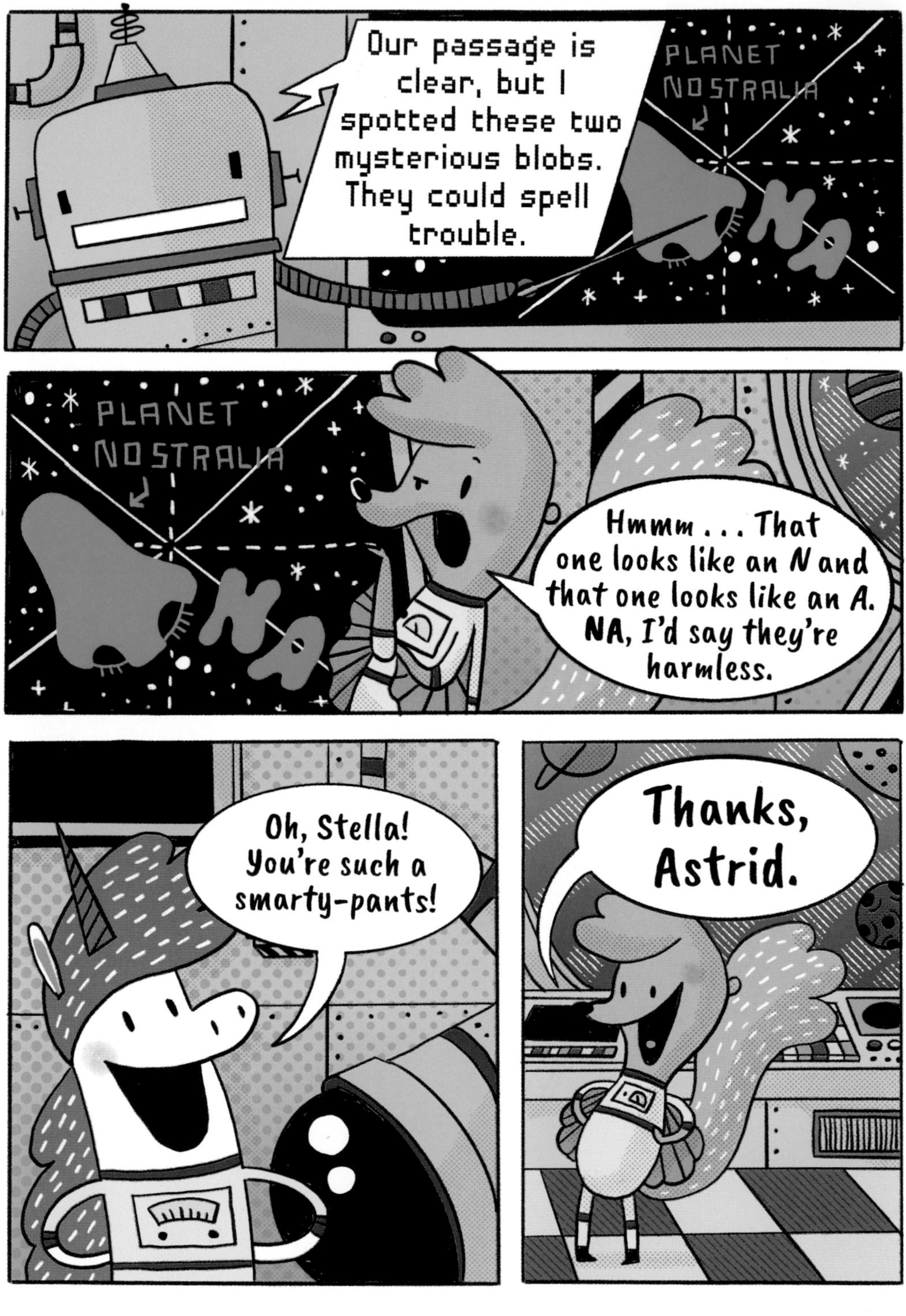
Our passage is clear, but I spotted these two mysterious blobs. They could spell trouble.
PLANET NOSTRALIA
NA
PLANET NOSTRALIA
NA
Hmmm . . . That one looks like an N and that one looks like an A. NA, I'd say they're harmless.
Oh, Stella! You're such a smarty-pants!
Thanks, Astrid.

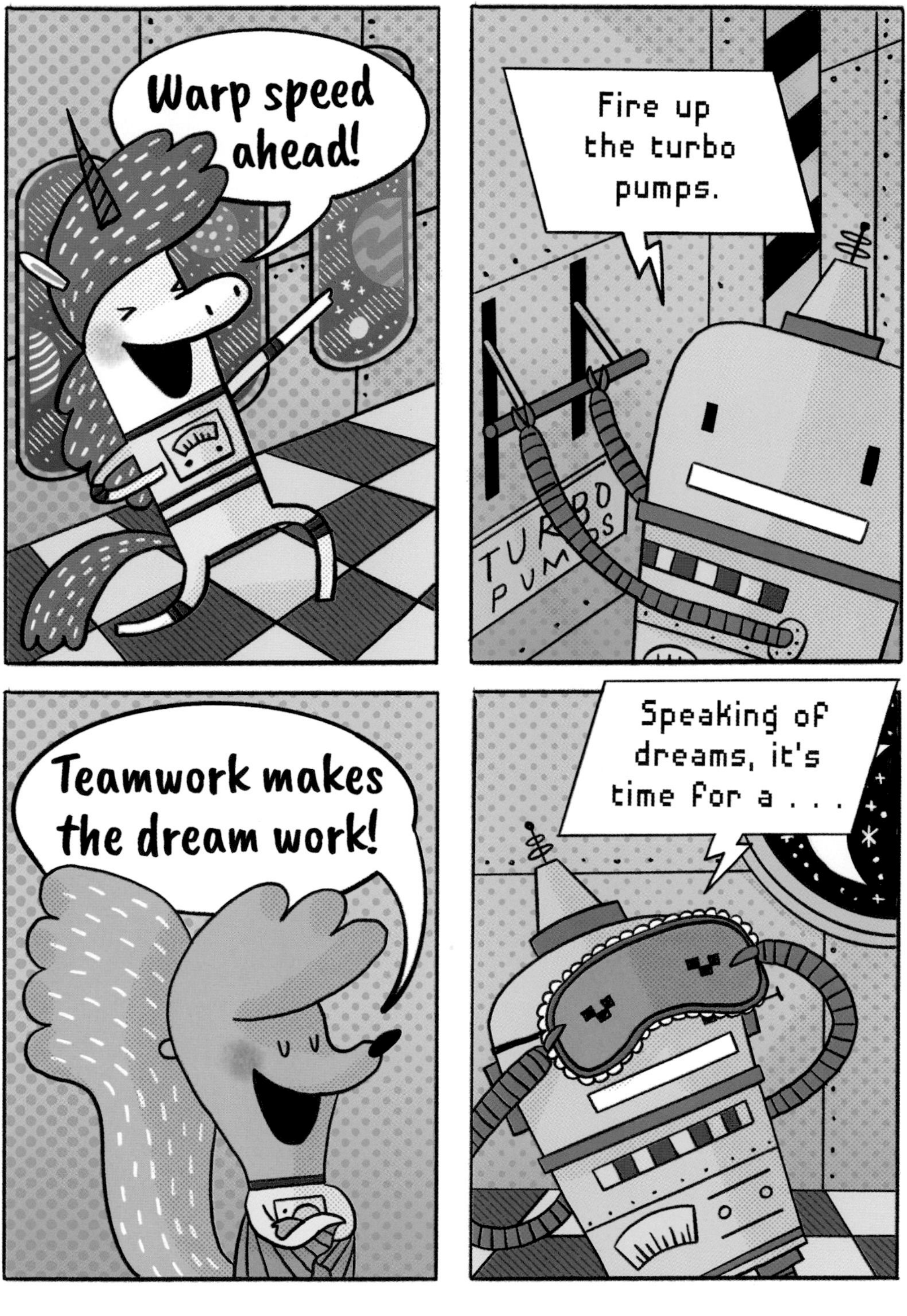
Warp speed ahead!
Fire up the turbo pumps.
TURBO PUMPS
Teamwork makes the dream work!
Speaking of dreams, it's time for a . . .

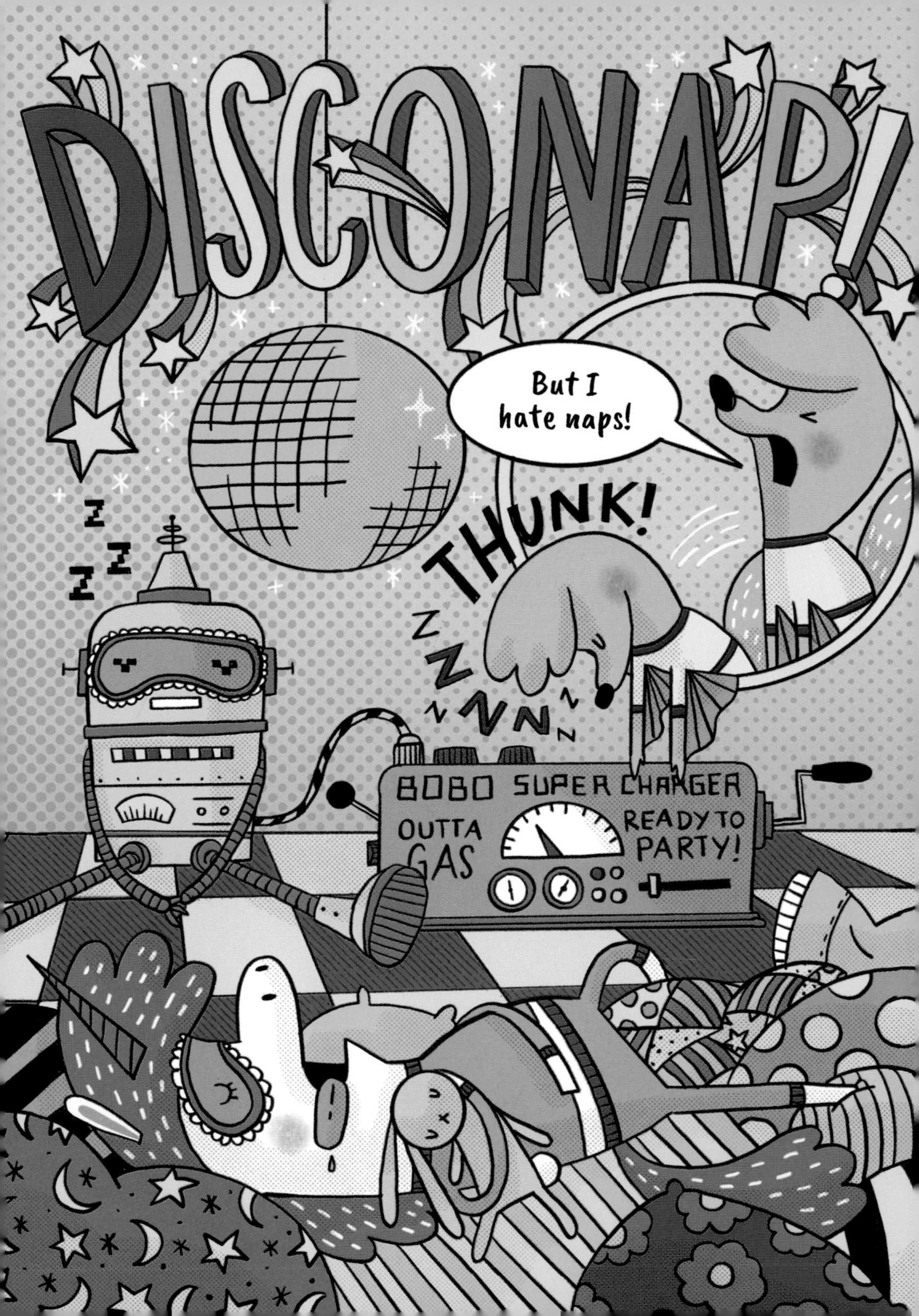
DISCO NAP!
But I hate naps!
THUNK!
BOBO SUPER CHARGER
OUTTA GAS
READY TO PARTY!

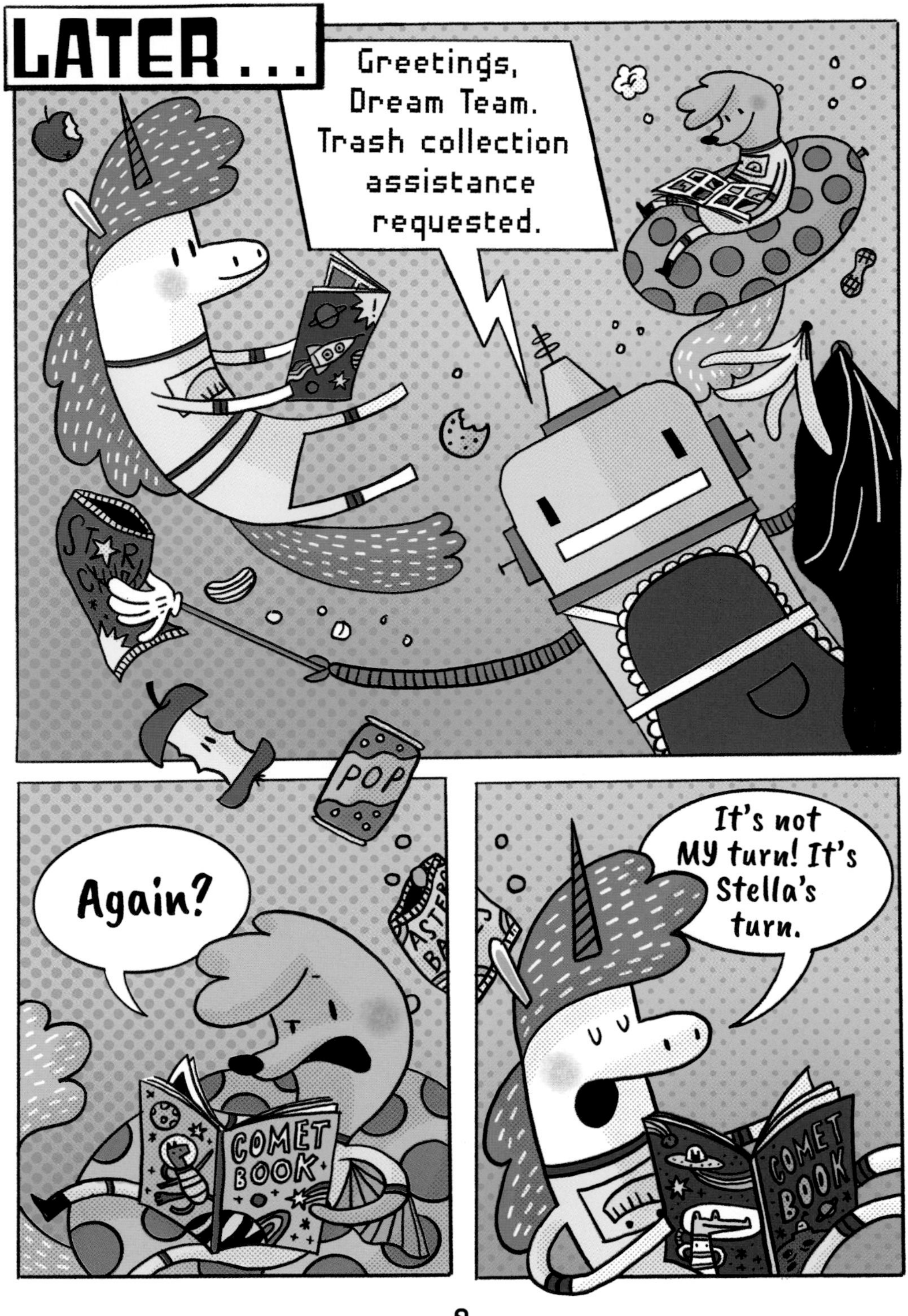
LATER . . .
Greetings, Dream Team. Trash collection assistance requested.
STAR CHIPS
POP
Again?
COMET BOOK
It's not MY turn! It's Stella's turn.
COMET BOOK

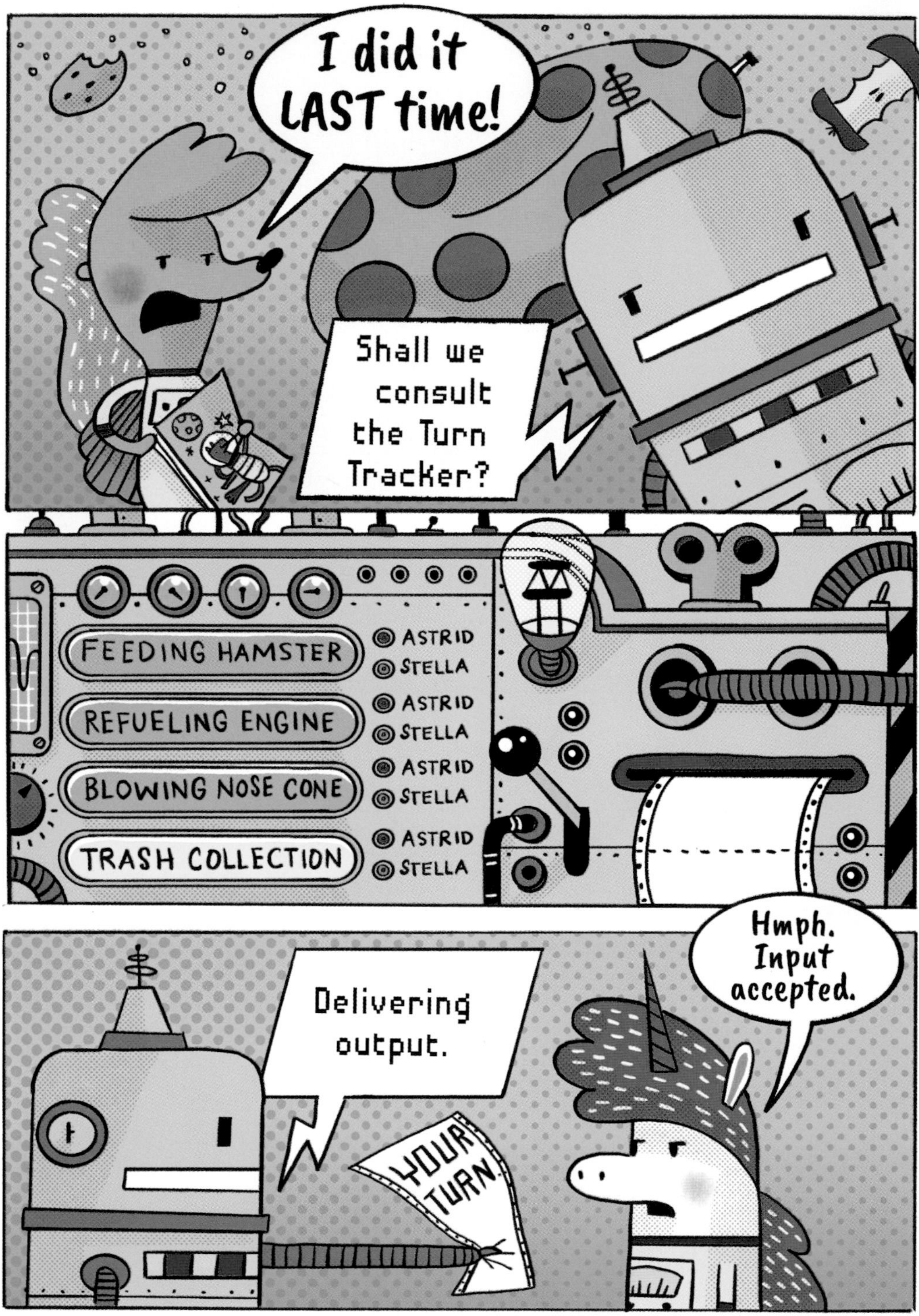
I did it LAST time!
Shall we consult the Turn Tracker?
FEEDING HAMSTER
ASTRID
STELLA
REFUELING ENGINE
ASTRID
STELLA
BLOWING NOSE CONE
ASTRID
STELLA
TRASH COLLECTION
ASTRID
STELLA
Delivering output.
YOUR TURN
Hmph. Input accepted.

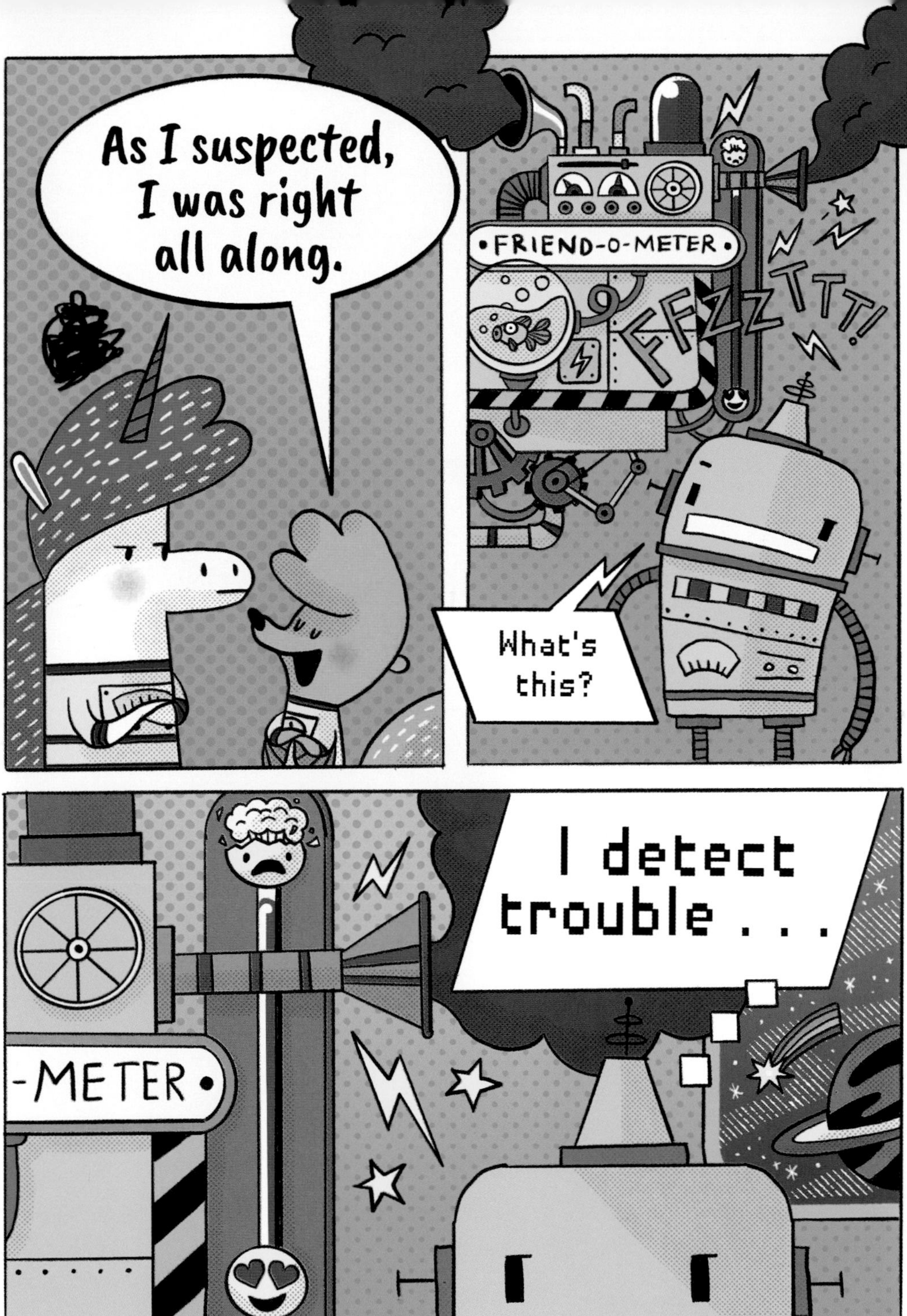

As I suspected, I was right all along.
FRIEND-O-METER
FFZZZTTT!
What's this?
-METER
I detect trouble . . .

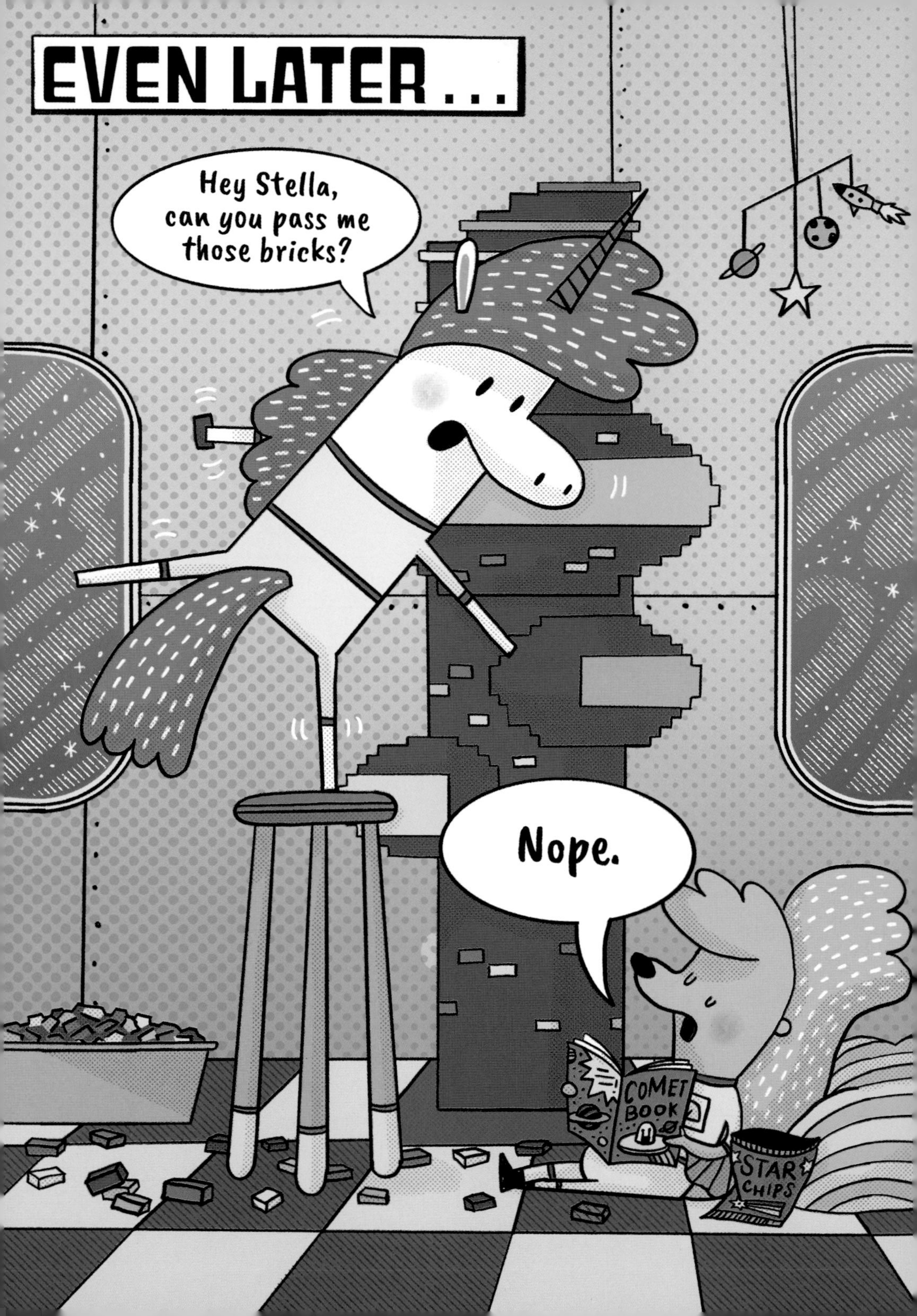
EVEN LATER . . .
Hey Stella, can you pass me those bricks?
Nope.
COMET BOOK
STAR CHIPS

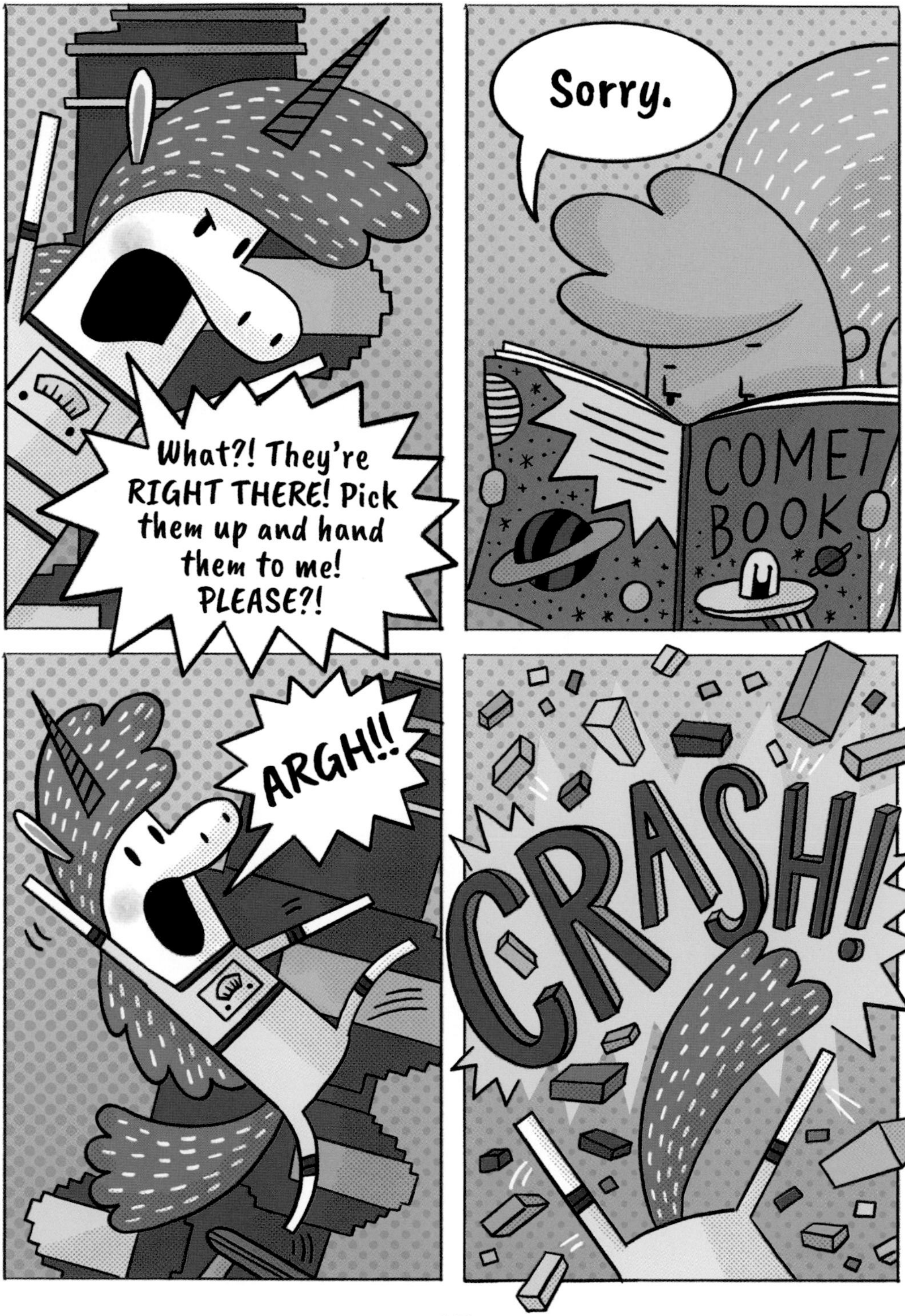
What?! They're RIGHT THERE! Pick them up and hand them to me! PLEASE?!
Sorry.
COMET BOOK
ARGH!!
CRASH!

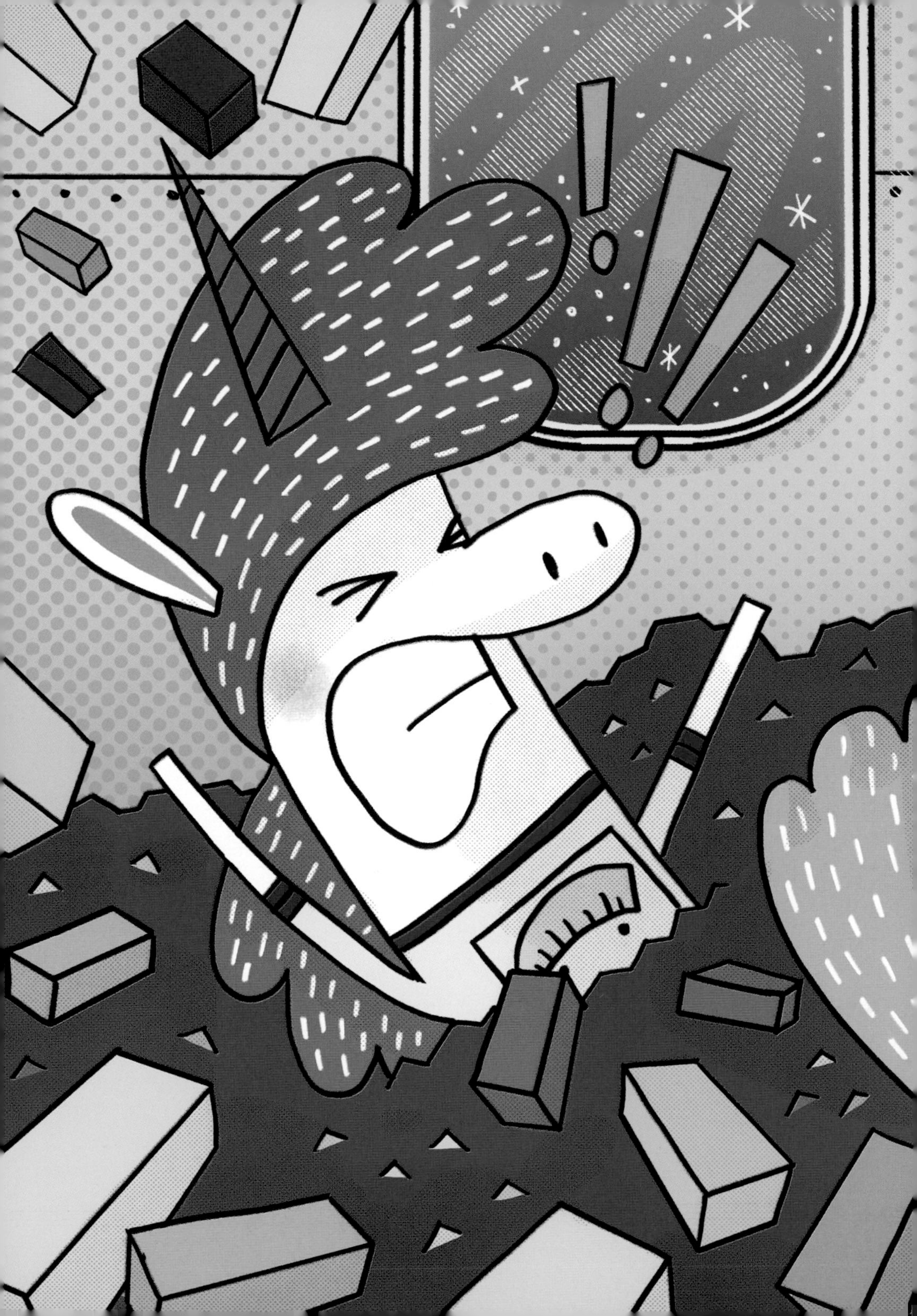
!!!

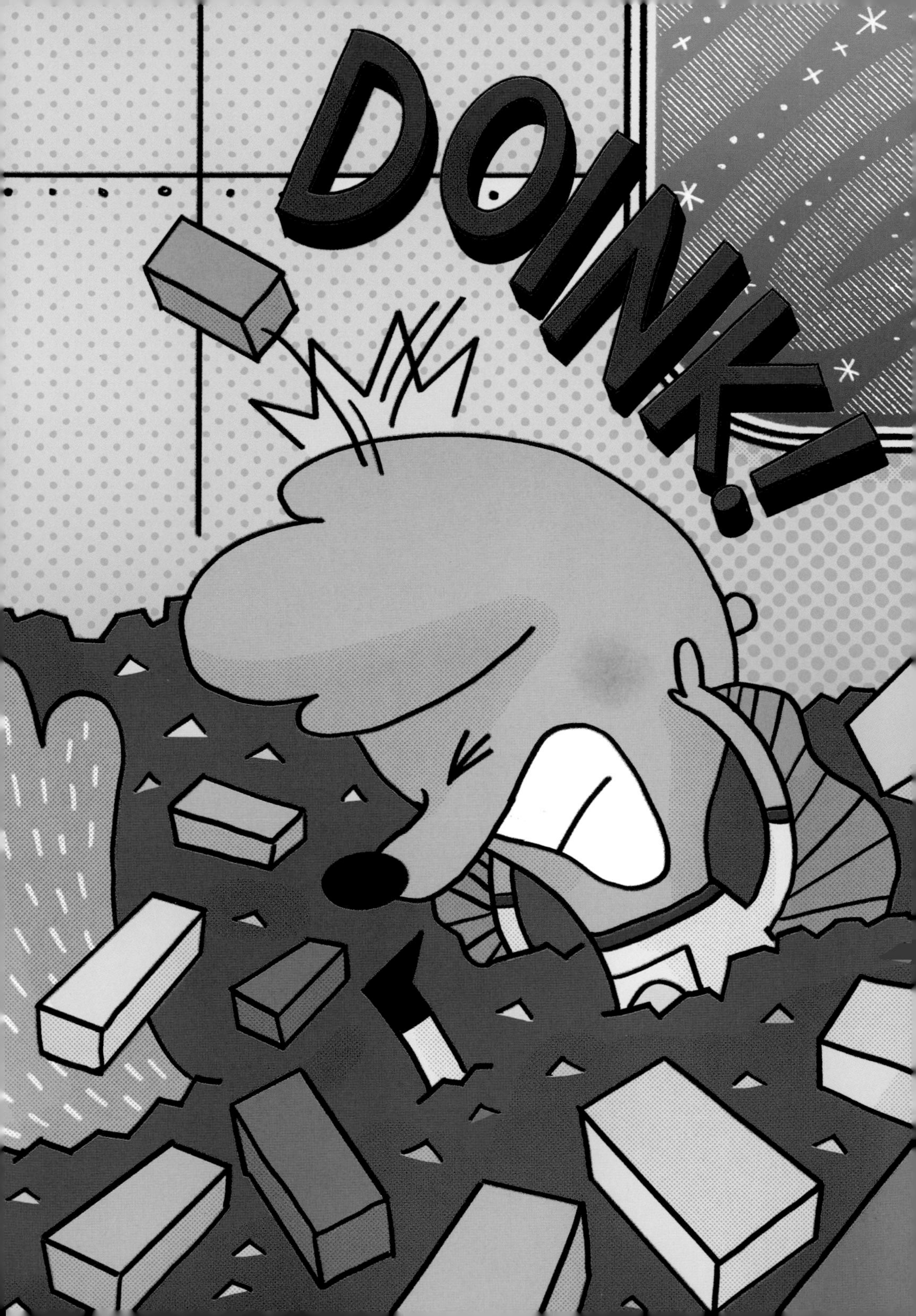
DOINK!

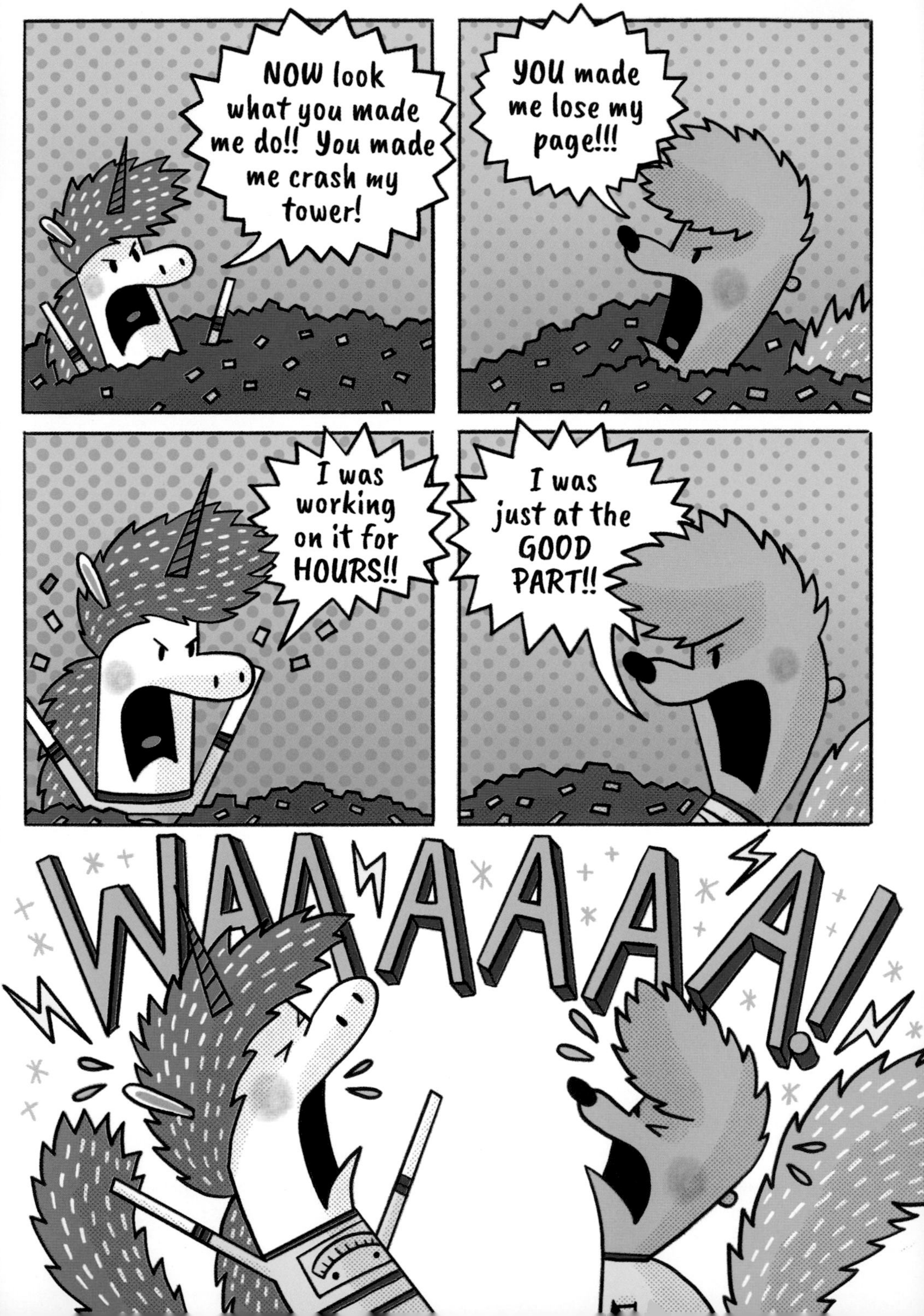
NOW look what you made me do!! You made me crash my tower!
YOU made me lose my page!!!
I was working on it for HOURS!!
I was just at the GOOD PART!!
WAAAAAA!!

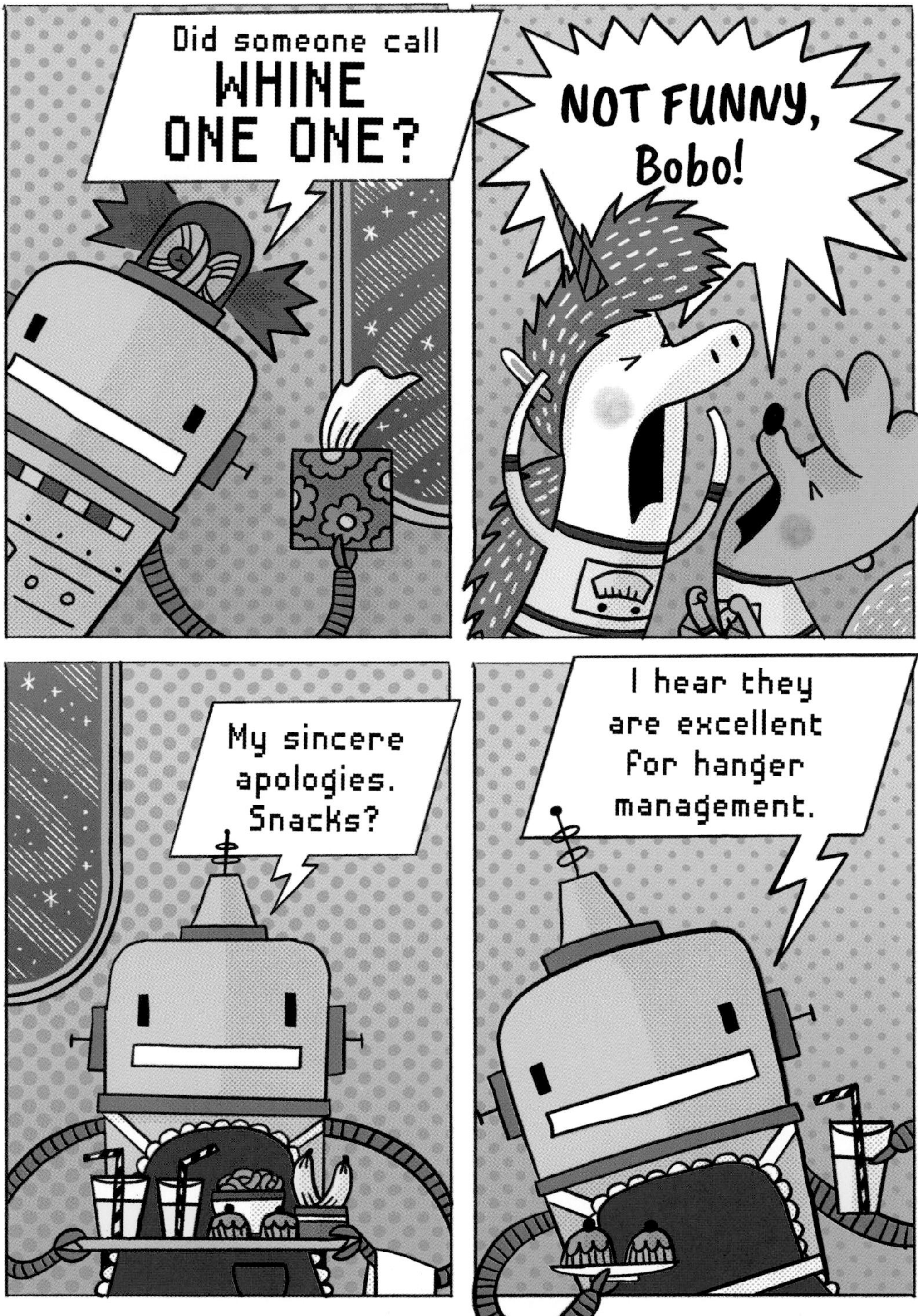
Did someone call WHINE ONE ONE?
NOT FUNNY, Bobo!
My sincere apologies. Snacks?
I hear they are excellent for hanger management.

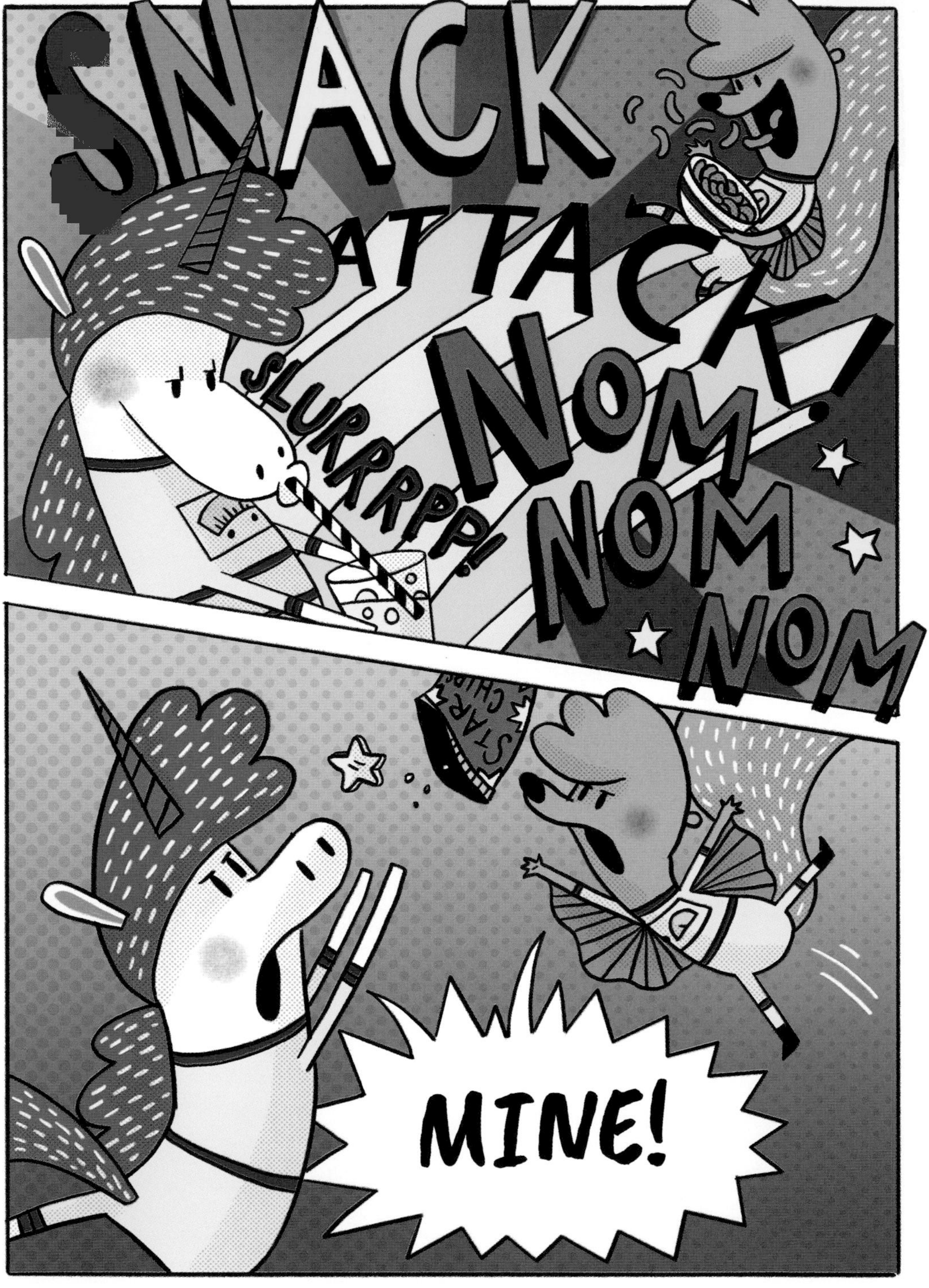
[redacted]NACK ATTACK!
SLURRRRPP!
NOM NOM NOM
STAR CHIPS
MINE!

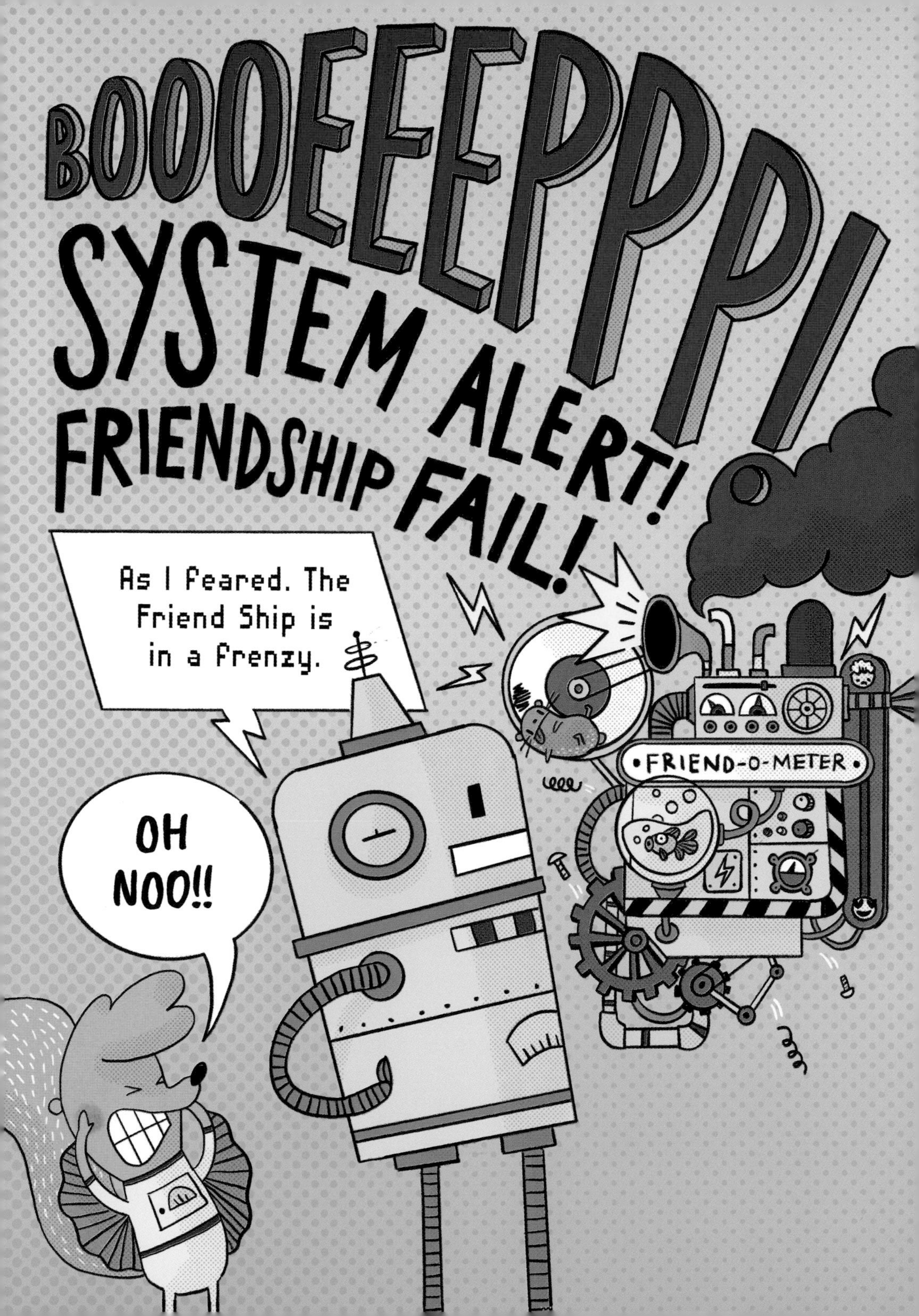
BOOOEEEEPPPP!
SYSTEM ALERT!
FRIENDSHIP FAIL!
As I feared. The Friend Ship is in a frenzy.
OH NOO!!
FRIEND-O-METER

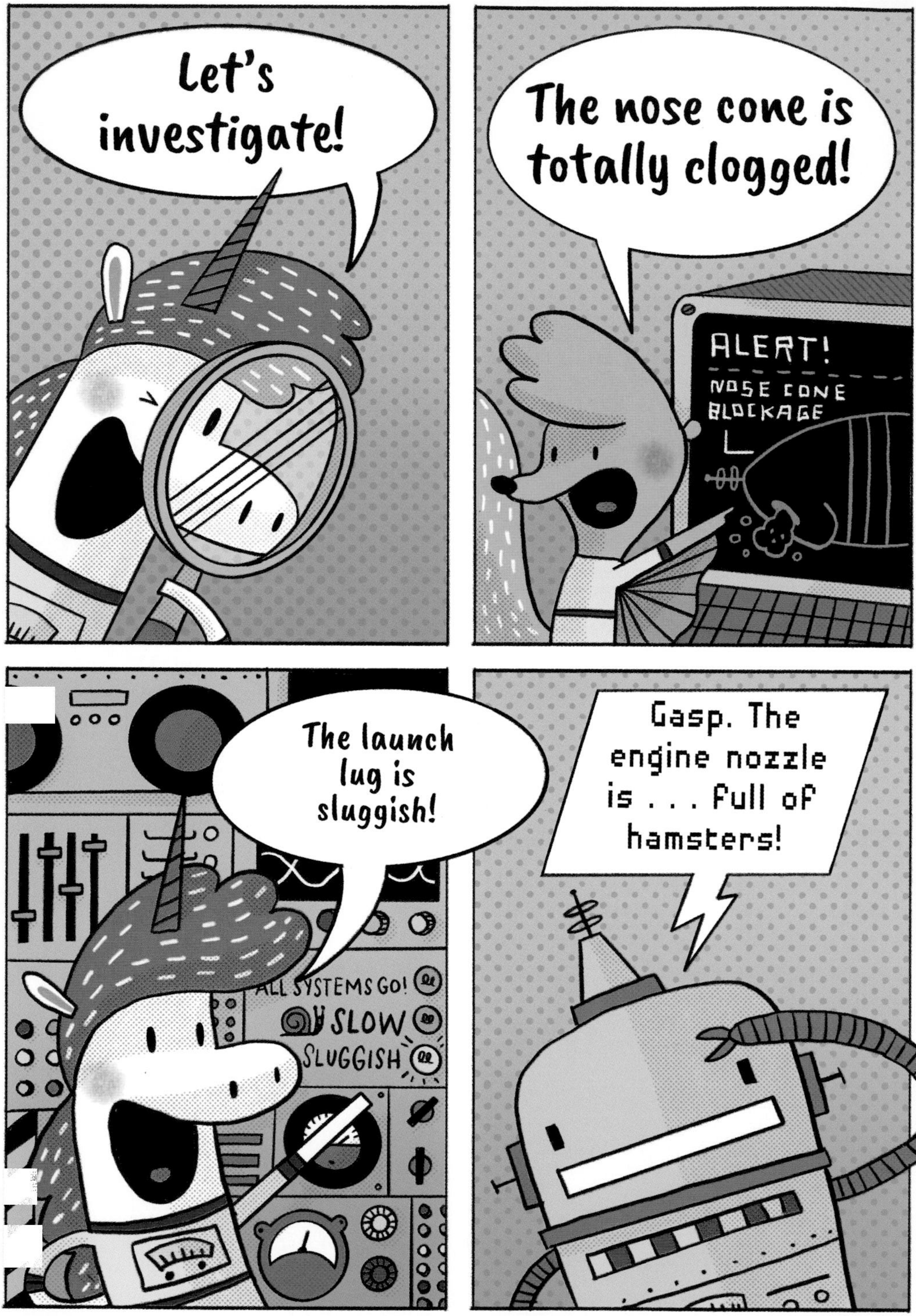
Let's investigate!
The nose cone is totally clogged!
ALERT!
NOSE CONE BLOCKAGE
The launch lug is sluggish!
ALL SYSTEMS GO!
SLOW
SLUGGISH
Gasp. The engine nozzle is . . . full of hamsters!

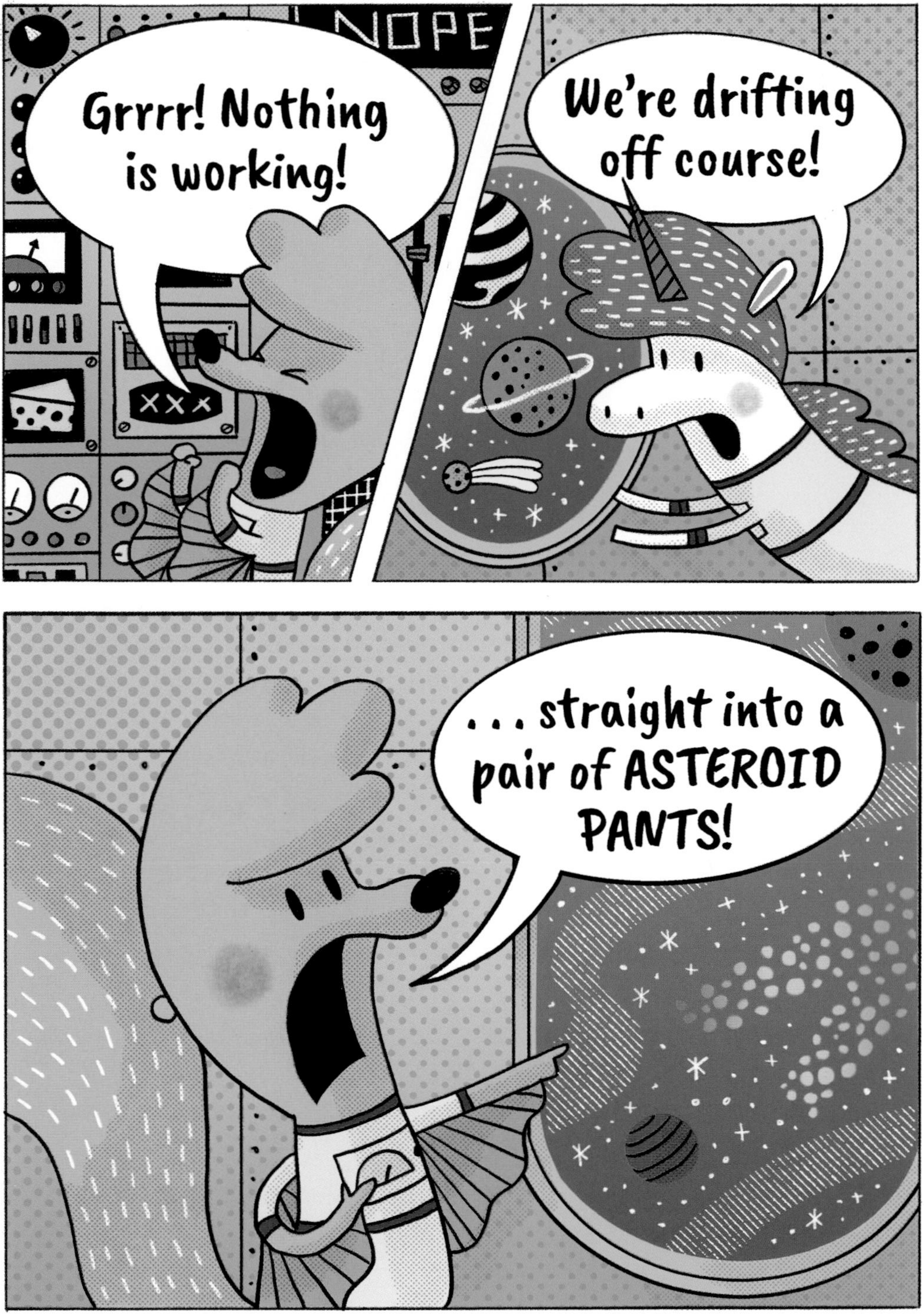
NOPE
Grrrr! Nothing is working!
We're drifting off course!
. . . straight into a pair of ASTEROID PANTS!

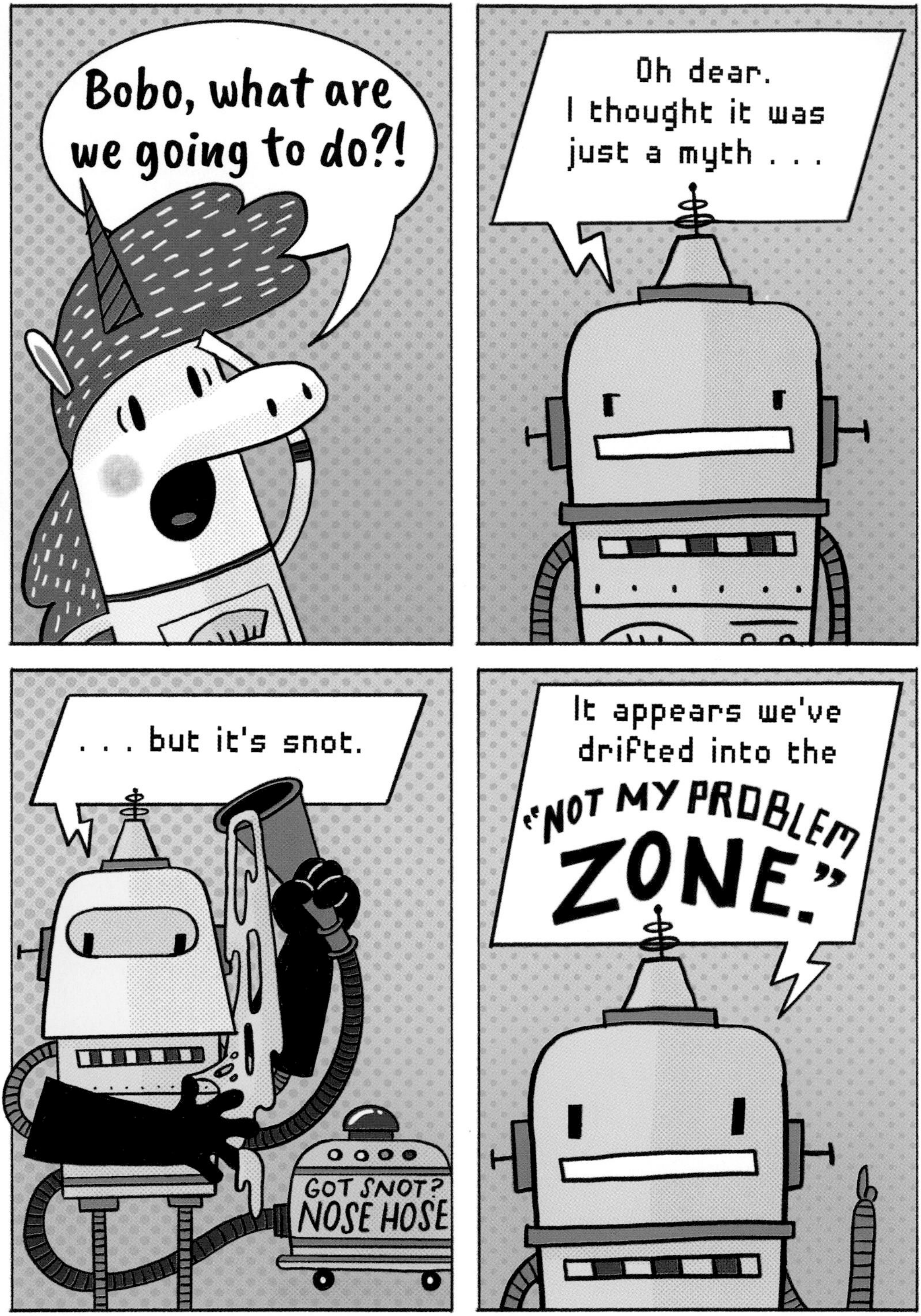
Bobo, what are we going to do?!
Oh dear. I thought it was just a myth . . .
. . . but it's snot.
GOT SNOT? NOSE HOSE
It appears we've drifted into the "NOT MY PROBLEM ZONE."

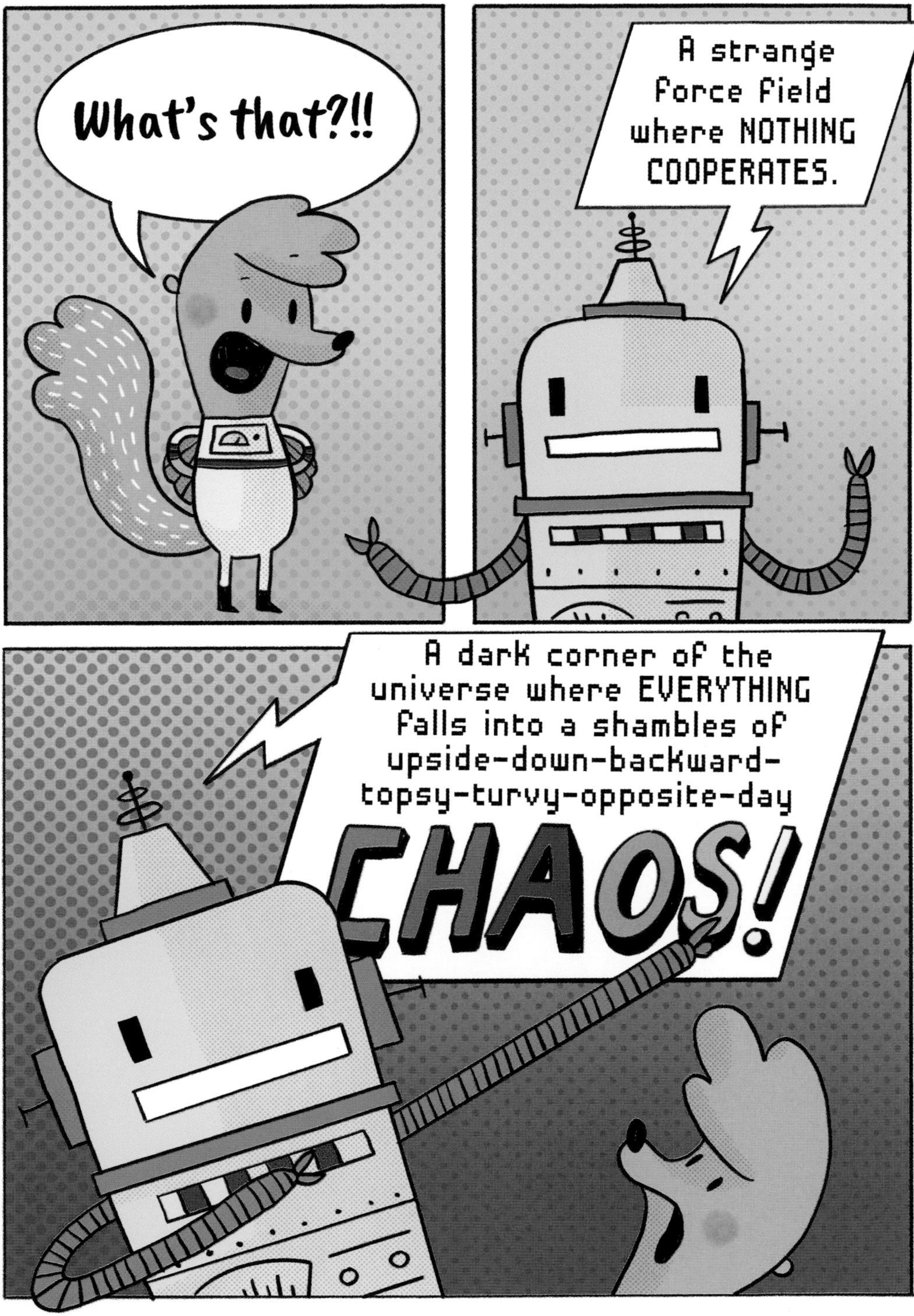
What's that?!!
A strange force field where NOTHING COOPERATES.
A dark corner of the universe where EVERYTHING falls into a shambles of upside-down-backward-topsy-turvy-opposite-day
CHAOS!

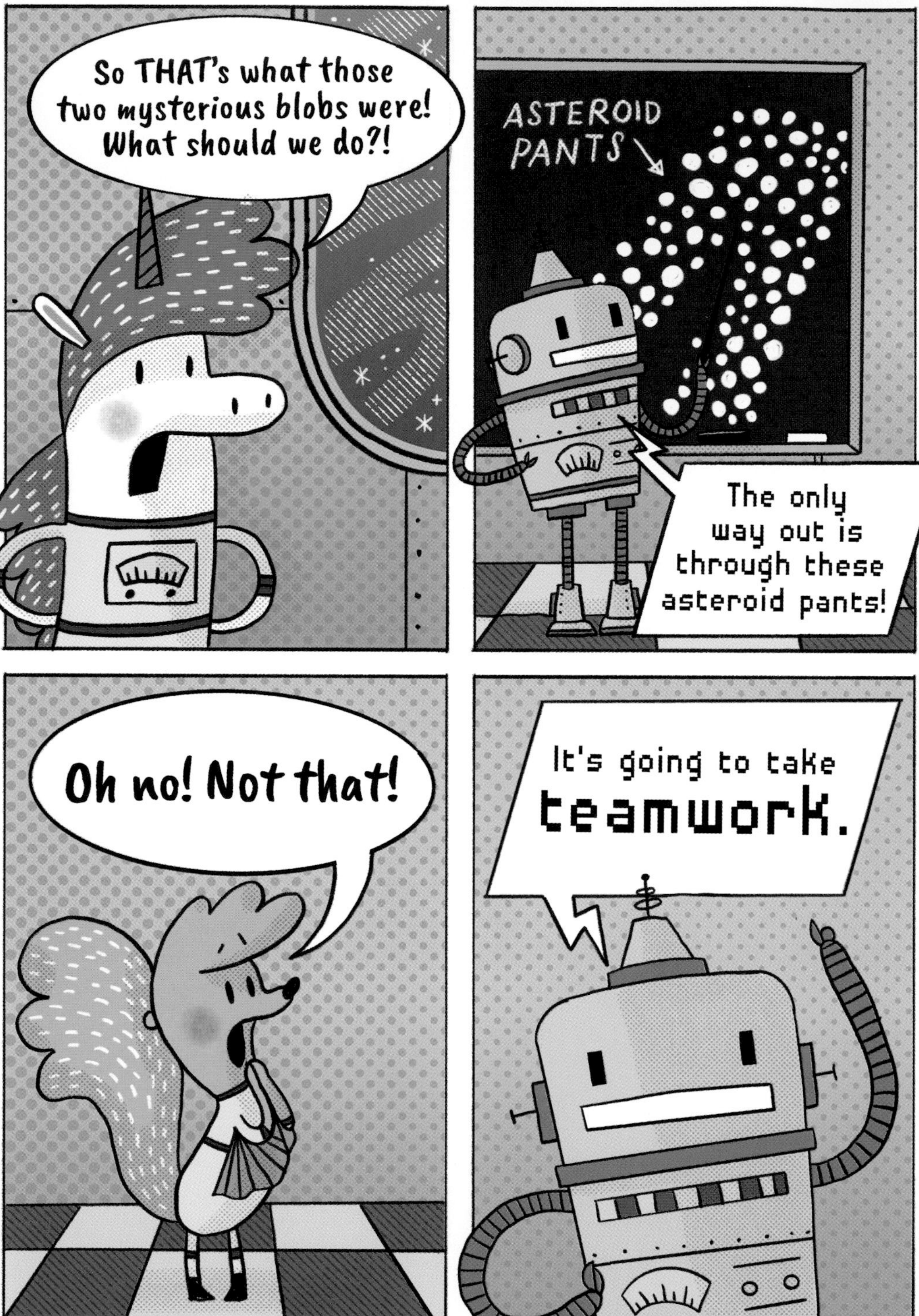
So THAT's what those two mysterious blobs were! What should we do?!
ASTEROID PANTS
The only way out is through these asteroid pants!
Oh no! Not that!
It's going to take teamwork.

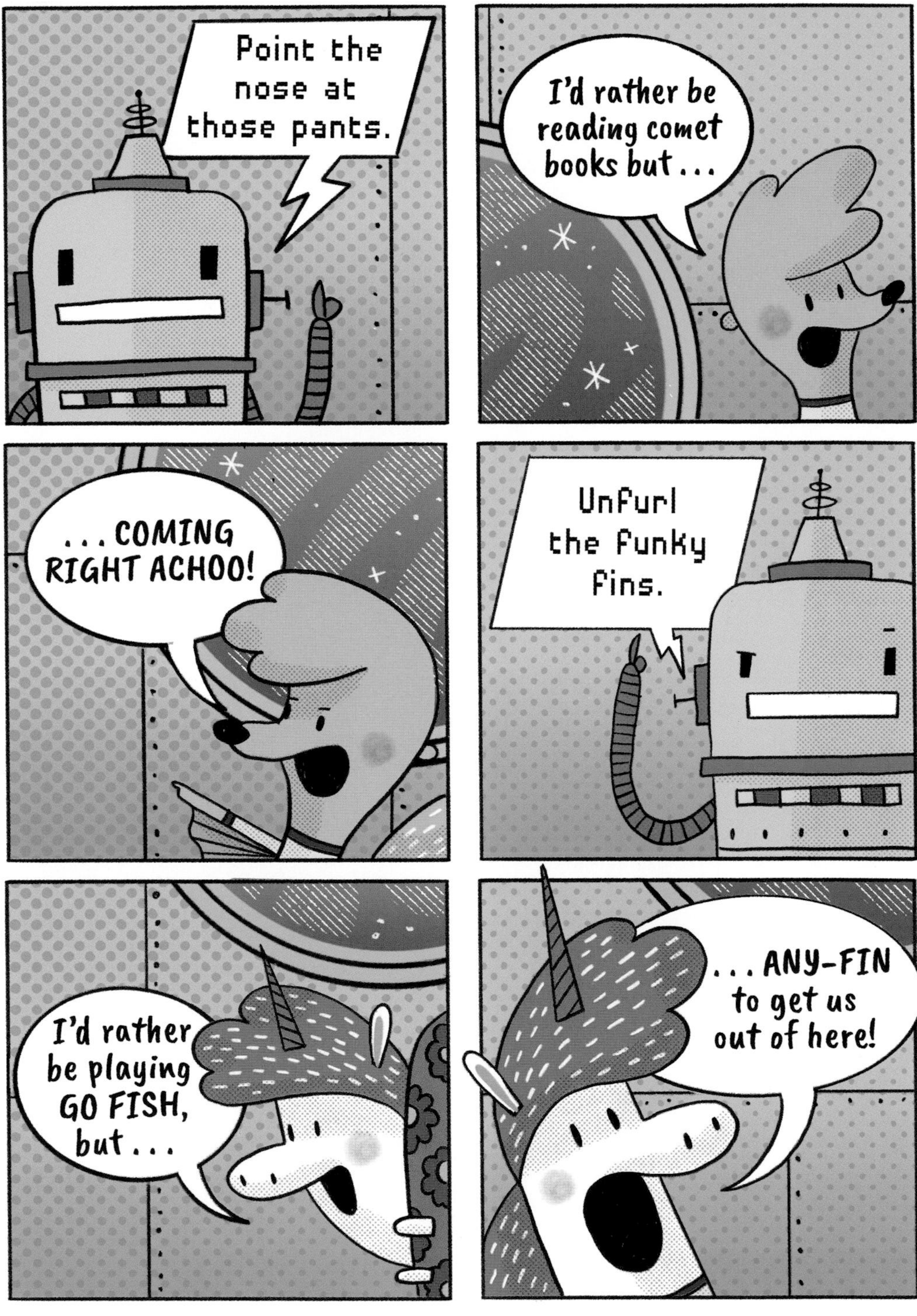
Point the nose at those pants.
I'd rather be reading comet books but . . .
. . . COMING RIGHT ACHOO!
Unfurl the funky fins.
I'd rather be playing GO FISH, but . . .
. . . ANY-FIN to get us out of here!

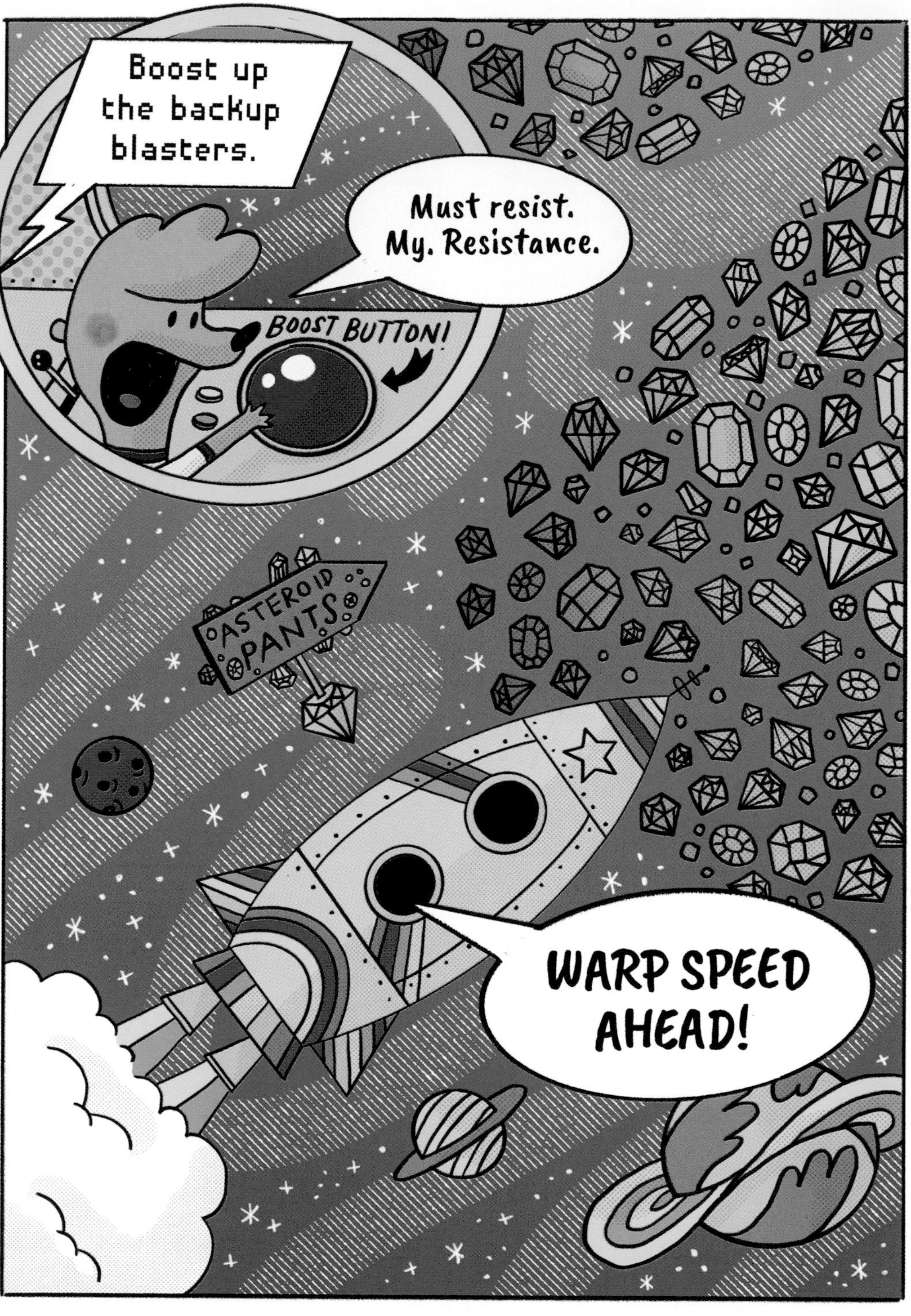
Boost up the backup blasters.
Must resist. My. Resistance.
BOOST BUTTON!
ASTEROID PANTS
WARP SPEED AHEAD!

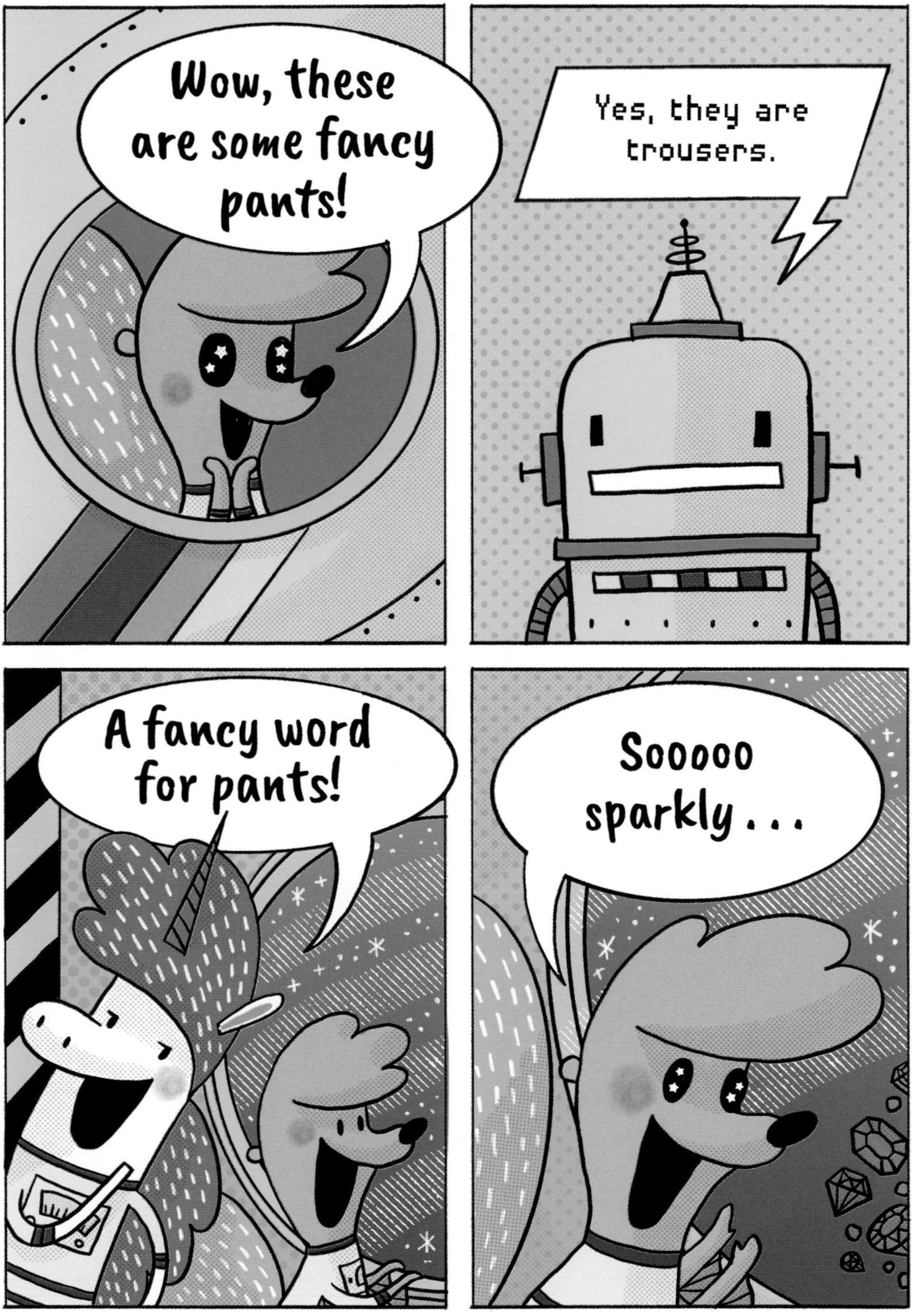
Wow, these are some fancy pants!
Yes, they are trousers.
A fancy word for pants!
Sooooo sparkly . . .

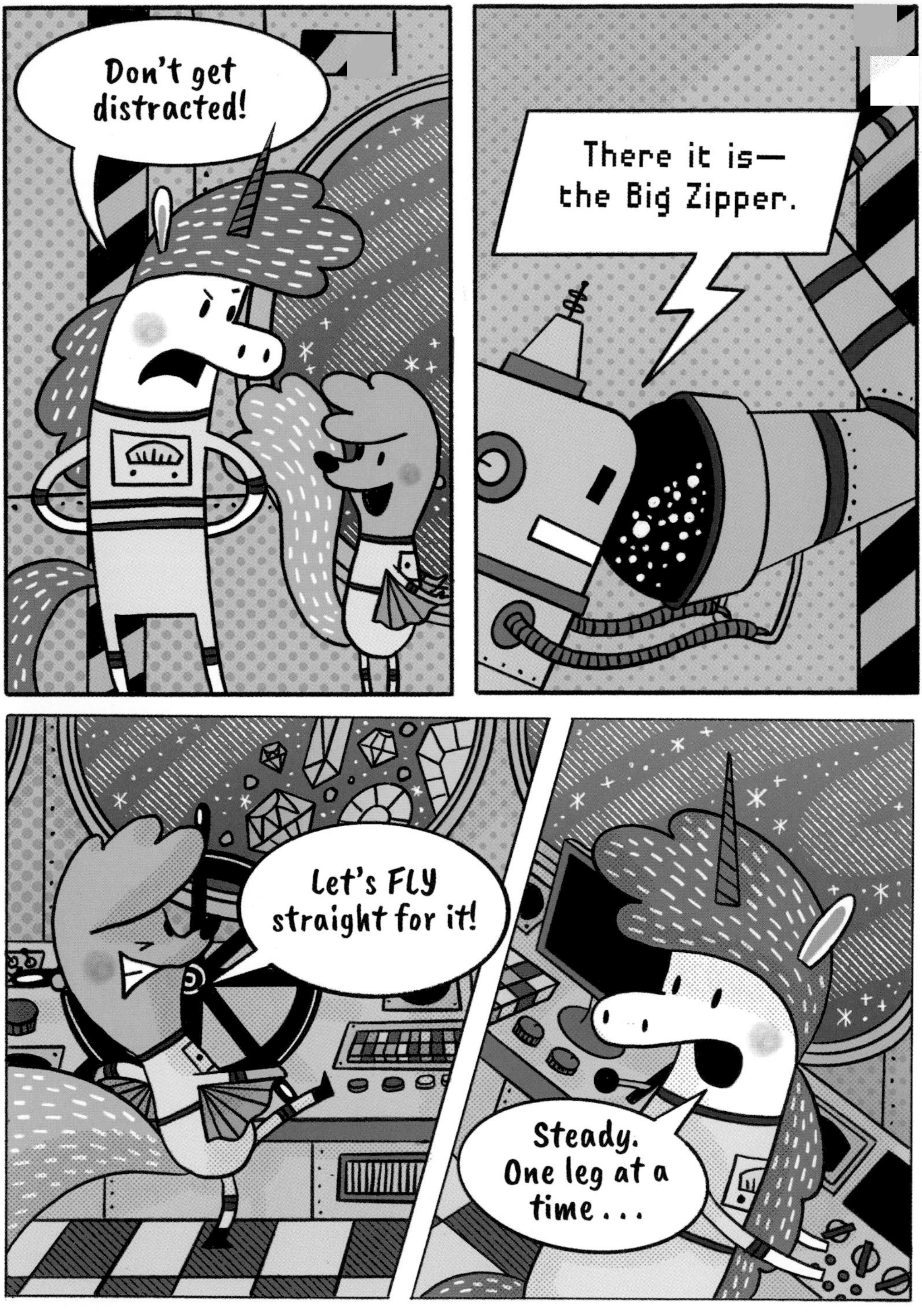
Don't get distracted!
There it is—the Big Zipper.
Let's FLY straight for it!
Steady. One leg at a time . . .

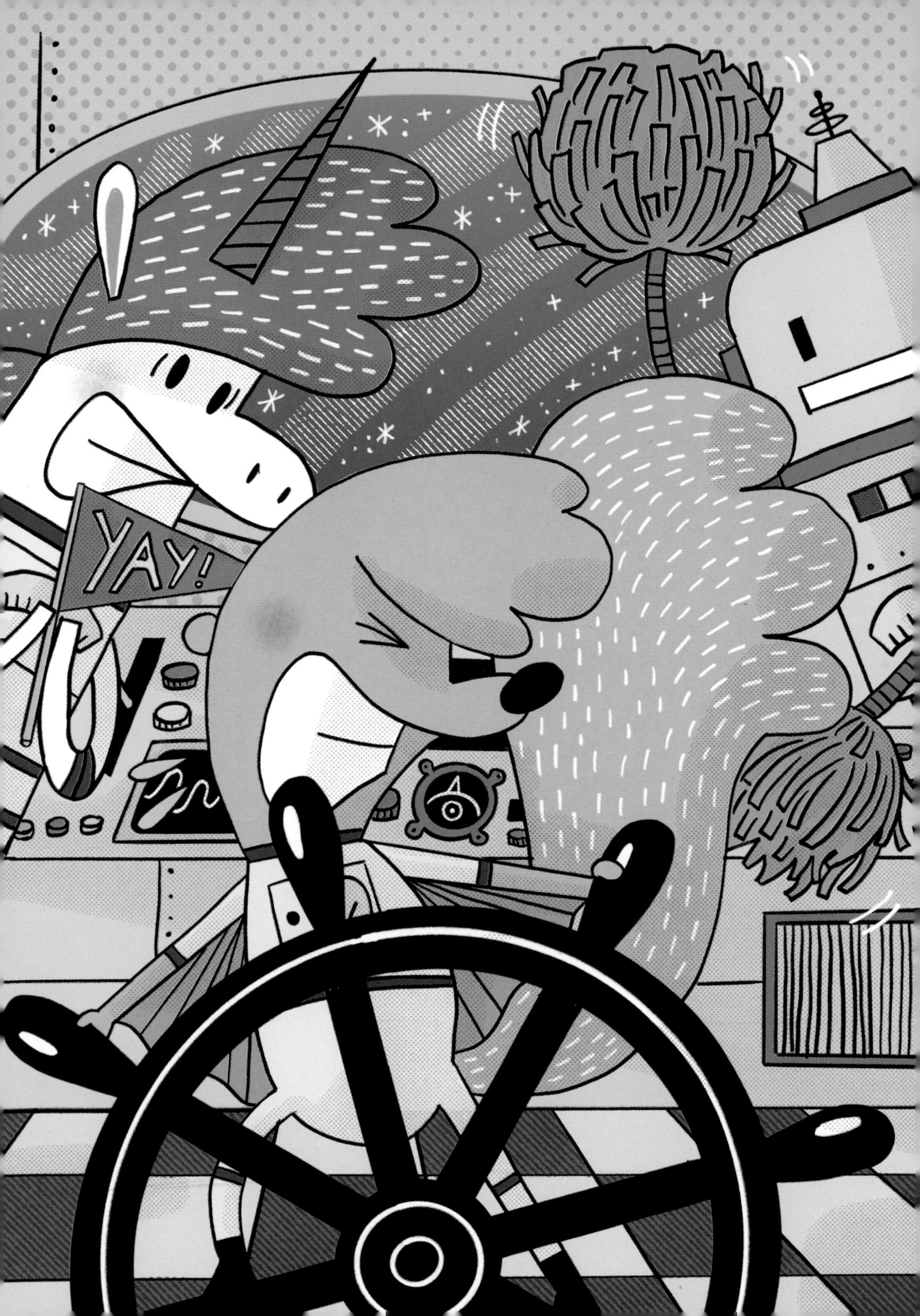
YAY!

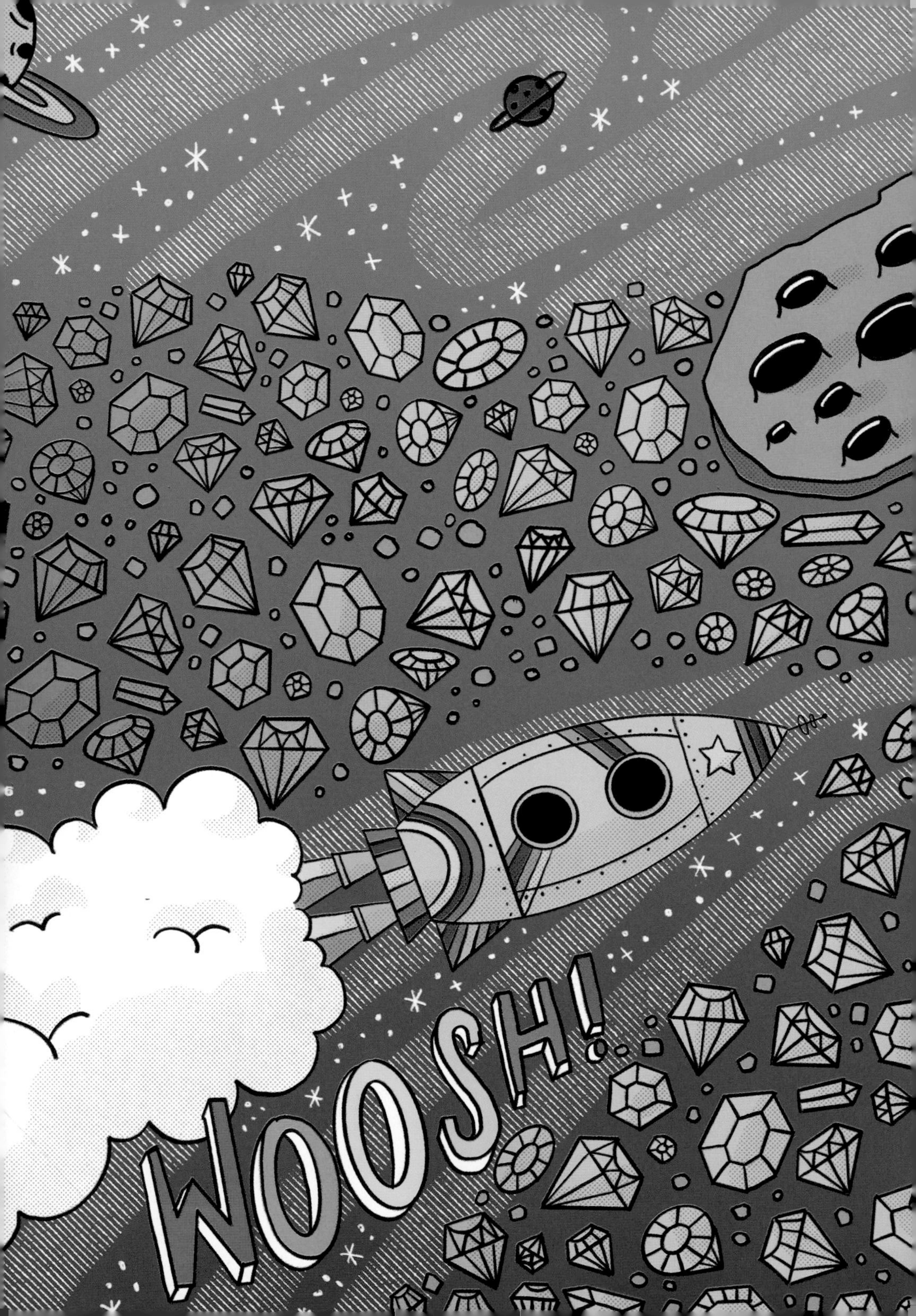
WOOSH!

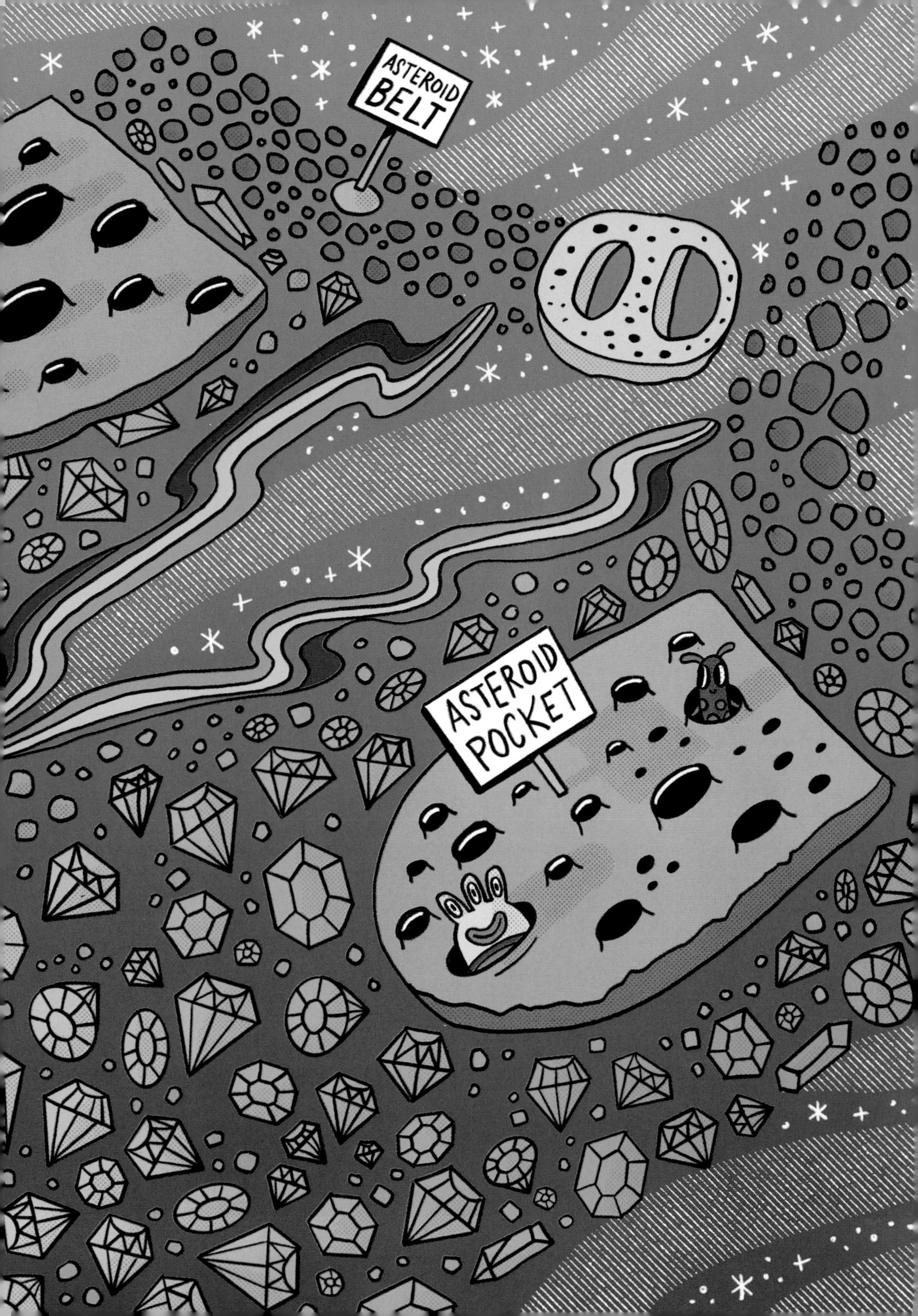
ASTEROID BELT
ASTEROID POCKET

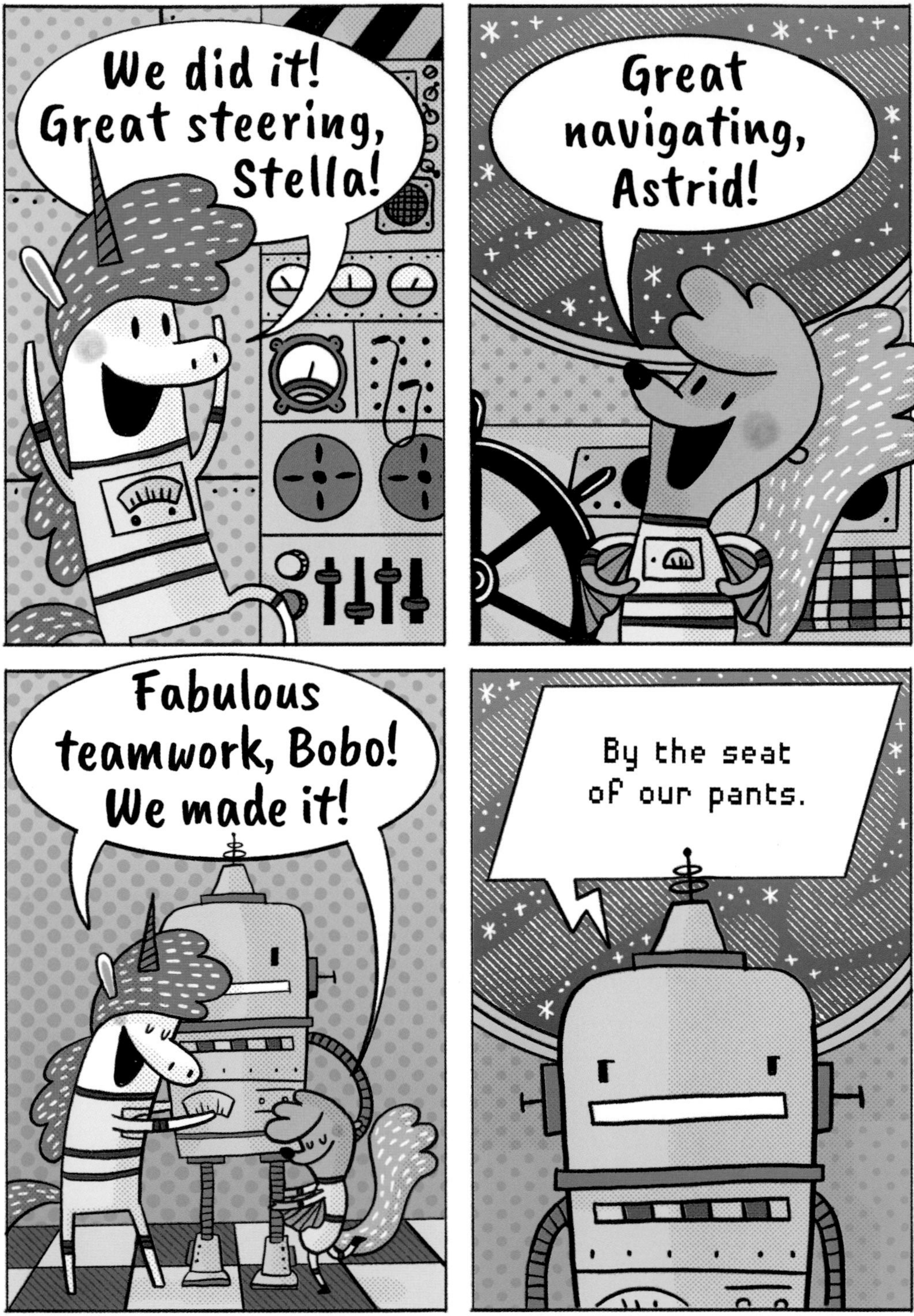
We did it! Great steering, Stella!
Great navigating, Astrid!
Fabulous teamwork, Bobo! We made it!
By the seat of our pants.

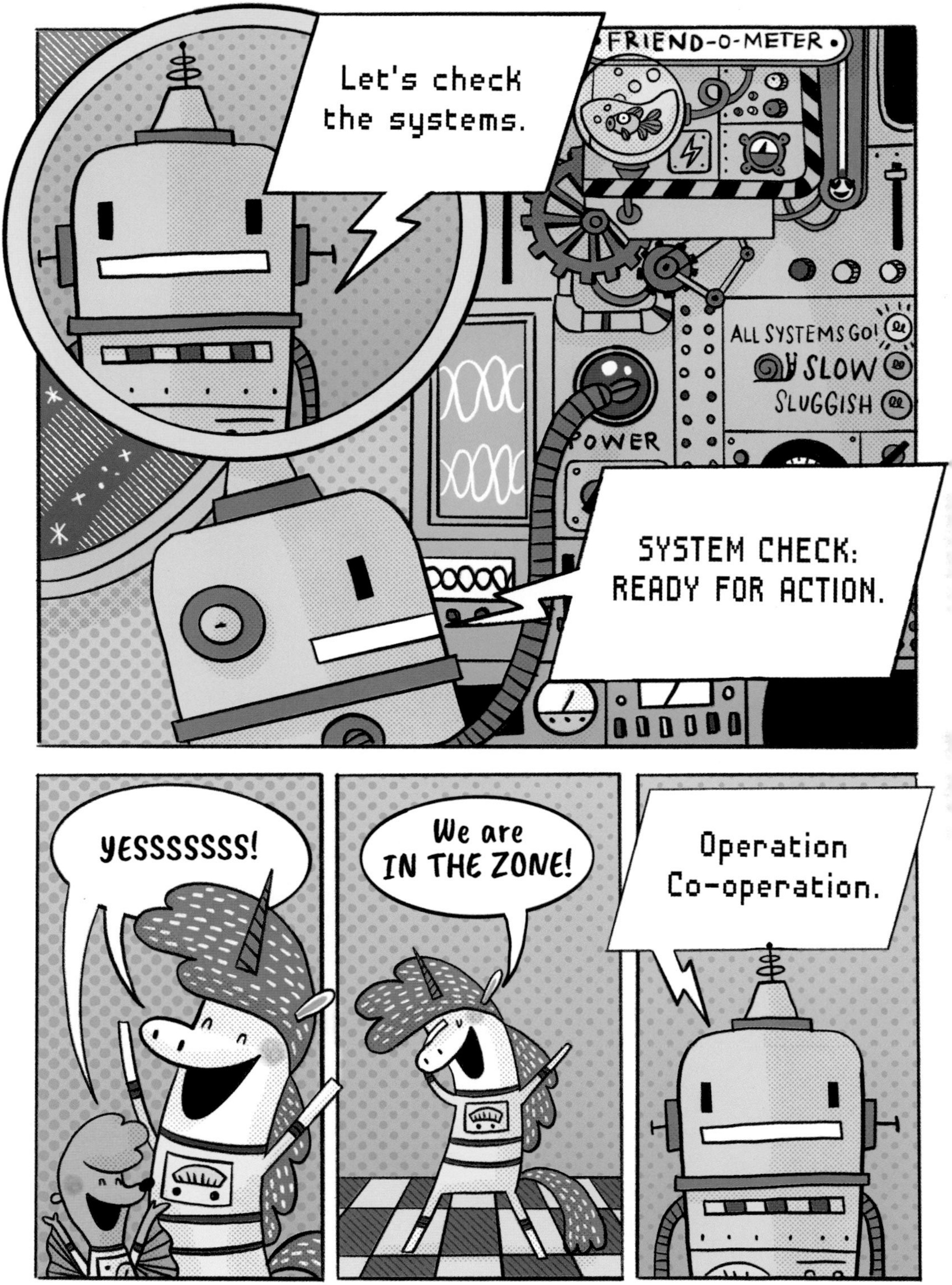

Let's check the systems.
FRIEND-O-METER
ALL SYSTEMS GO!
SLOW
SLUGGISH
POWER
SYSTEM CHECK: READY FOR ACTION.
YESSSSSSS!
We are IN THE ZONE!
Operation Co-operation.

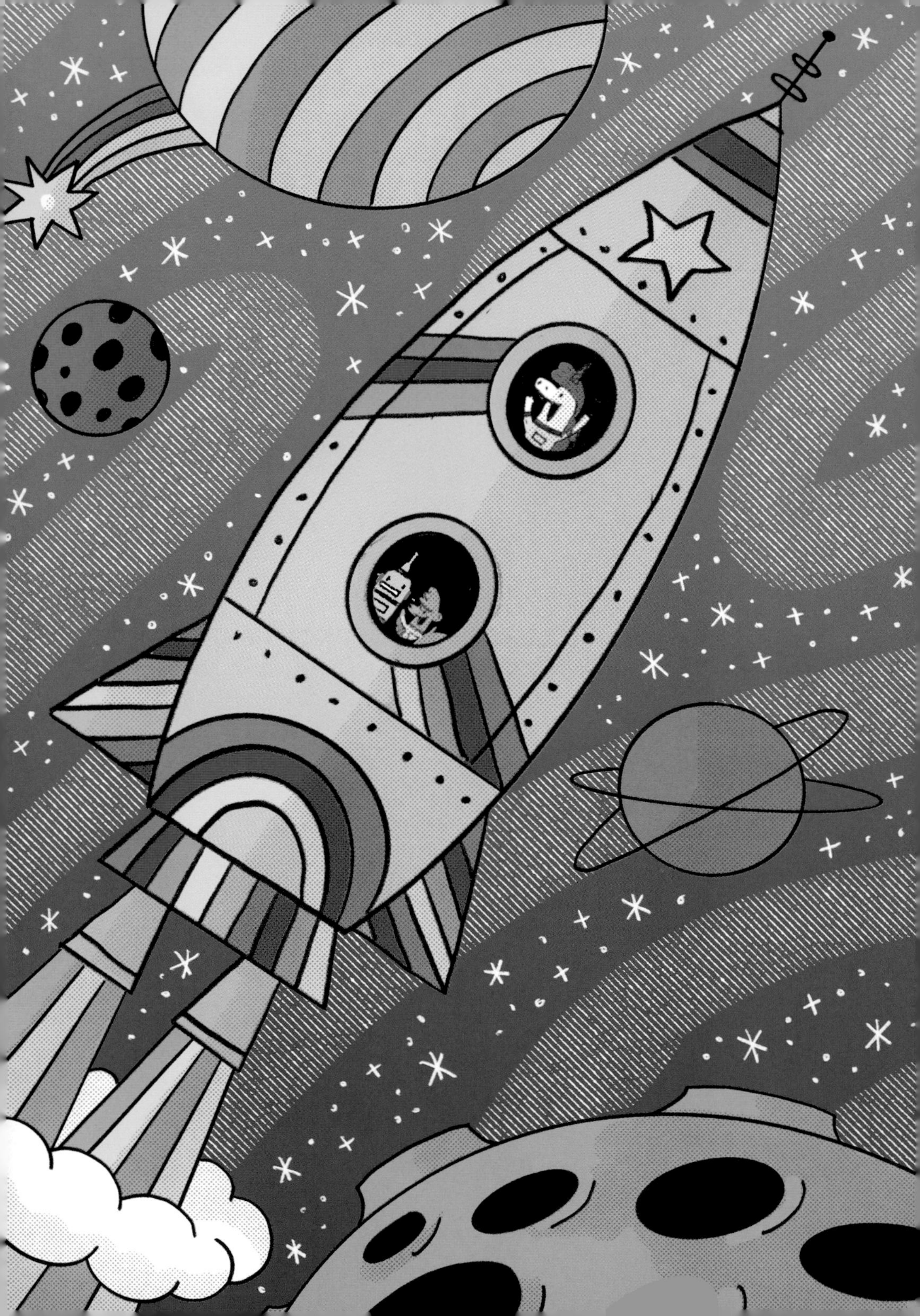

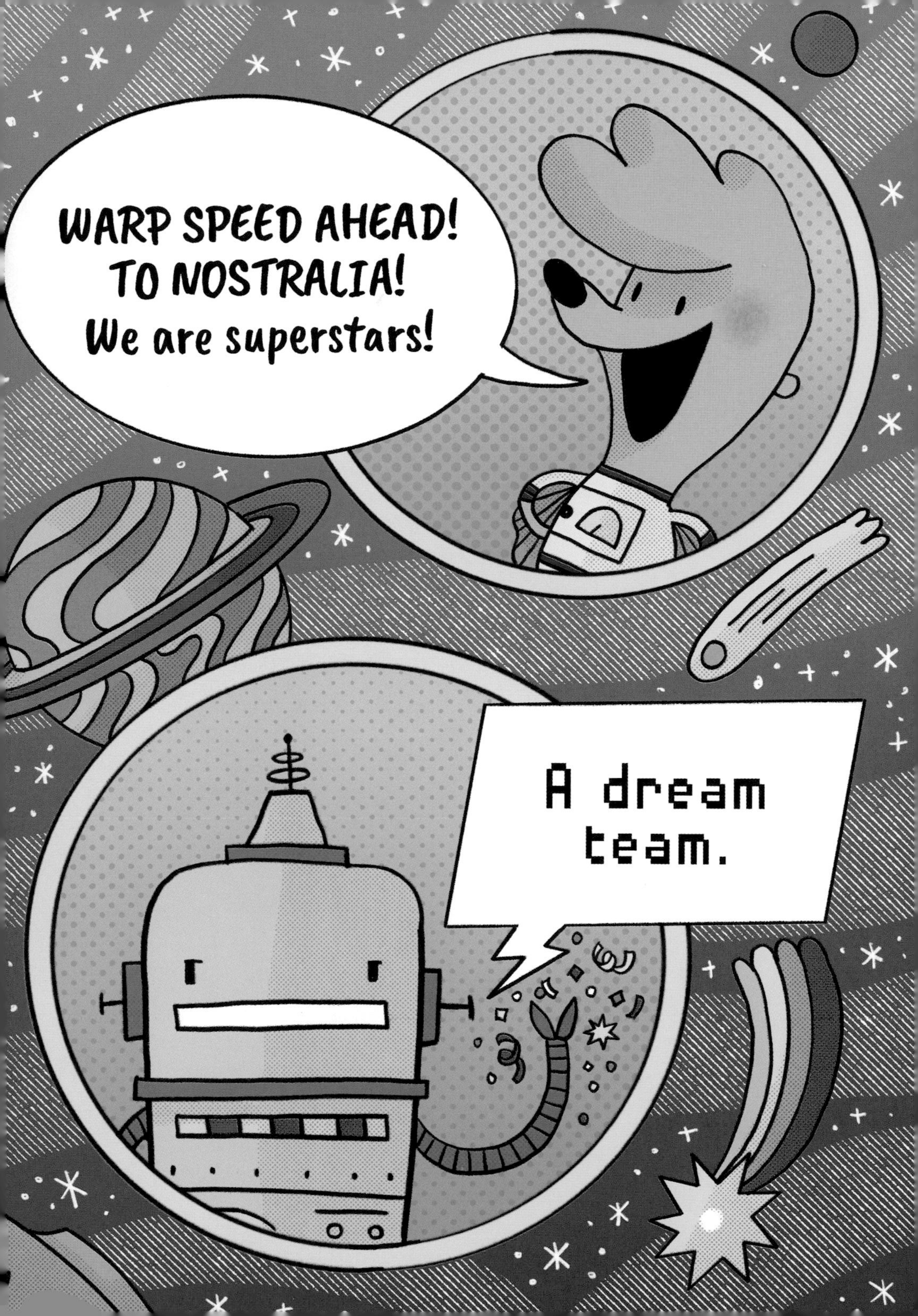
WARP SPEED AHEAD! TO NOSTRALIA! We are superstars!
A dream team.

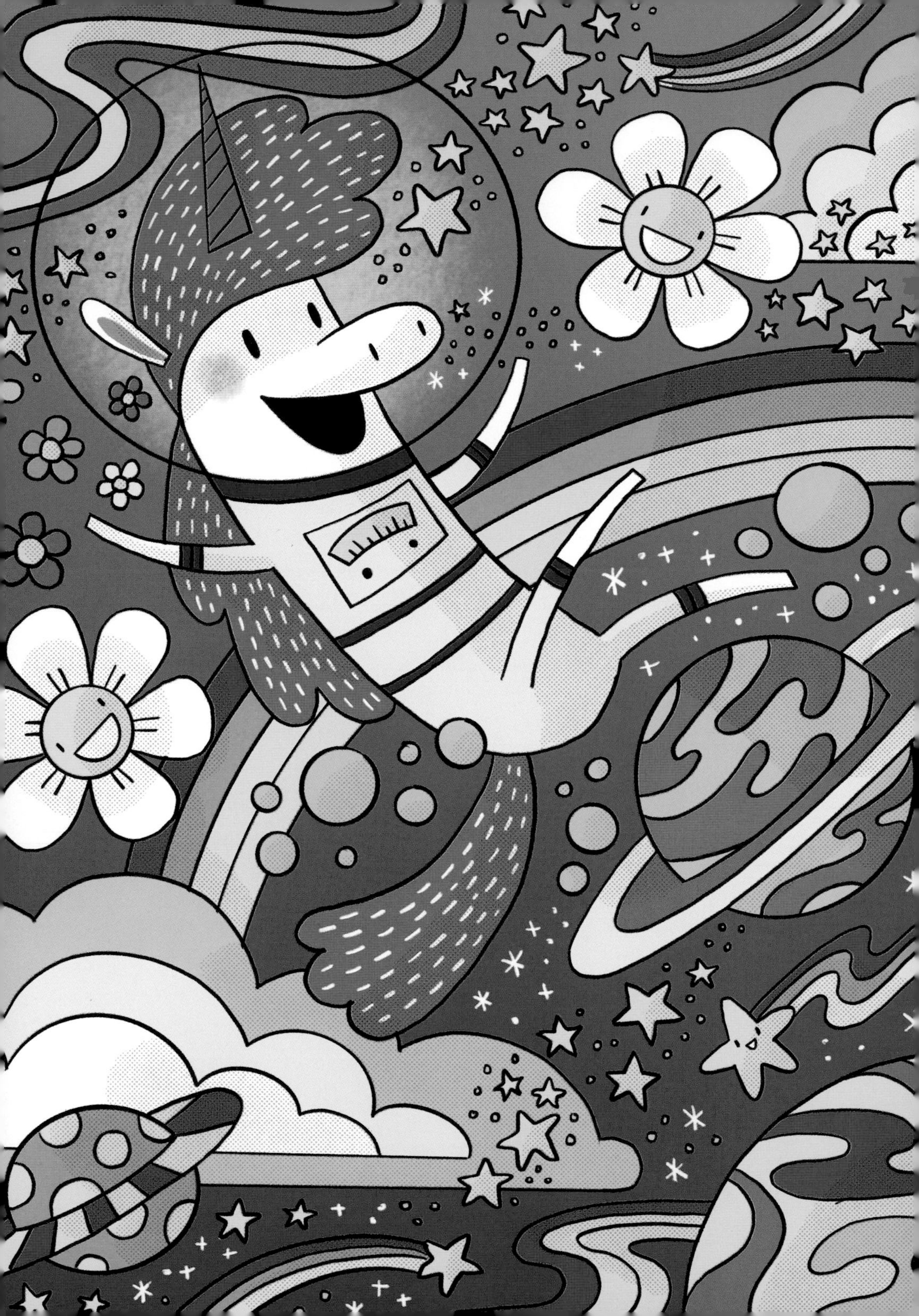

CHAPTER TWO

HAPPY PLACE

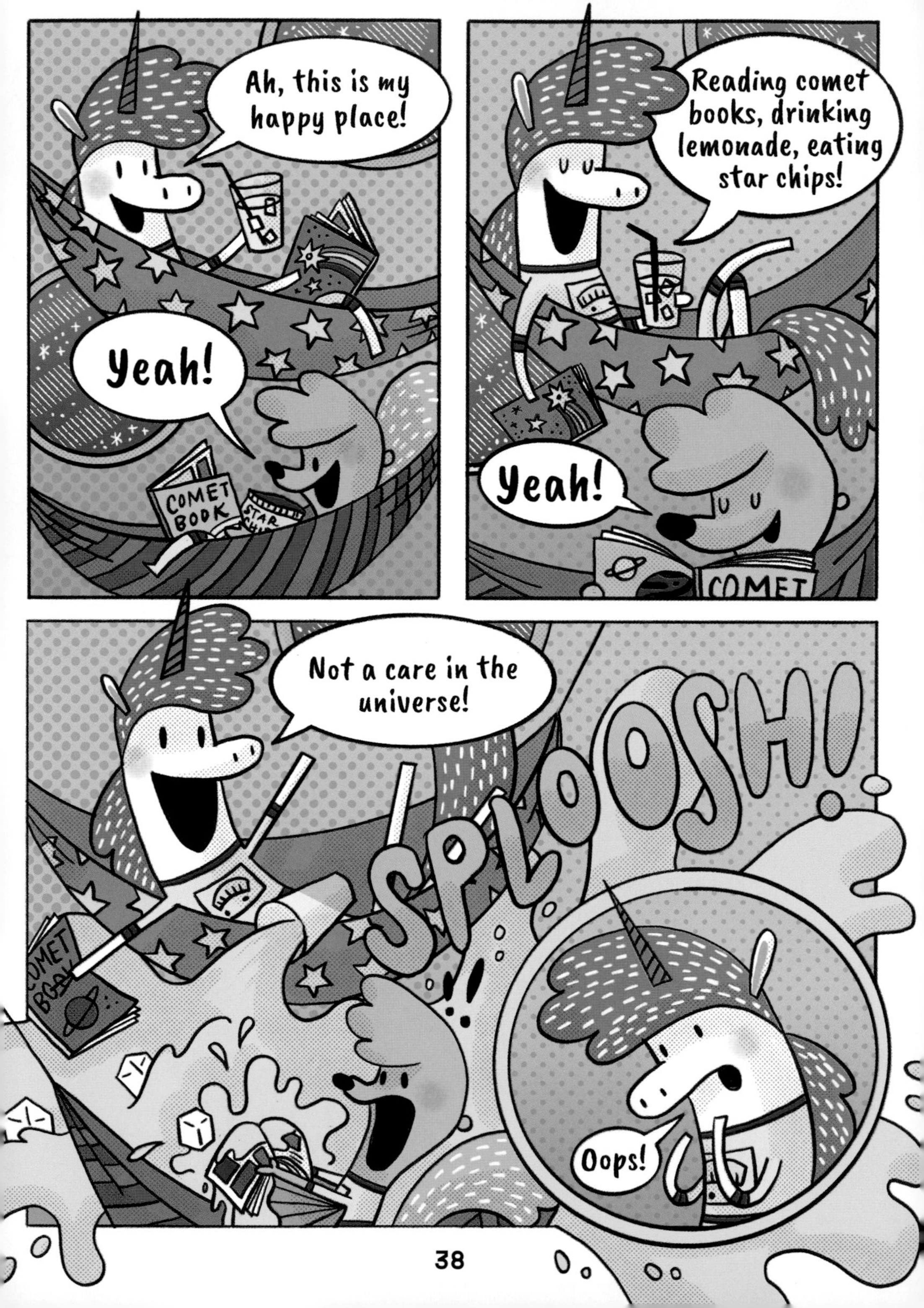
Ah, this is my happy place!
Yeah!
COMET BOOK
STAR
Reading comet books, drinking lemonade, eating star chips!
Yeah!
COMET
Not a care in the universe!
SPLOOSH!!
COMET BOOK
Oops!

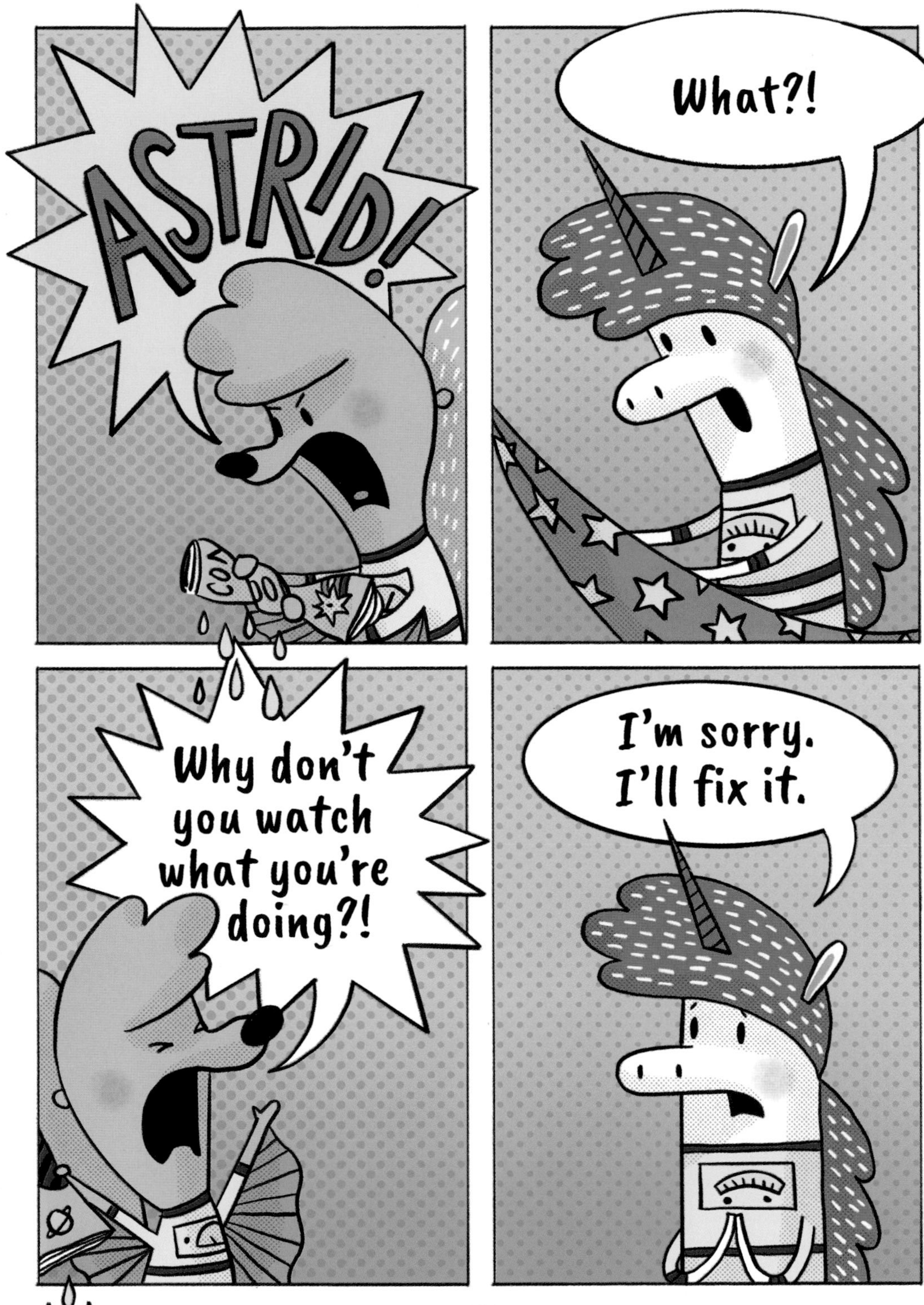
ASTRID!
What?!
Why don't you watch what you're doing?!
I'm sorry. I'll fix it.

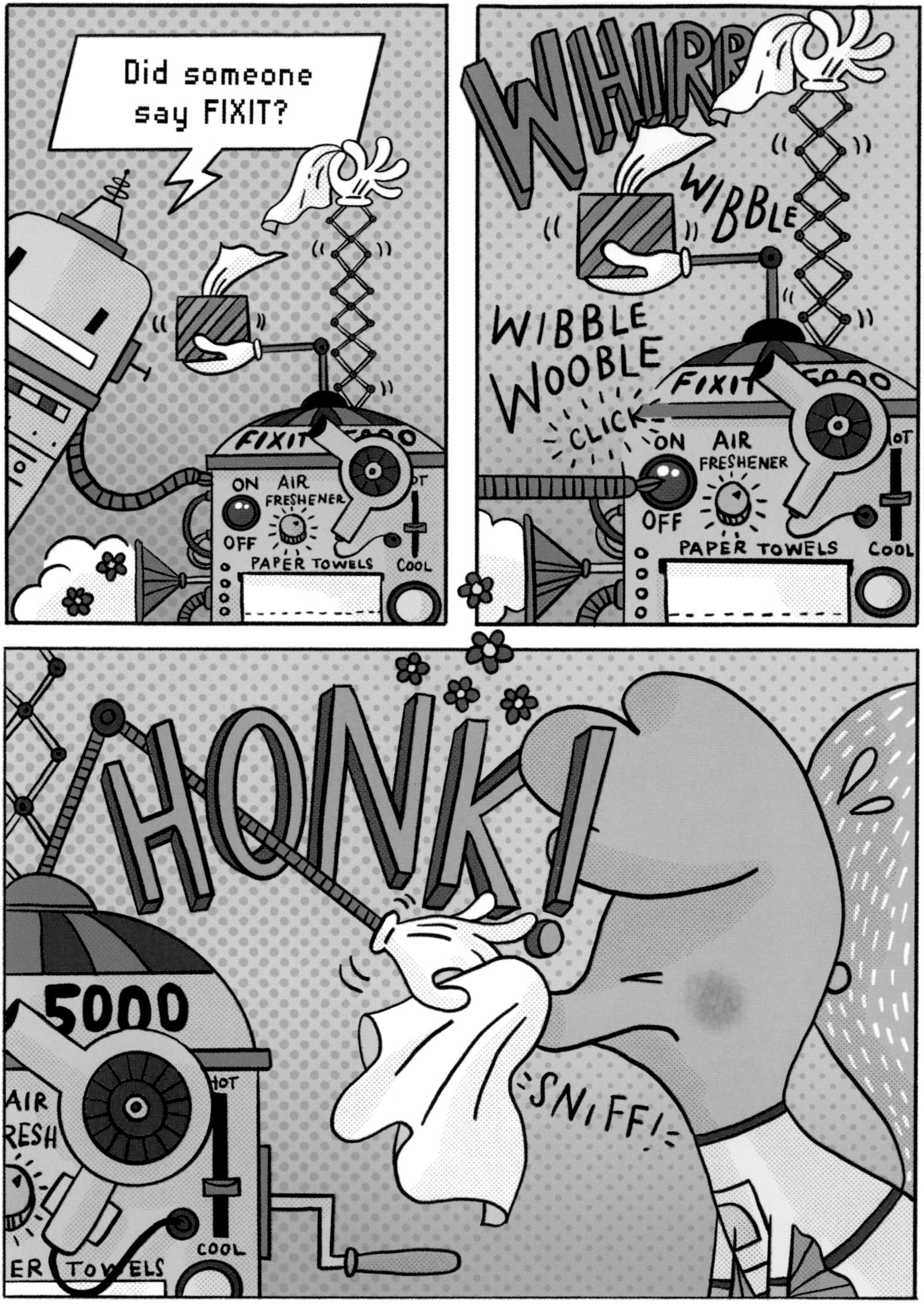
Did someone say FIXIT?
FIXIT 5000
ON
OFF
AIR FRESHENER
PAPER TOWELS
HOT
COOL
WHIRR
WIBBLE
WIBBLE WOOBLE
CLICK
HONK!
5000
AIR
RESH
ER TOWELS
HOT
COOL
SNIFF!

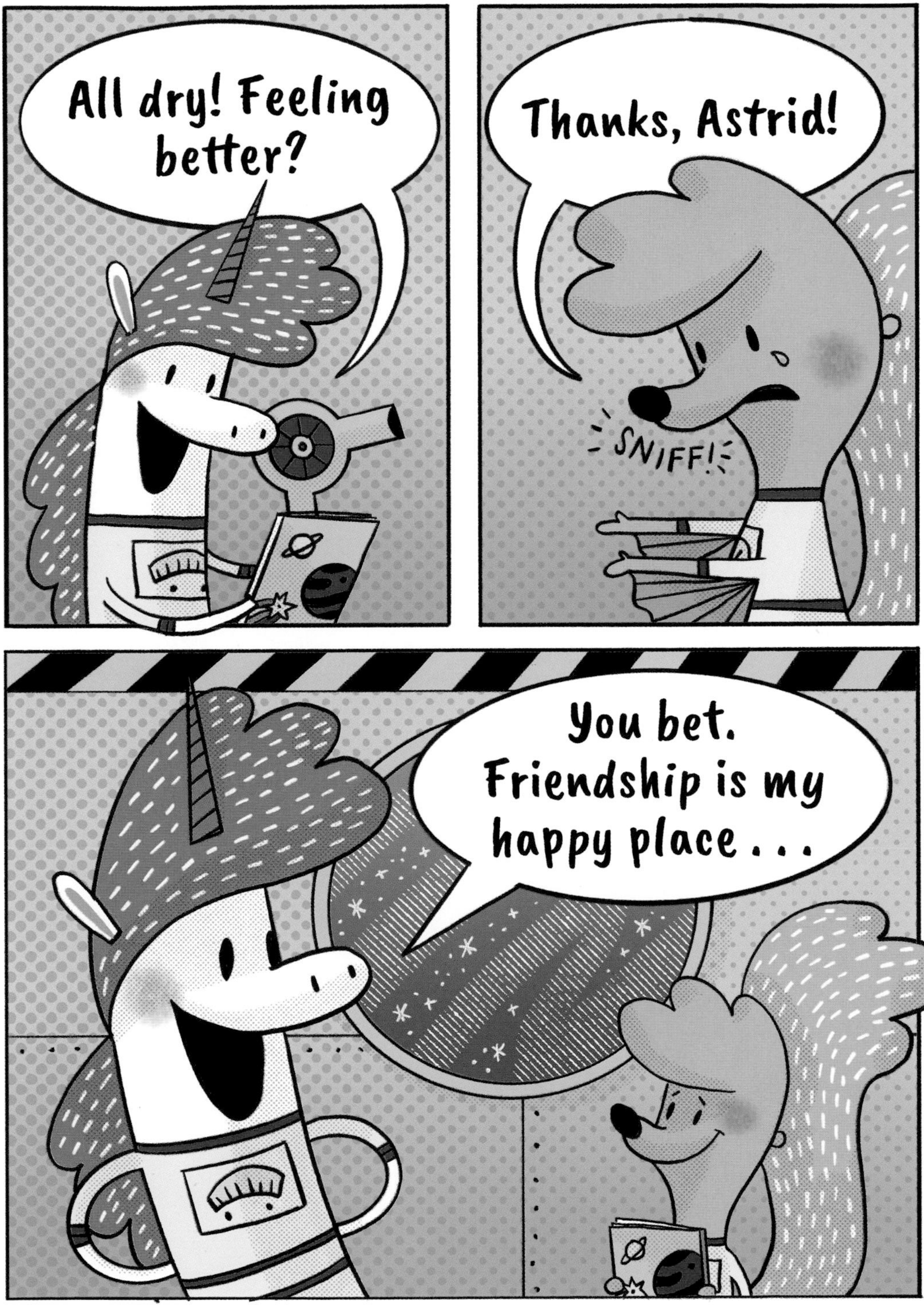
All dry! Feeling better?
Thanks, Astrid!
SNIFF!
You bet. Friendship is my happy place . . .

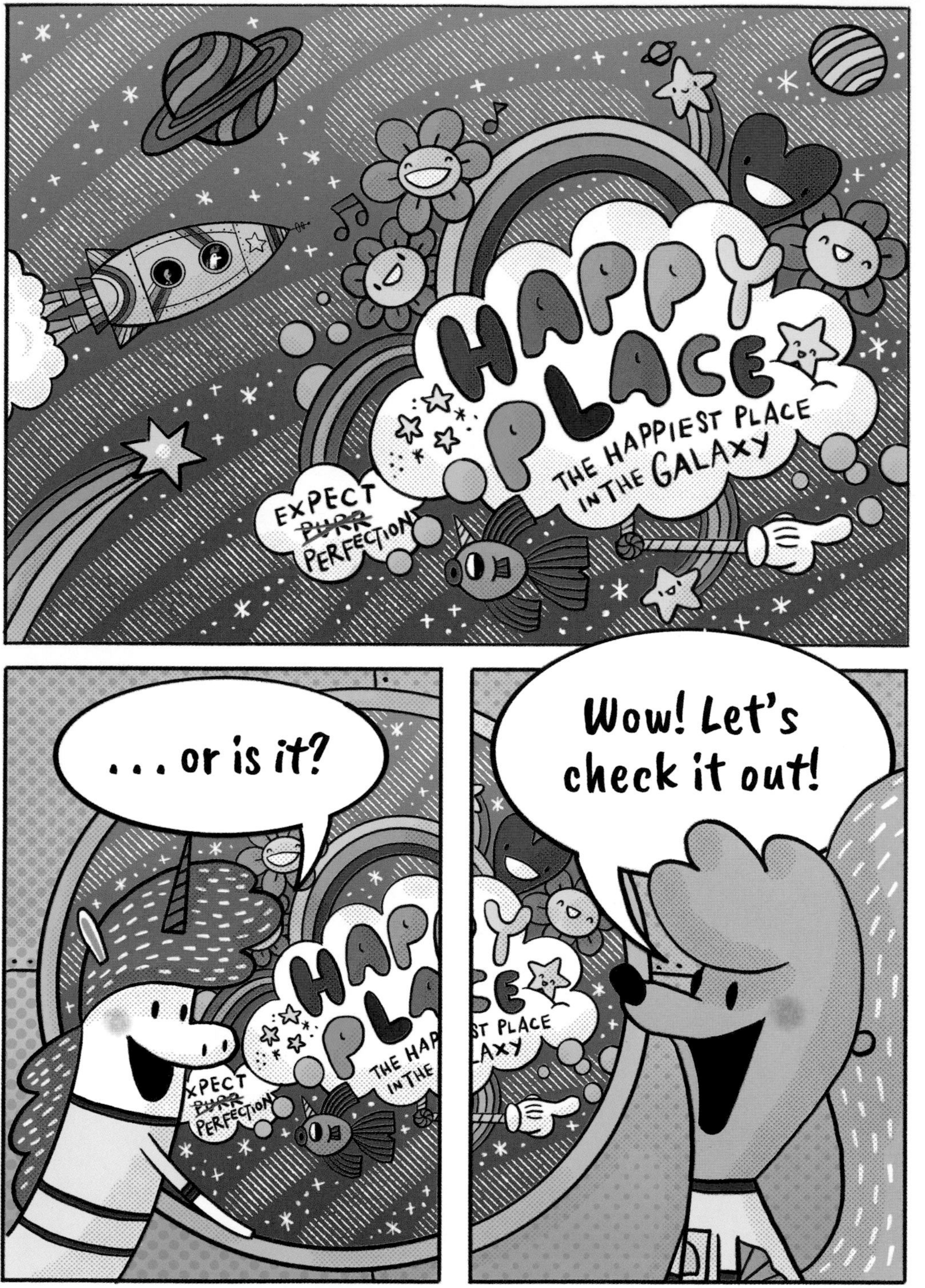
HAPPY PLACE
THE HAPPIEST PLACE IN THE GALAXY
EXPECT ~~PURR~~ PERFECTION
. . . or is it?
Wow! Let's check it out!

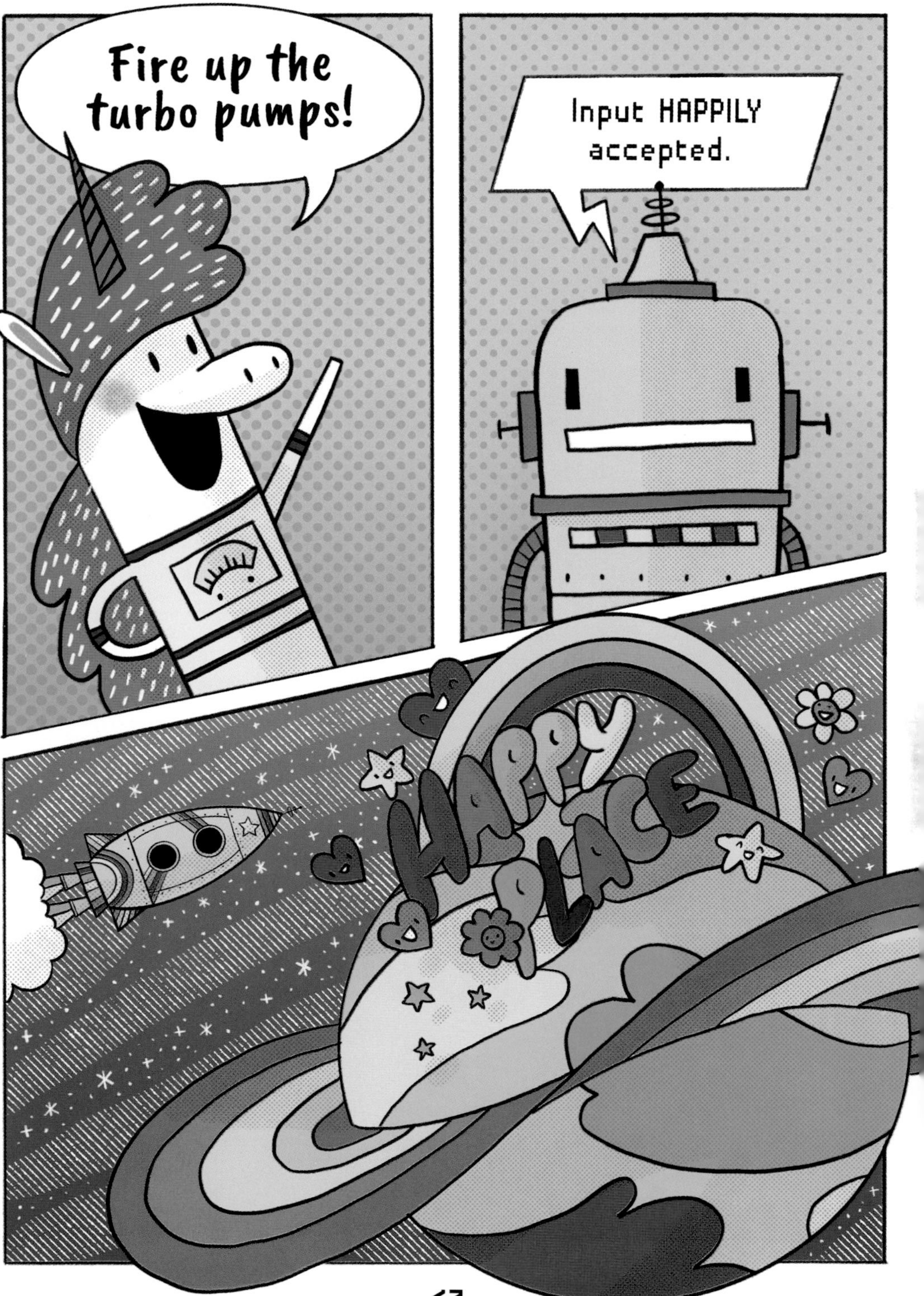

Fire up the turbo pumps!
Input HAPPILY accepted.
HAPPY PLACE

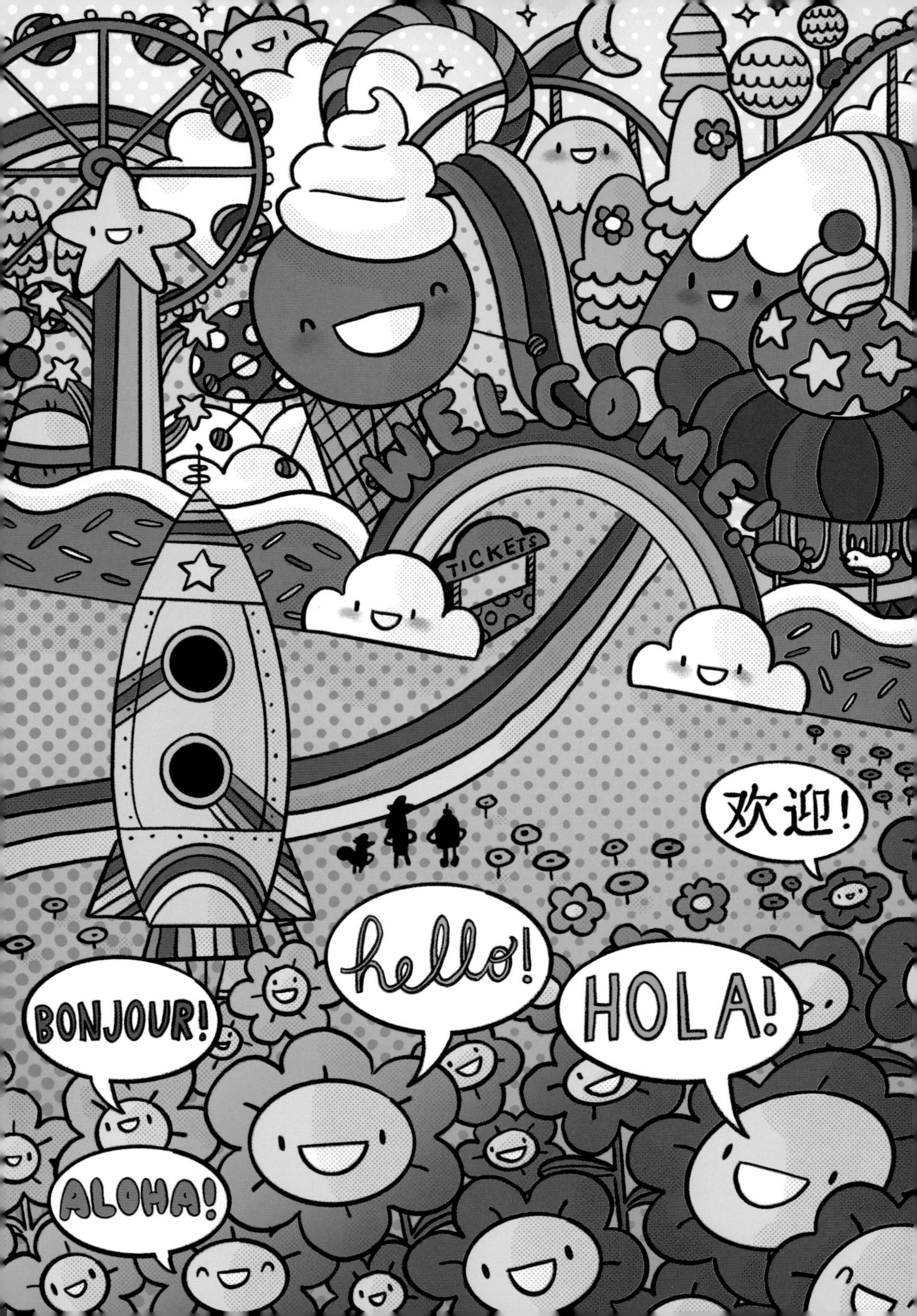
WELCOME!
TICKETS
欢迎!
hello!
HOLA!
BONJOUR!
ALOHA!

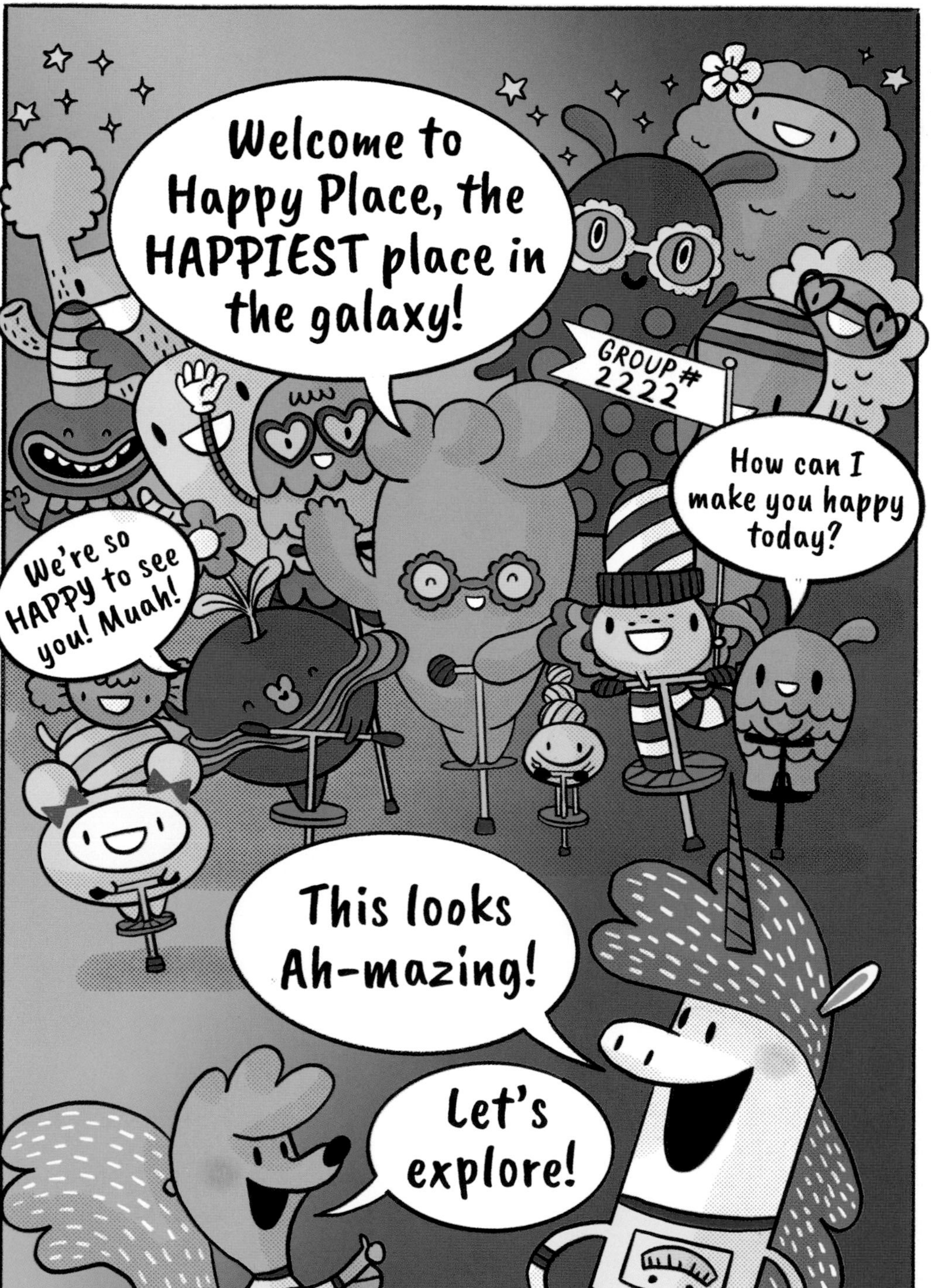
Welcome to Happy Place, the HAPPIEST place in the galaxy!
GROUP # 2222
We're so HAPPY to see you! Muah!
How can I make you happy today?
This looks Ah-mazing!
Let's explore!

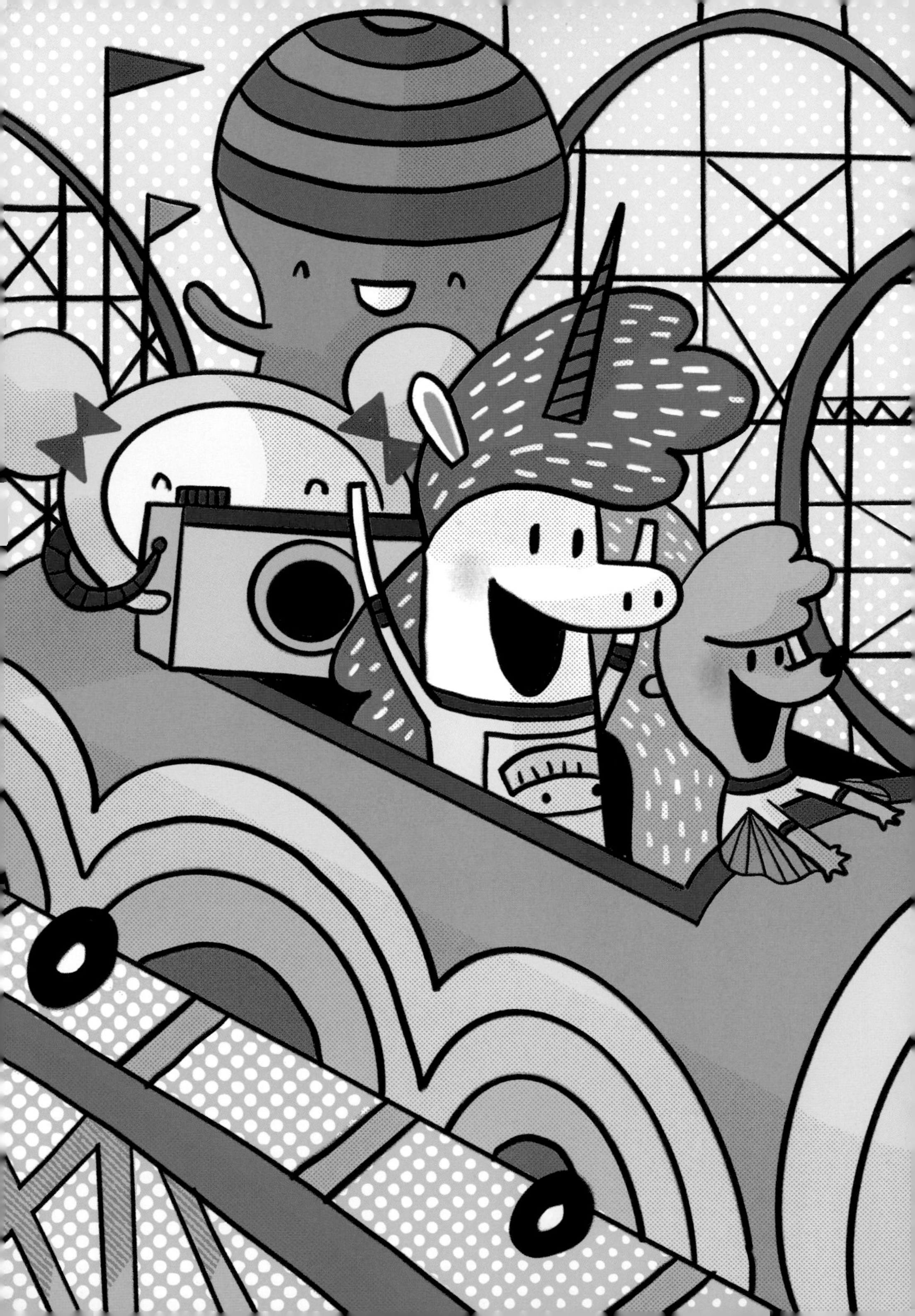

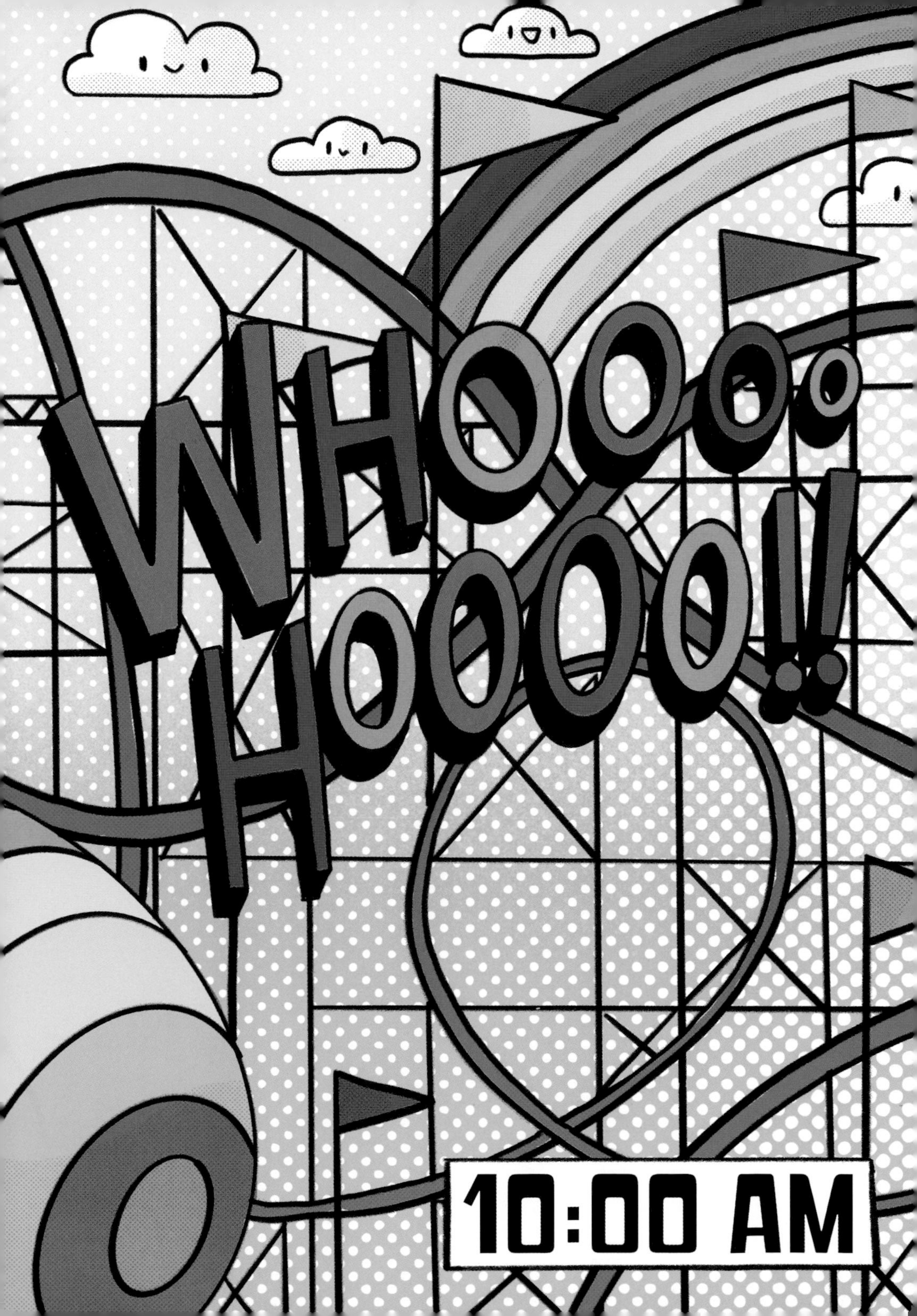
WHOOOo
HOOOO!!!
10:00 AM

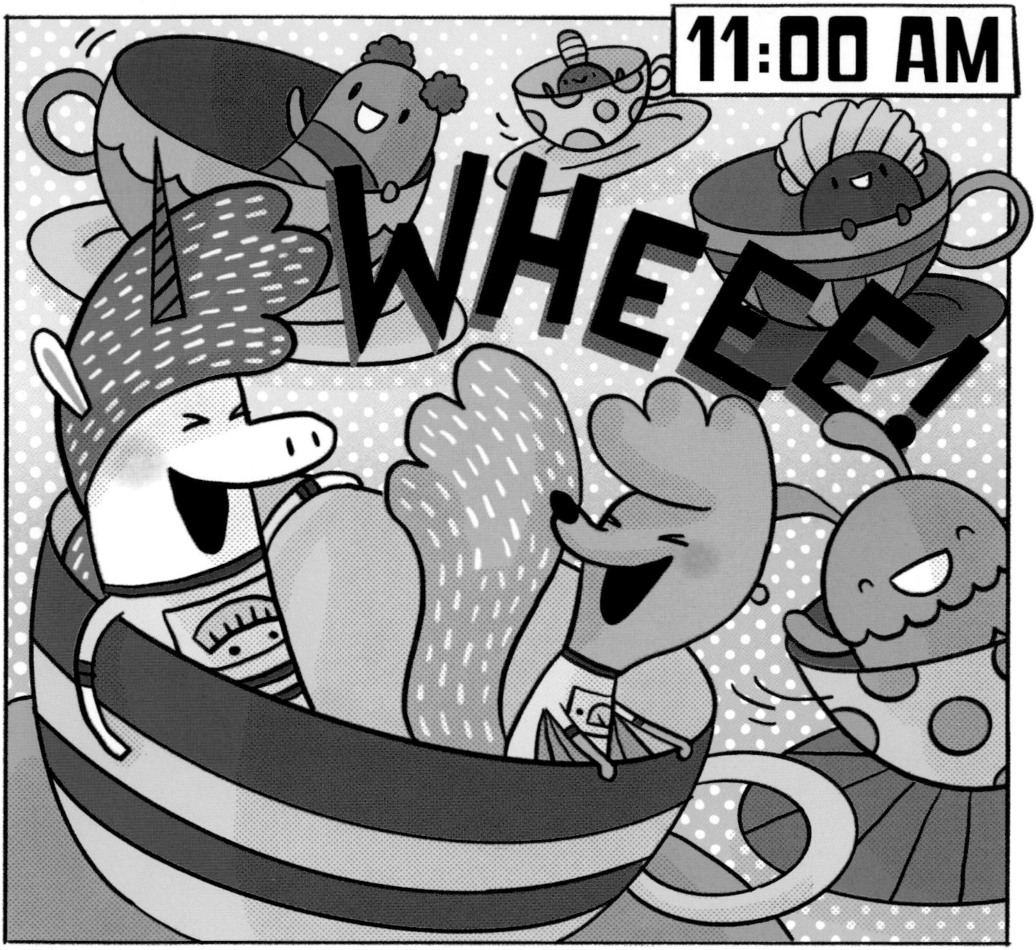
11:00 AM
WHEEE!

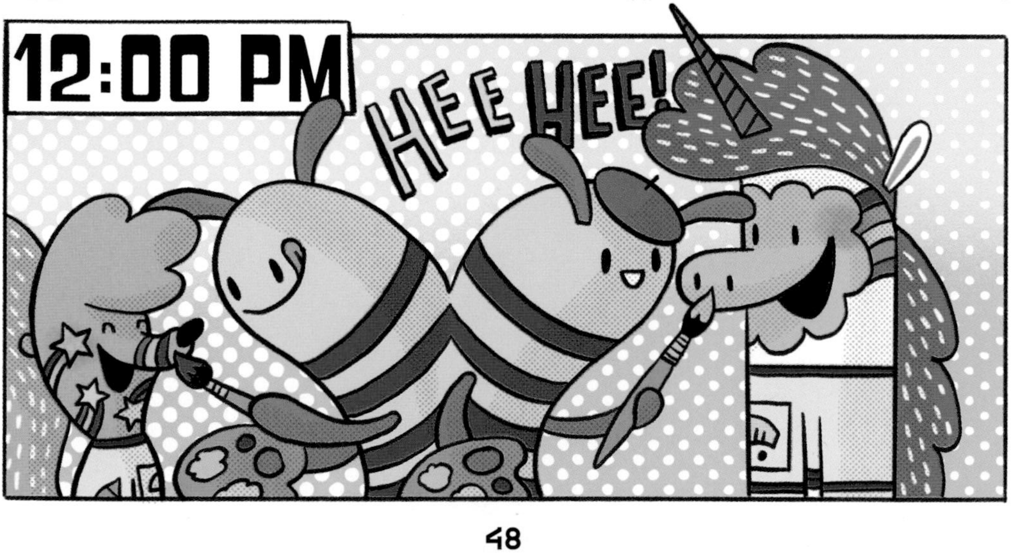
12:00 PM
HEE HEE!

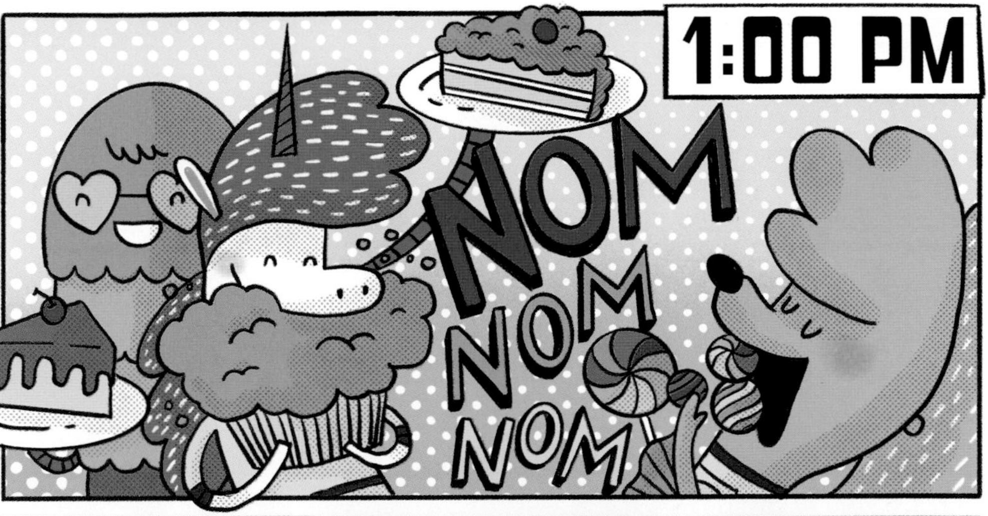
1:00 PM
NOM
NOM
NOM
NOM

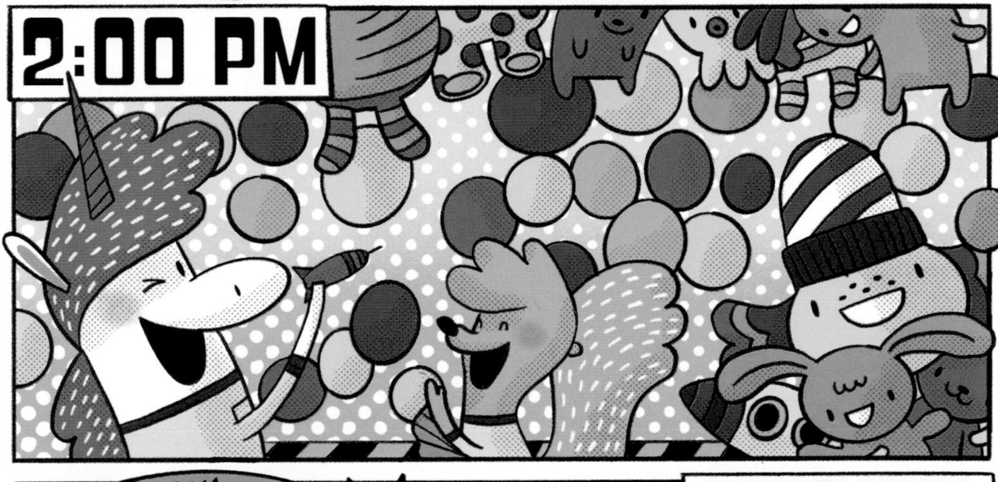
2:00 PM

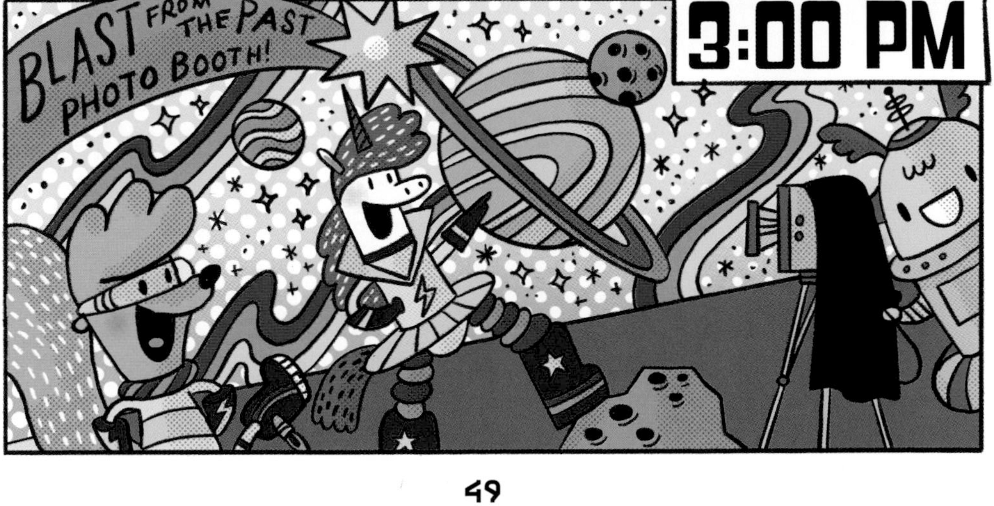
BLAST FROM THE PAST PHOTO BOOTH!
3:00 PM

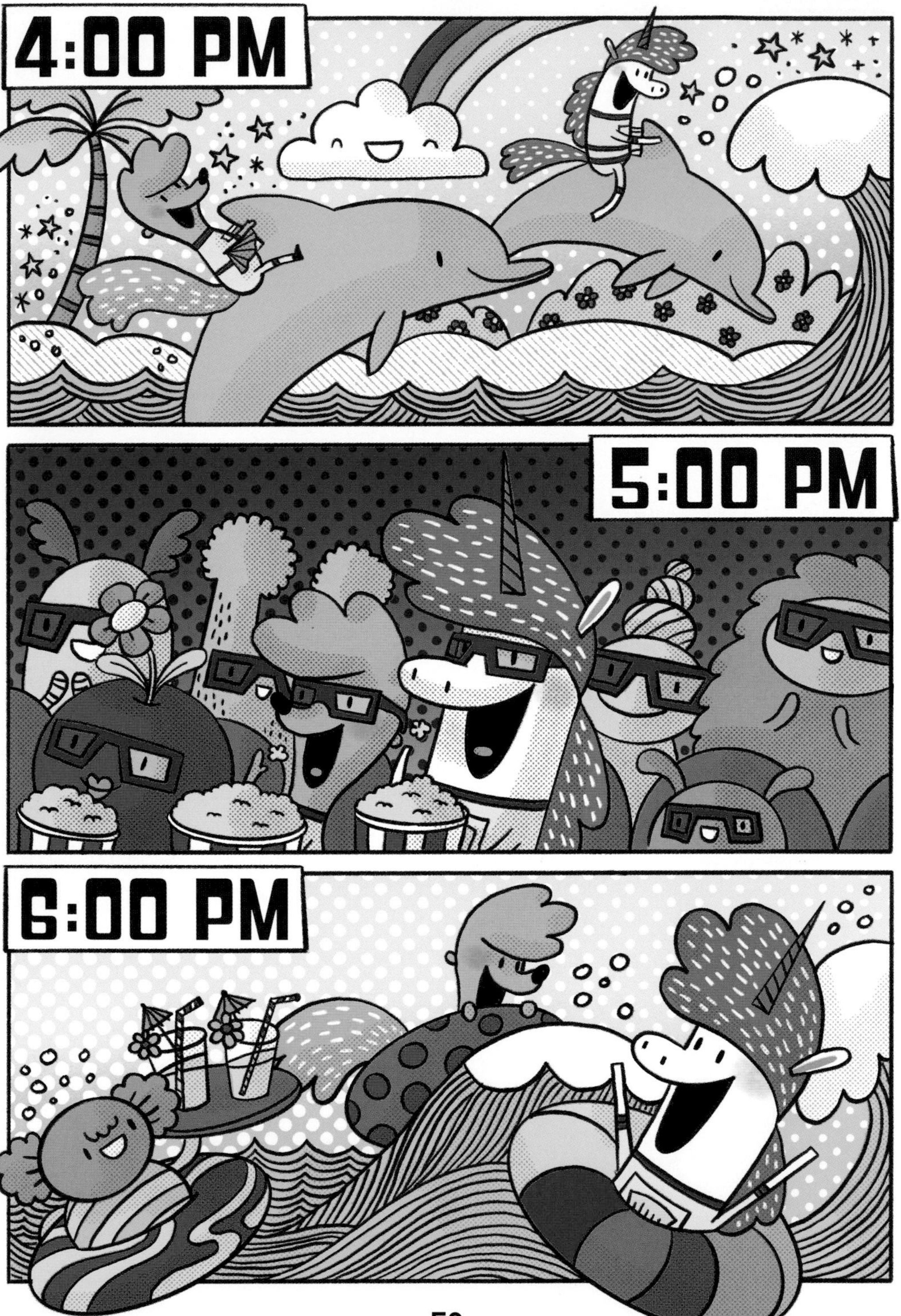
4:00 PM
5:00 PM
6:00 PM

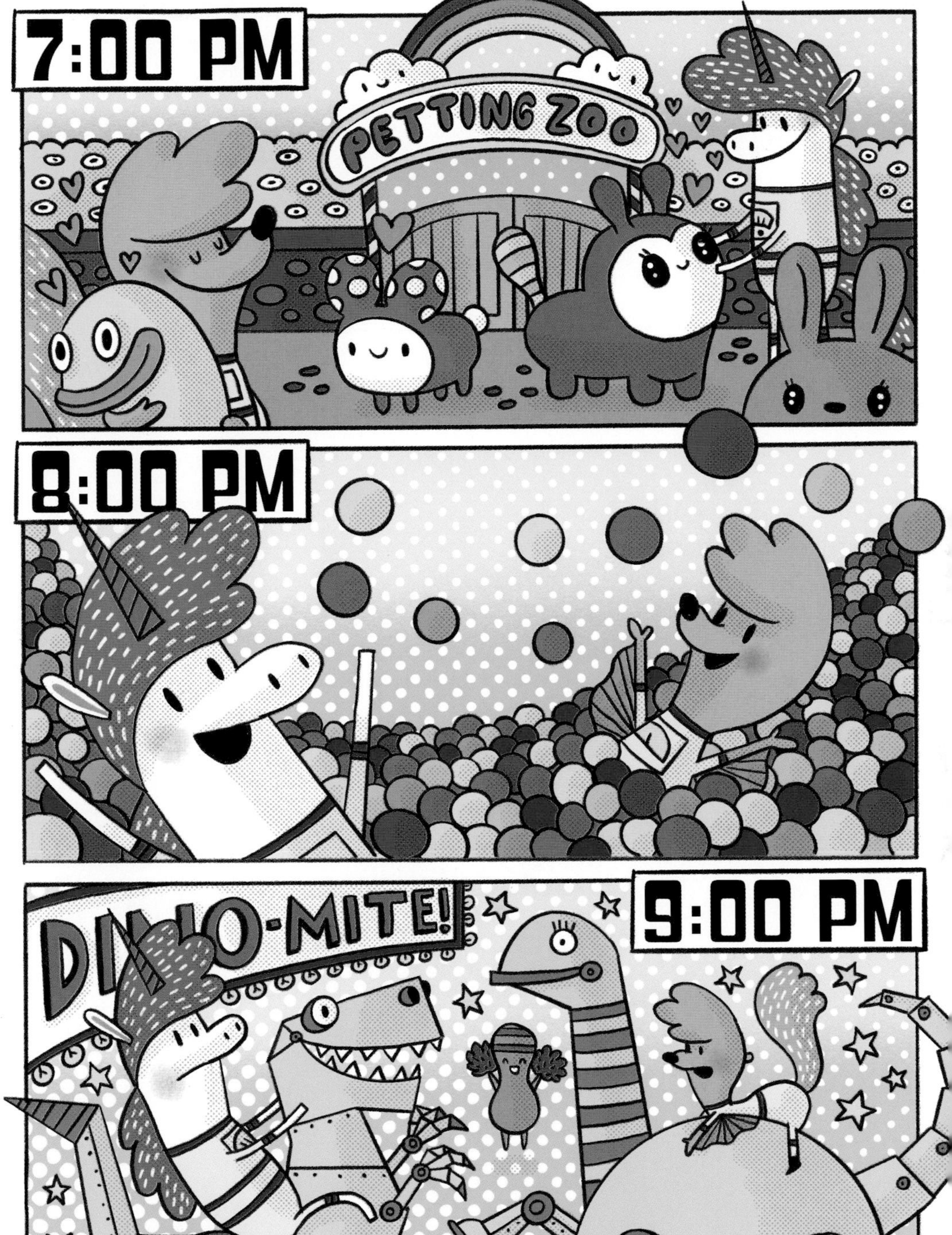
7:00 PM
PETTING ZOO
8:00 PM
DI O-MITE!
9:00 PM

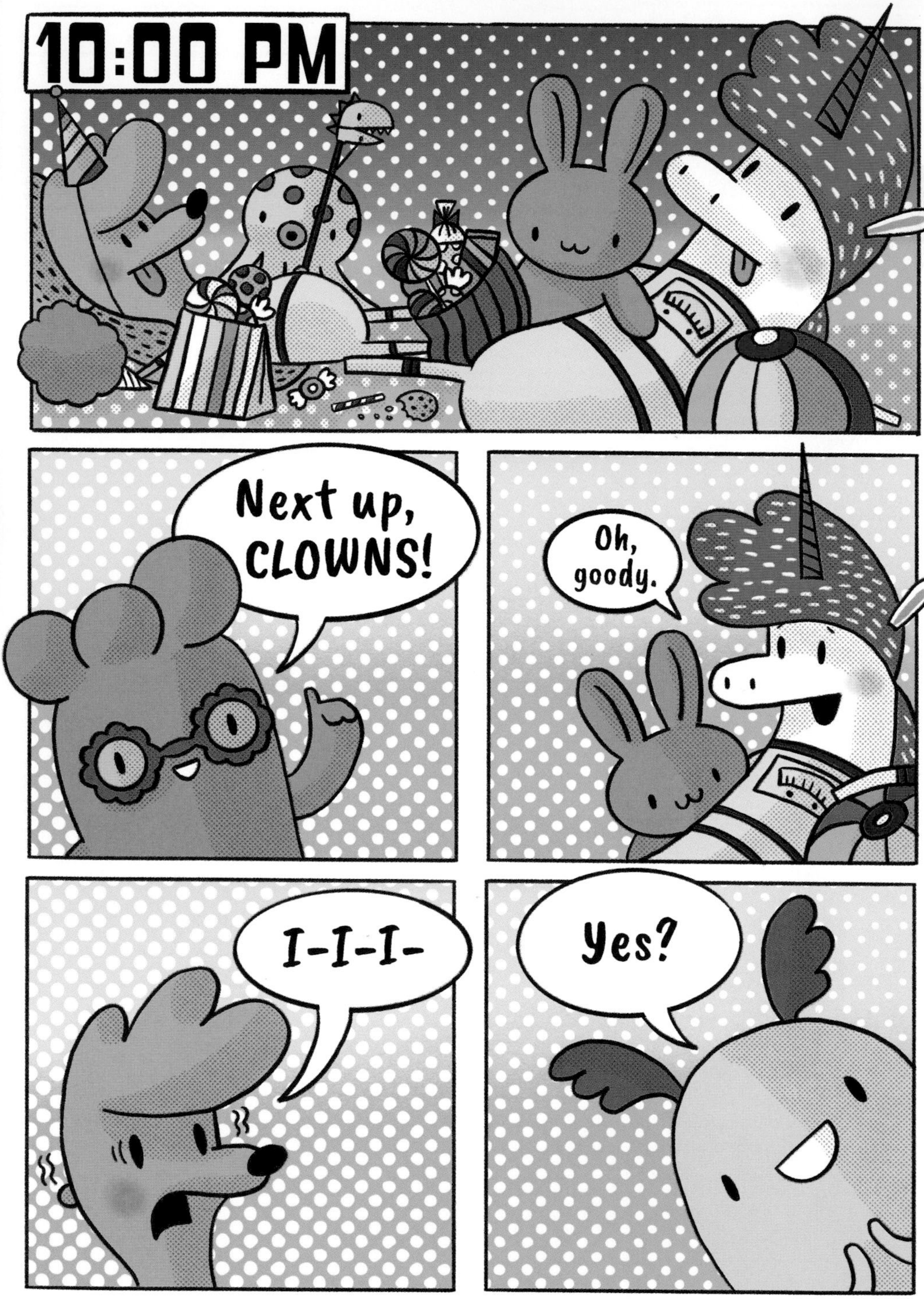
10:00 PM
Next up, CLOWNS!
Oh, goody.
I-I-I-
Yes?

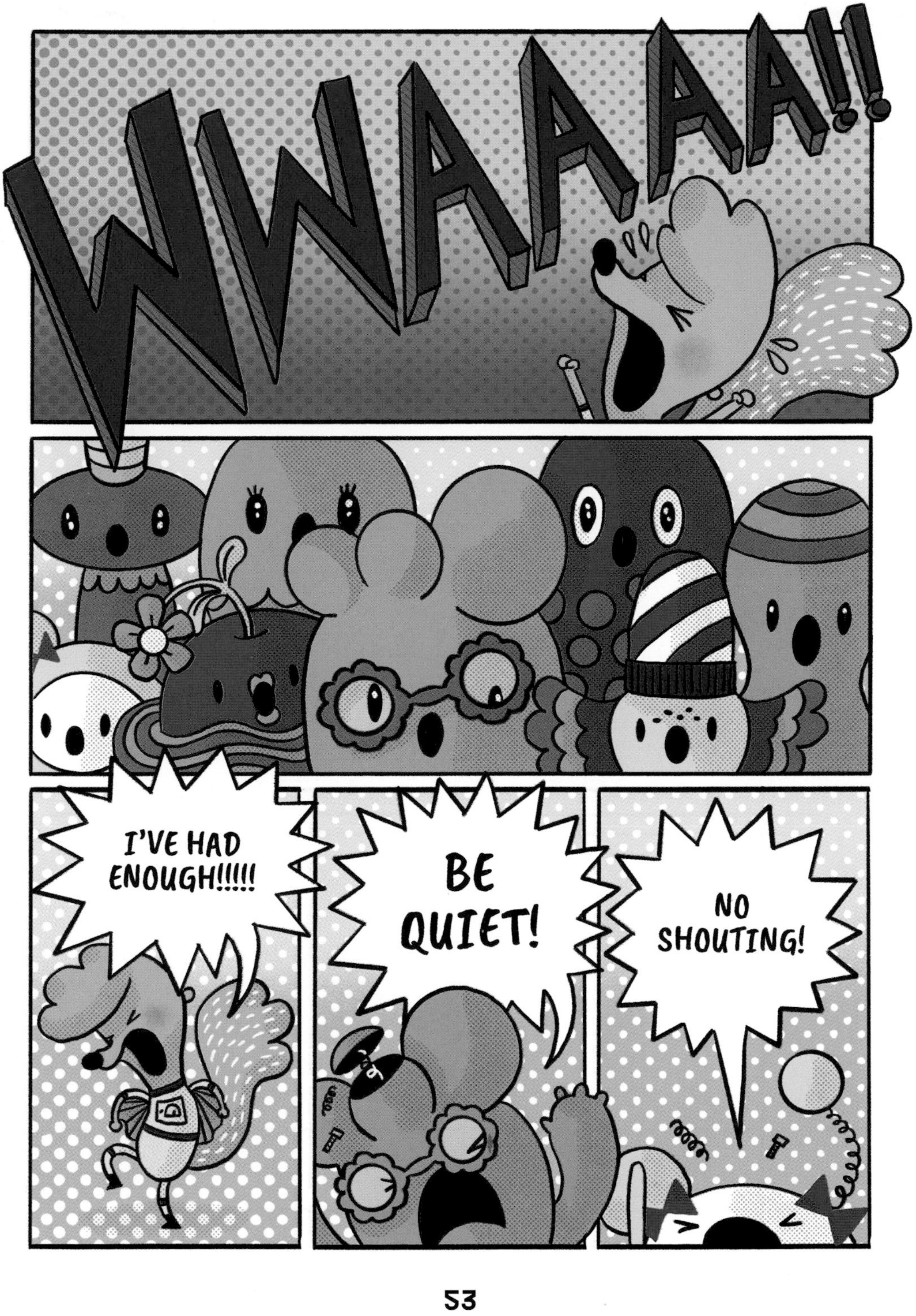
WWAAAAA!!!
I'VE HAD ENOUGH!!!!!
BE QUIET!
NO SHOUTING!

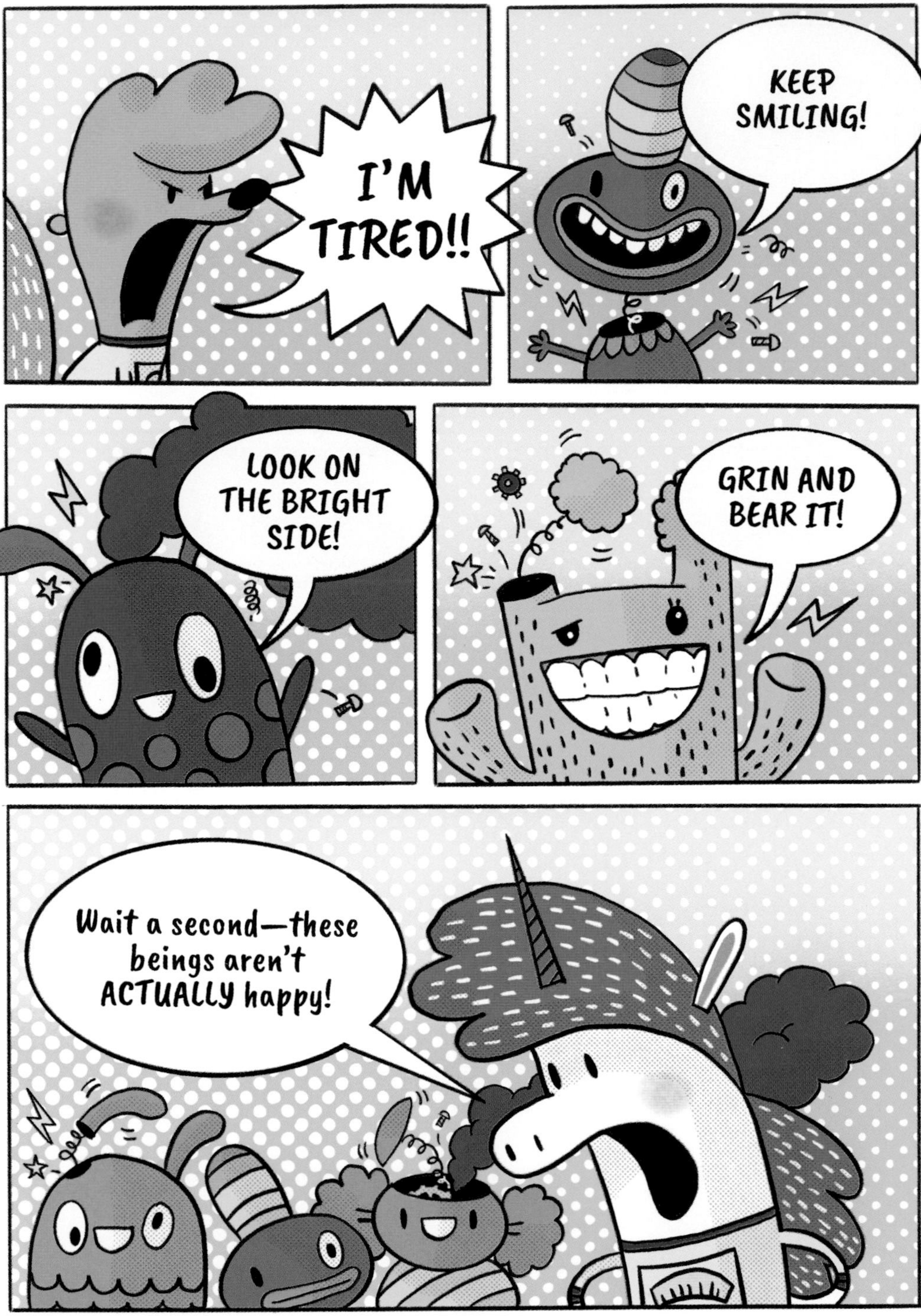
I'M TIRED!!
KEEP SMILING!
LOOK ON THE BRIGHT SIDE!
GRIN AND BEAR IT!
Wait a second—these beings aren't ACTUALLY happy!

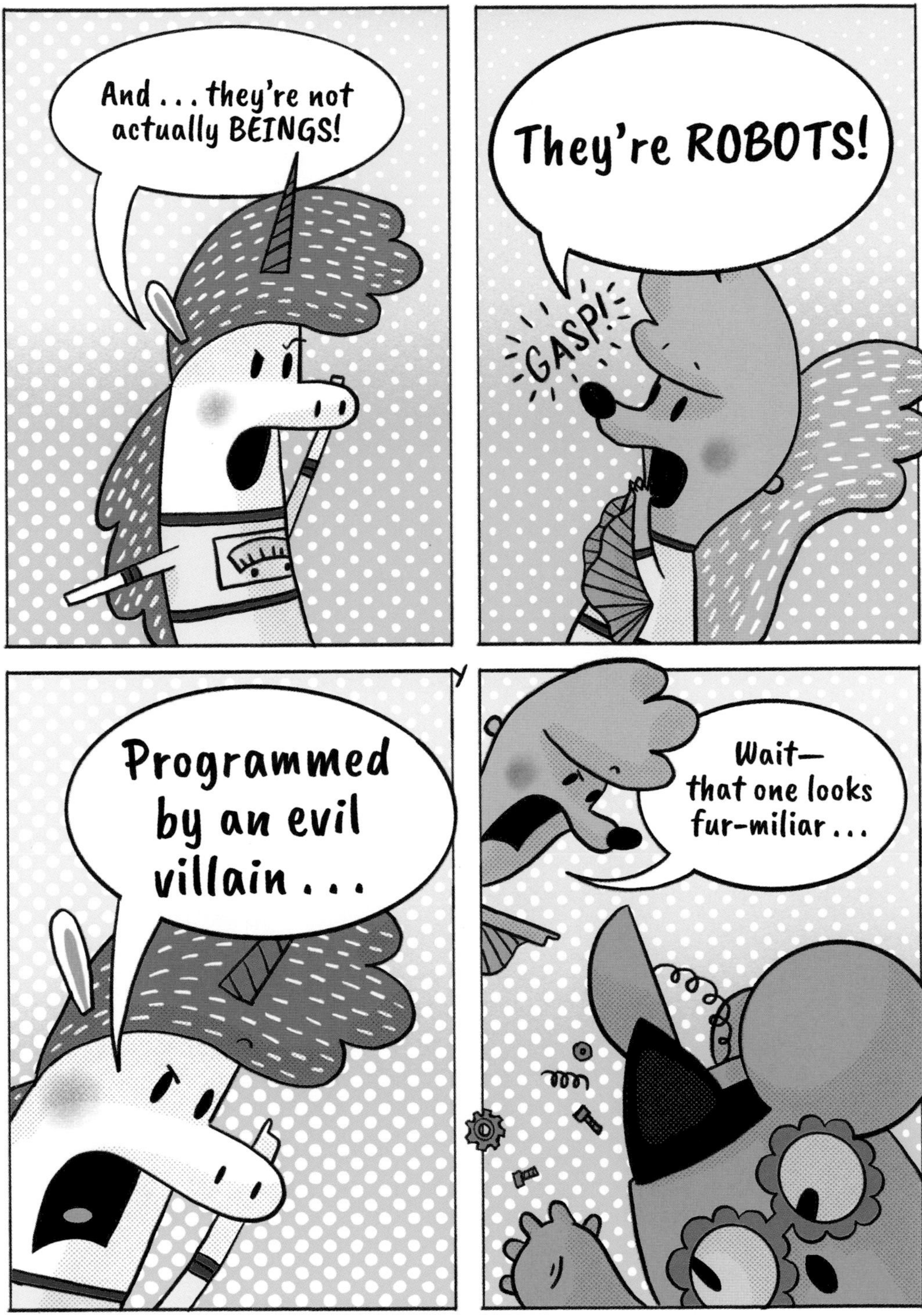
And . . . they're not actually BEINGS!
They're ROBOTS!
GASP!
Programmed by an evil villain . . .
Wait— that one looks fur-miliar . . .

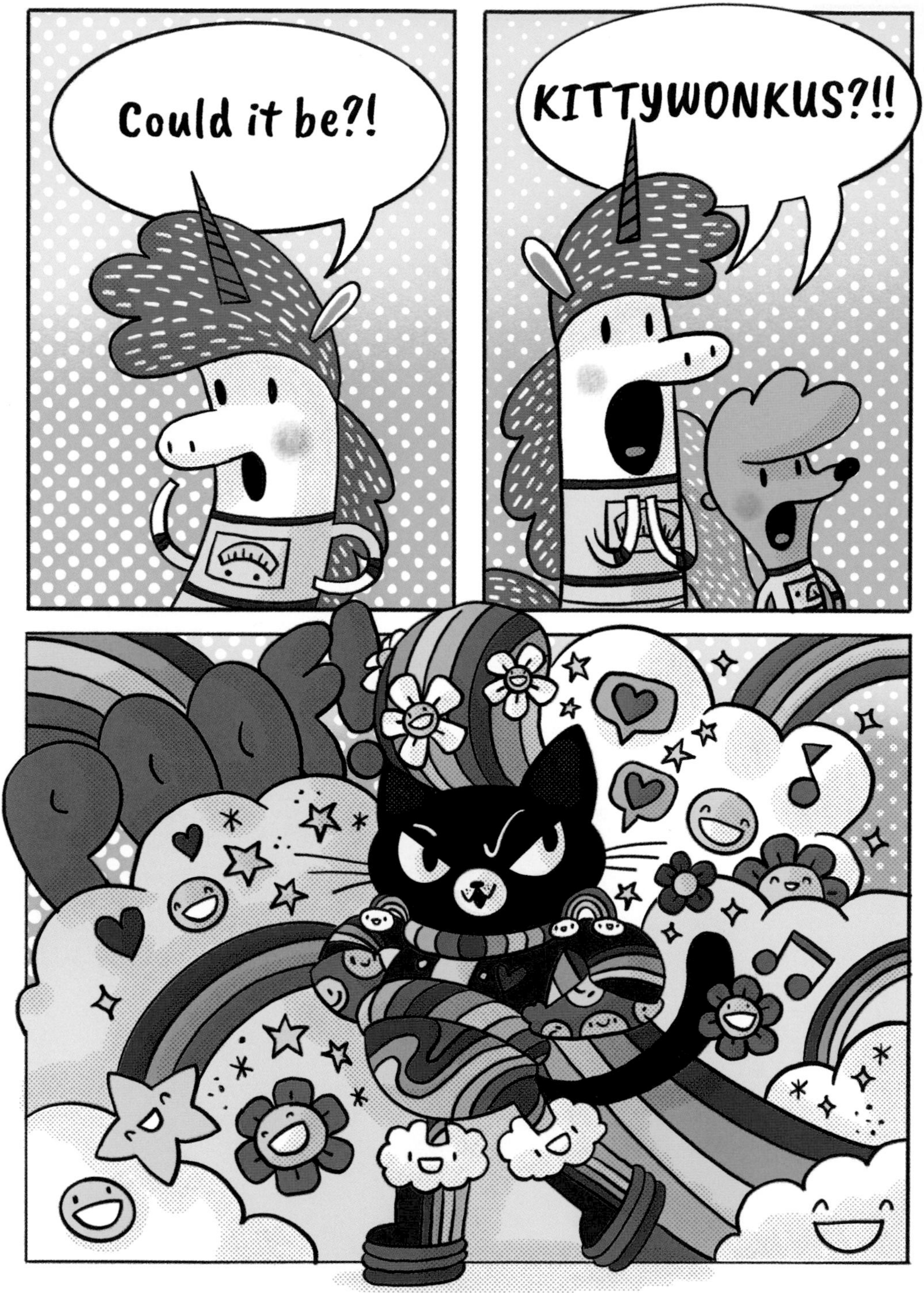
Could it be?!
KITTYWONKUS?!!

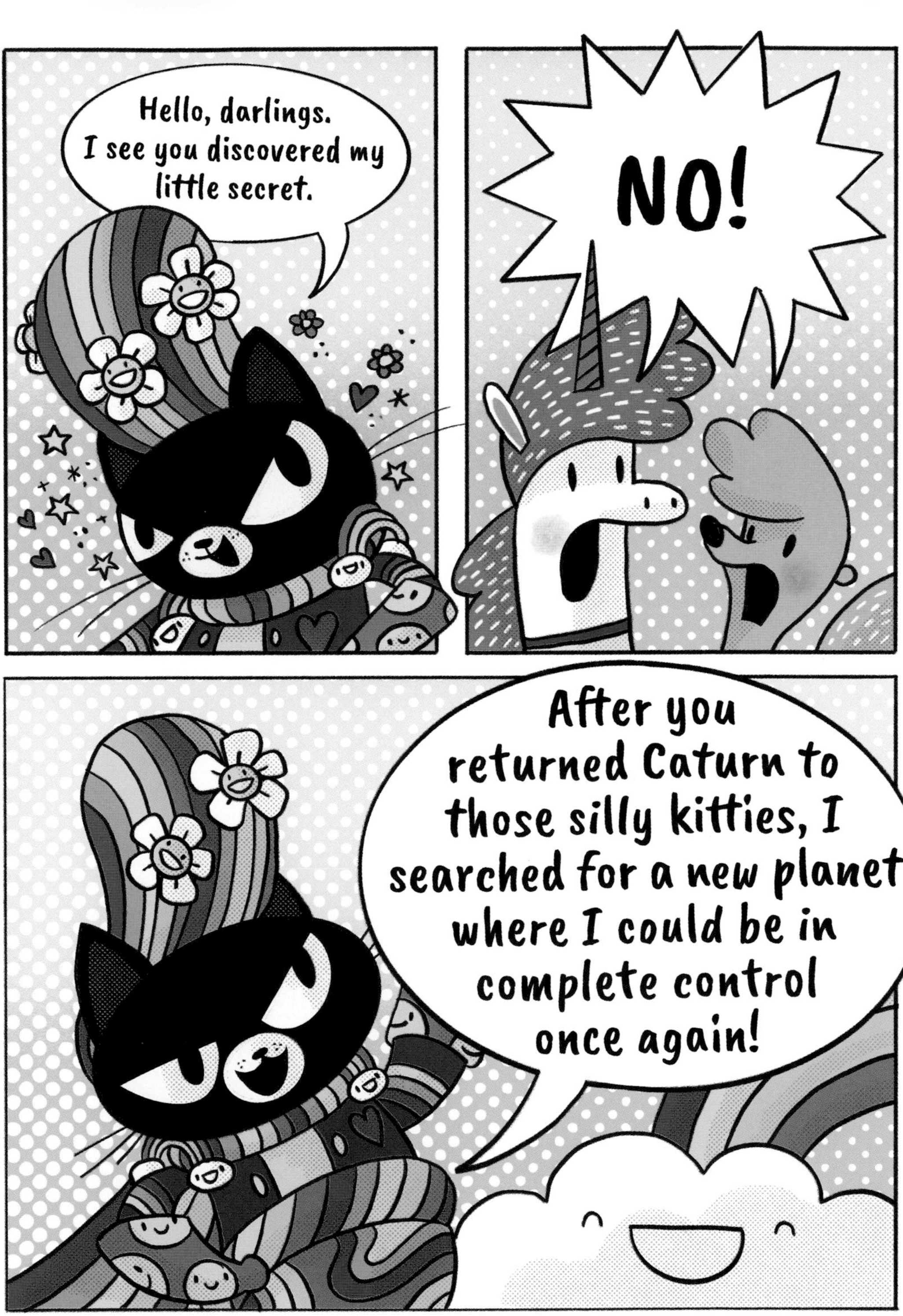
Hello, darlings. I see you discovered my little secret.
NO!
After you returned Caturn to those silly kitties, I searched for a new planet where I could be in complete control once again!

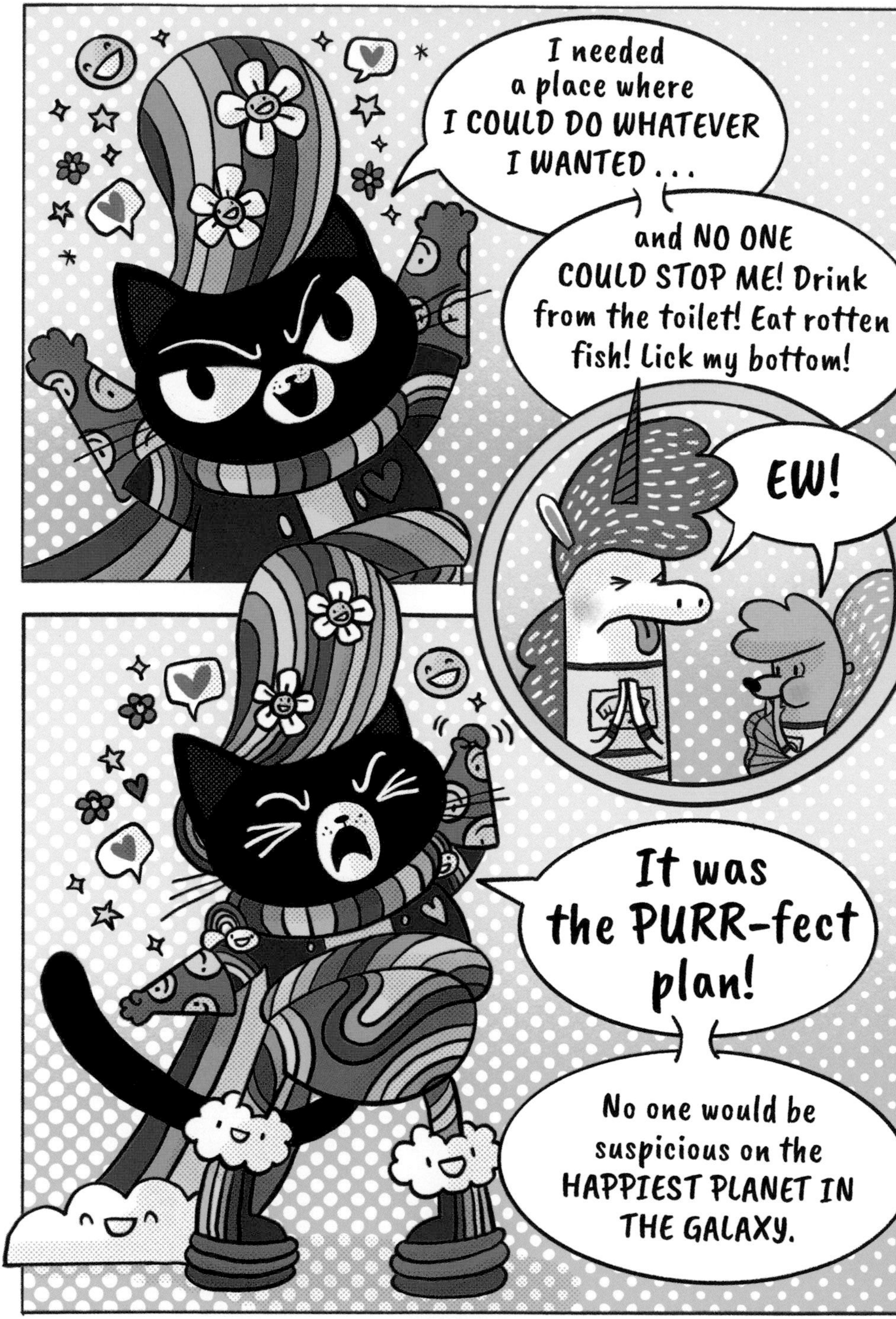
I needed a place where I COULD DO WHATEVER I WANTED . . .
and NO ONE COULD STOP ME! Drink from the toilet! Eat rotten fish! Lick my bottom!
EW!
It was the PURR-fect plan!
No one would be suspicious on the HAPPIEST PLANET IN THE GALAXY.

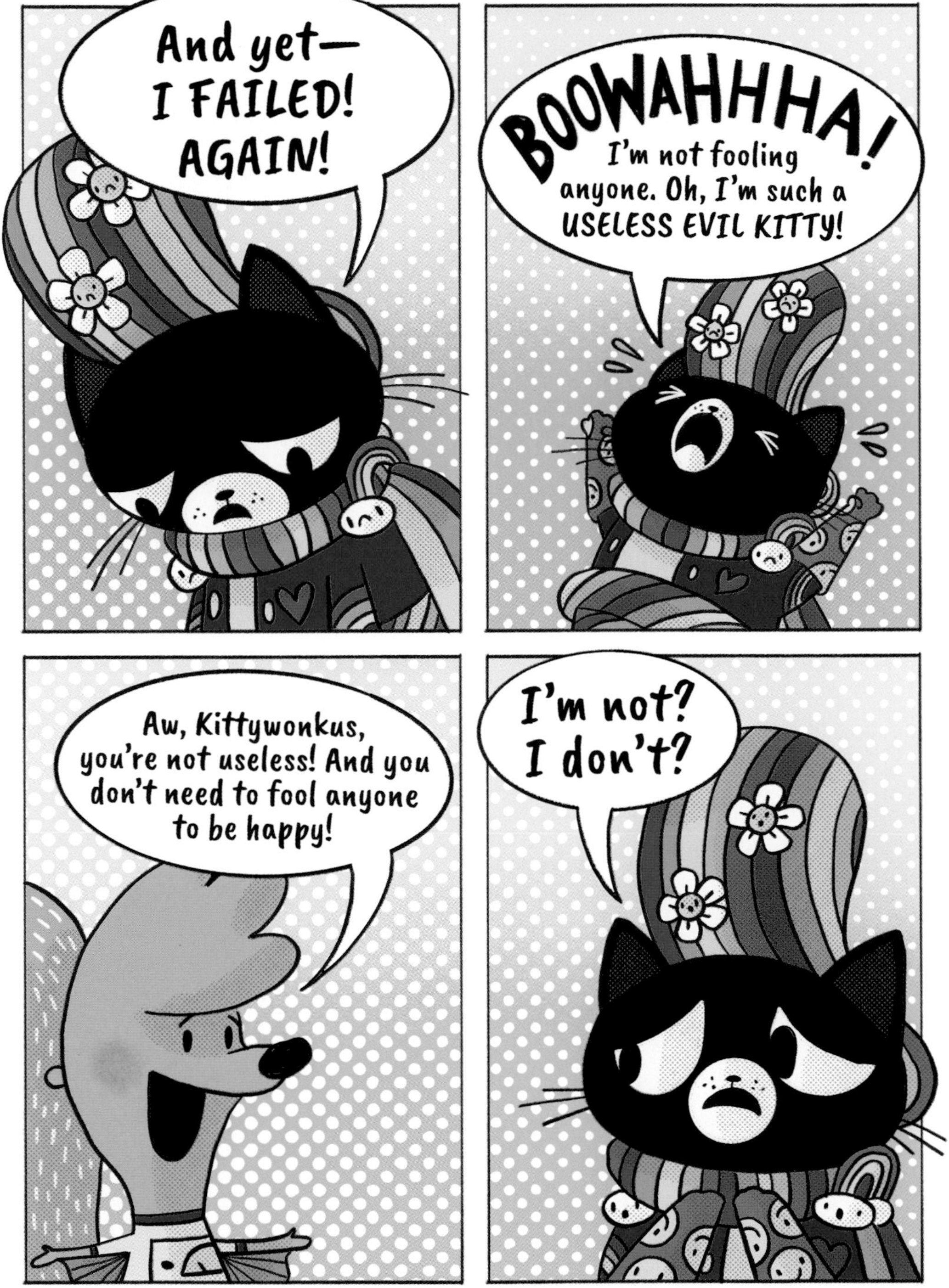
And yet—
I FAILED!
AGAIN!
BOOWAHHHA!
I'm not fooling anyone. Oh, I'm such a USELESS EVIL KITTY!
Aw, Kittywonkus, you're not useless! And you don't need to fool anyone to be happy!
I'm not?
I don't?

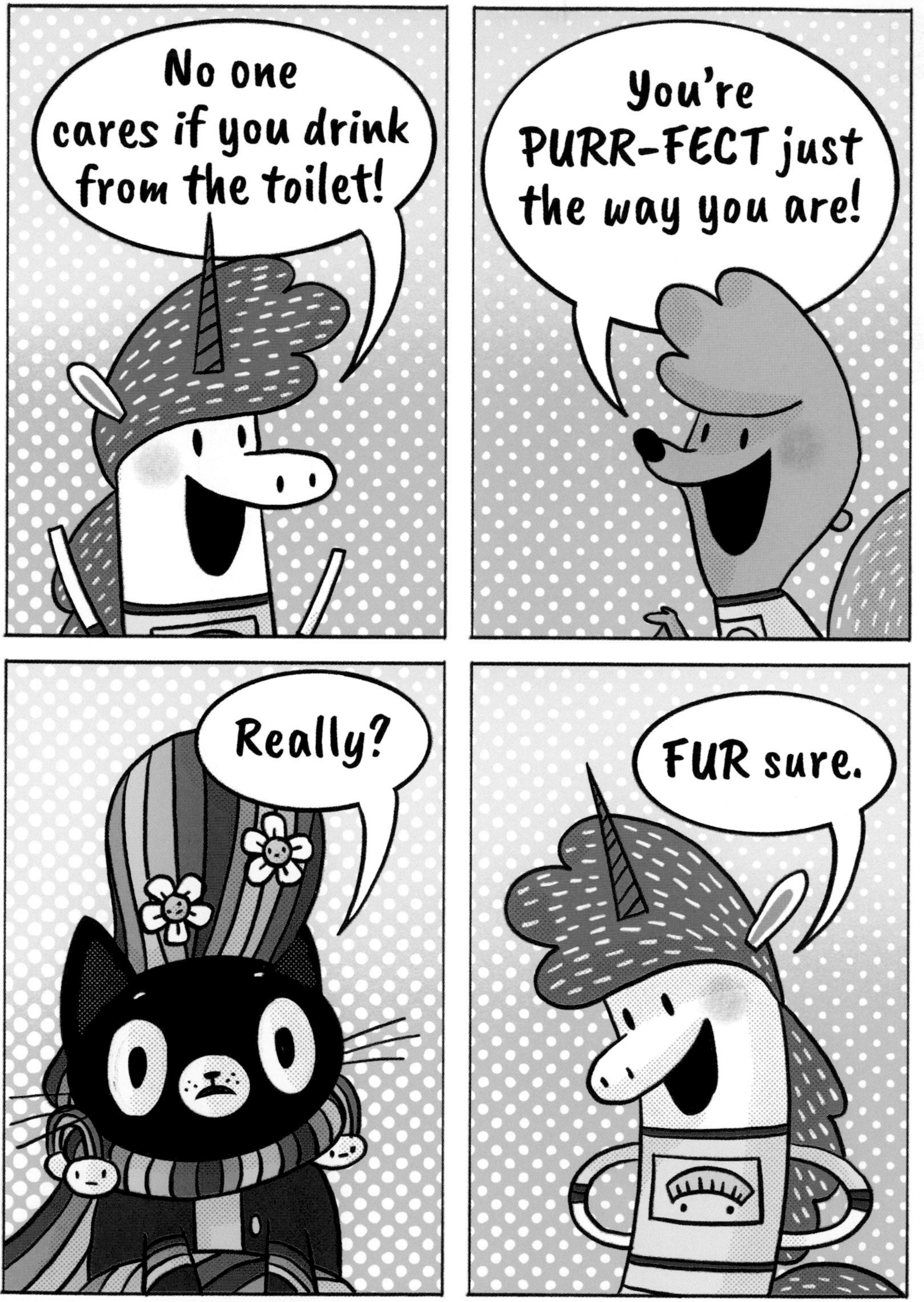
No one cares if you drink from the toilet!
You're PURR-FECT just the way you are!
Really?
FUR sure.

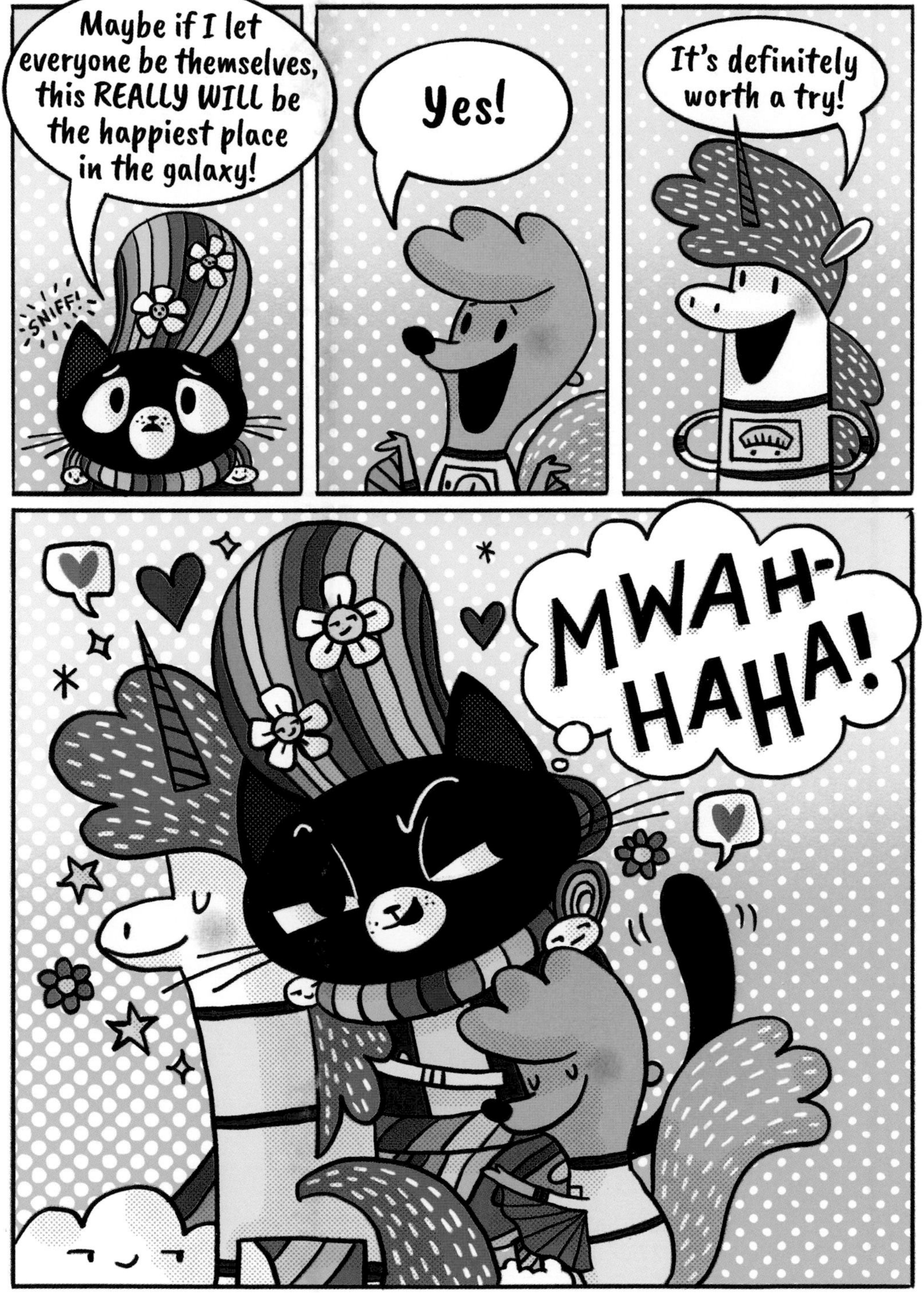
Maybe if I let everyone be themselves, this REALLY WILL be the happiest place in the galaxy!
SNIFF!
Yes!
It's definitely worth a try!
MWAH-HAHA!

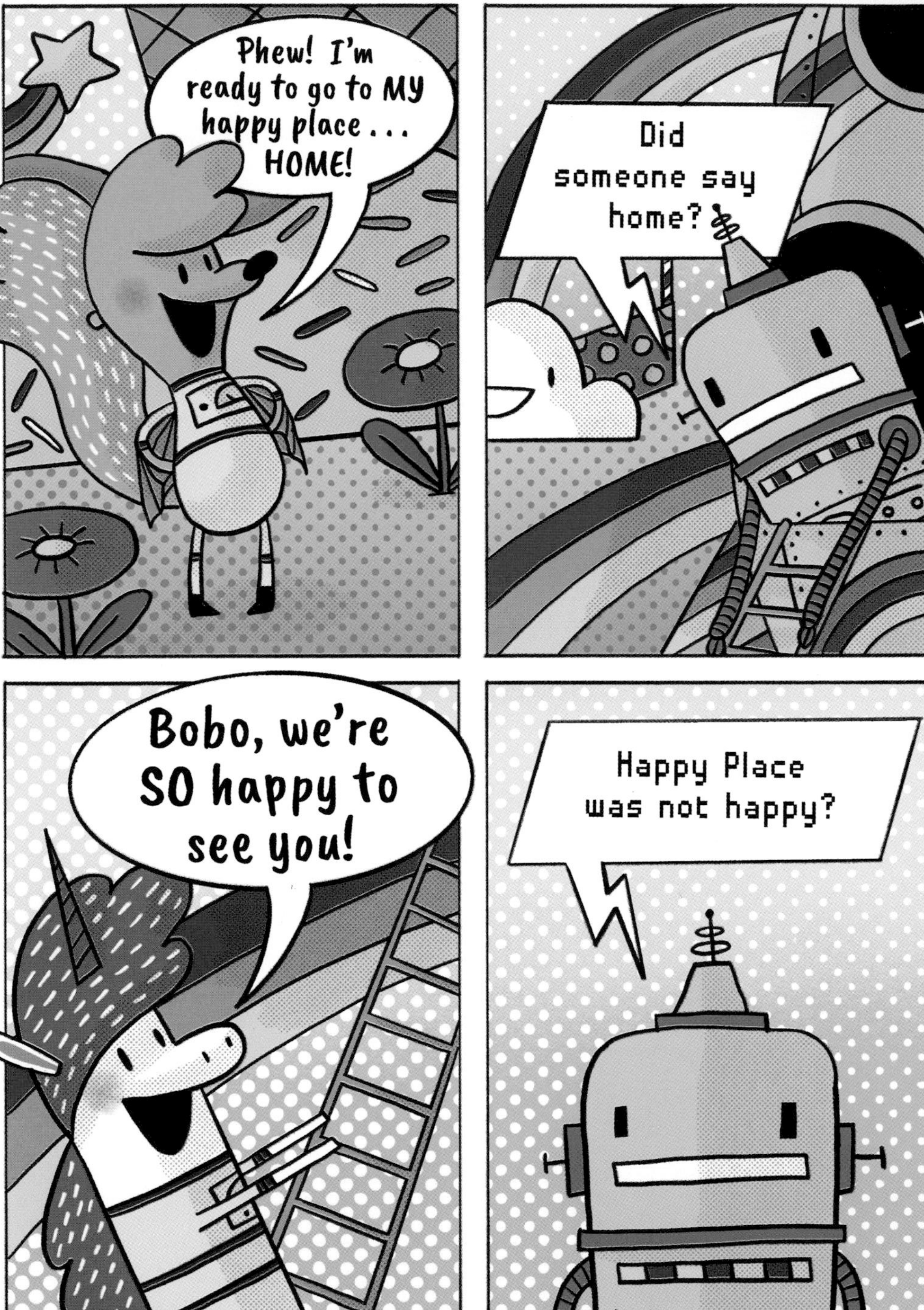
Phew! I'm ready to go to MY happy place . . . HOME!
Did someone say home?
Bobo, we're SO happy to see you!
Happy Place was not happy?

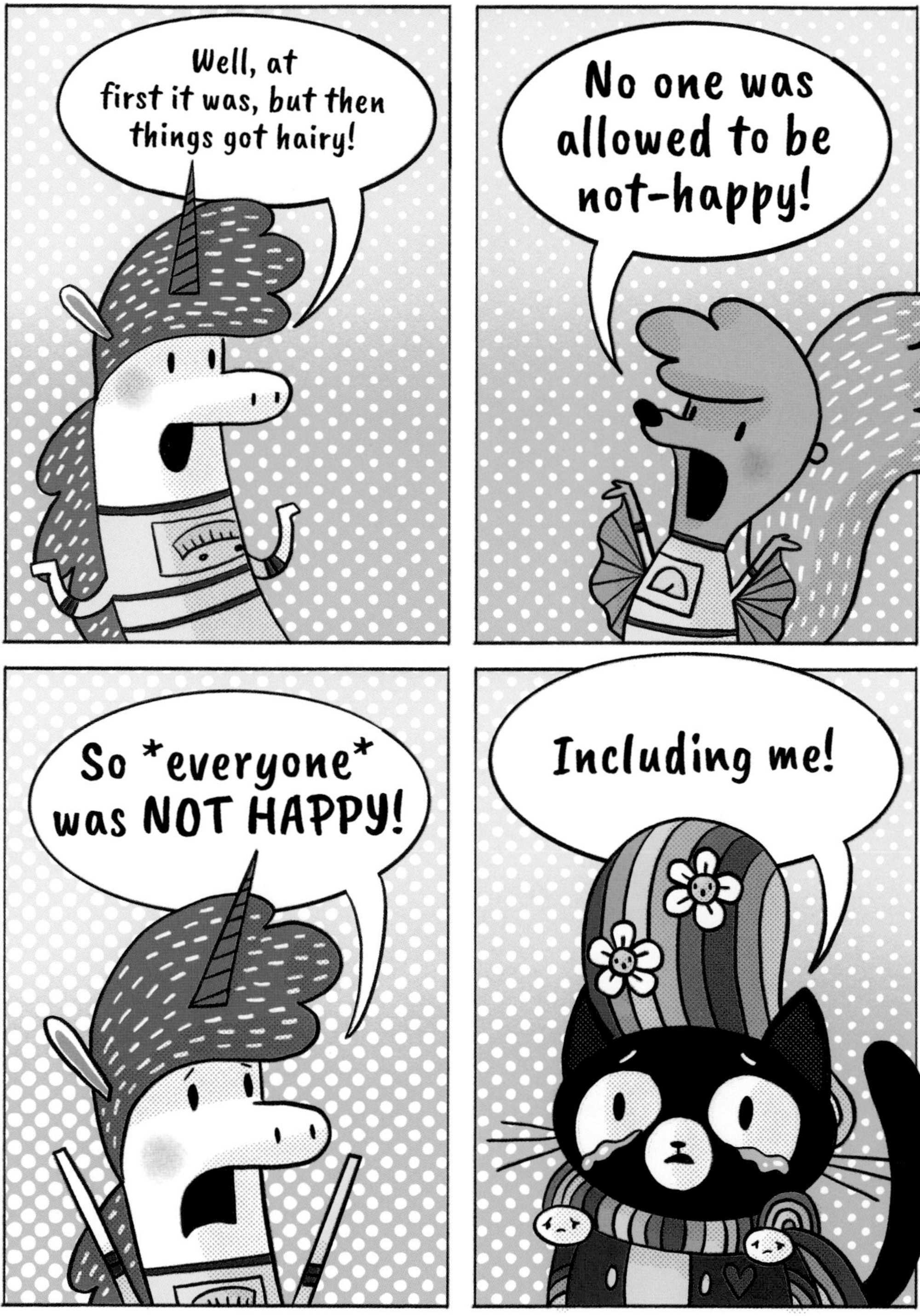

Well, at first it was, but then things got hairy!
No one was allowed to be not-happy!
So *everyone* was NOT HAPPY!
Including me!

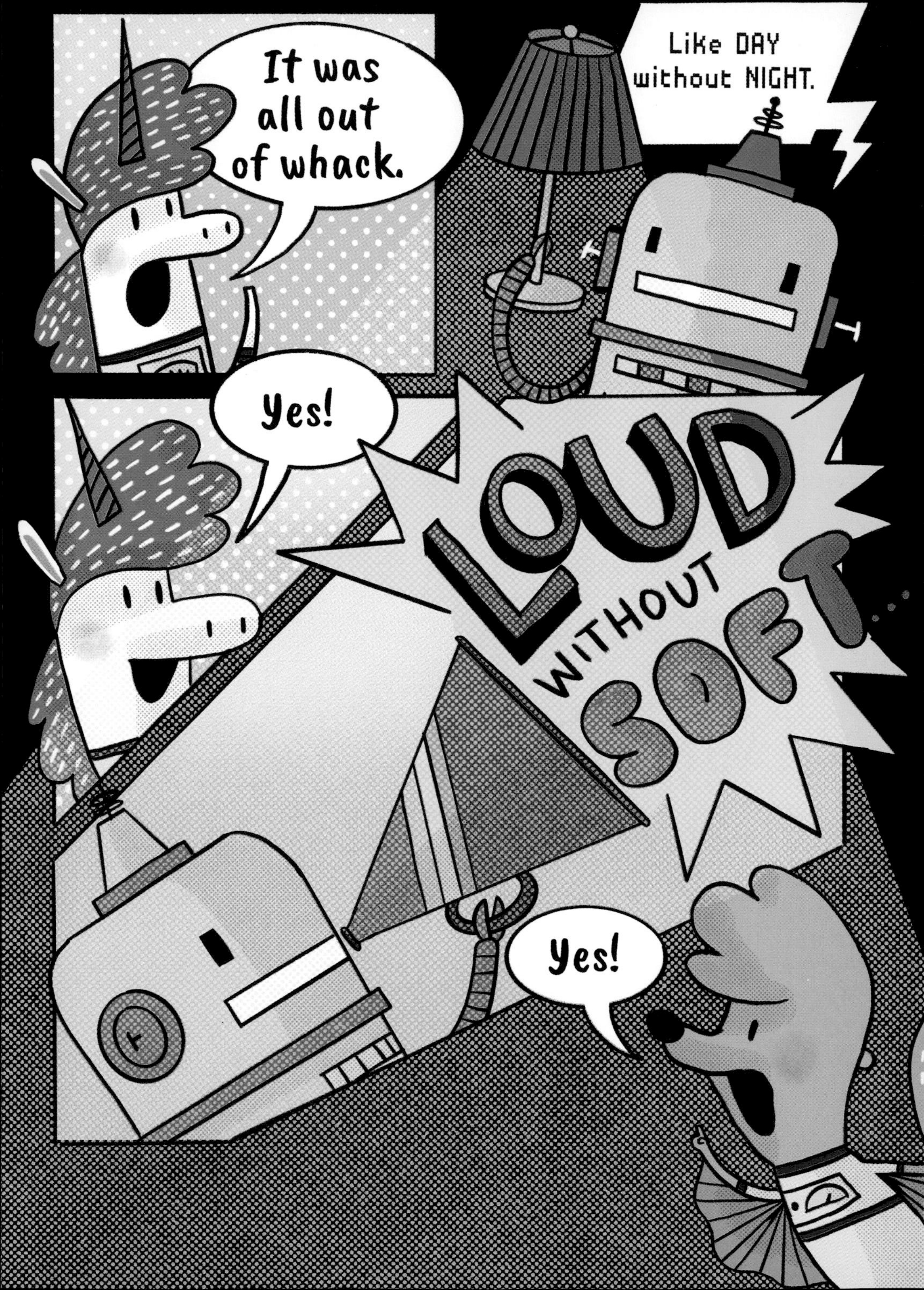

It was all out of whack.
Like DAY without NIGHT.
Yes!
LOUD WITHOUT SOFT...
Yes!

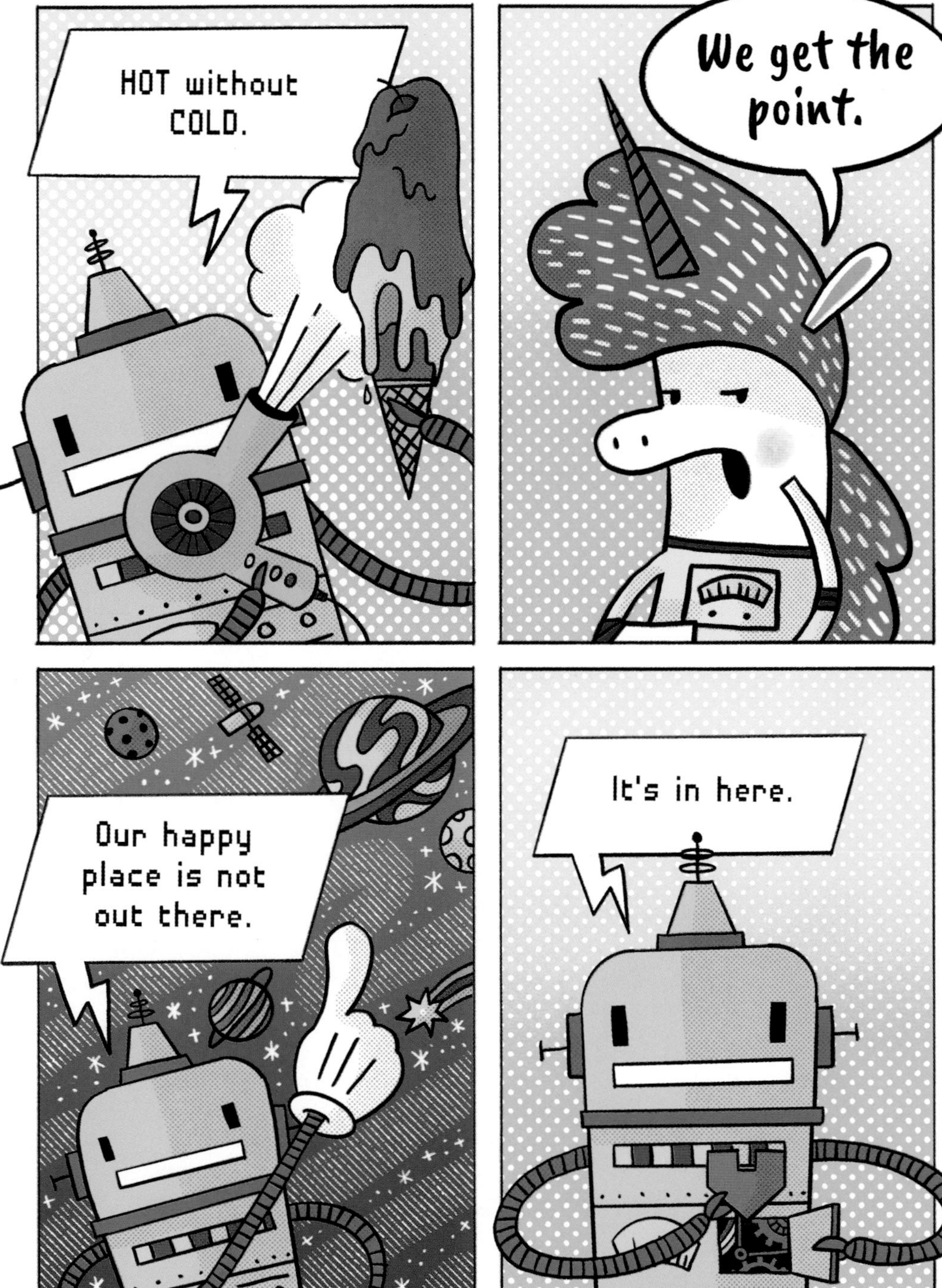

HOT without COLD.
We get the point.
Our happy place is not out there.
It's in here.

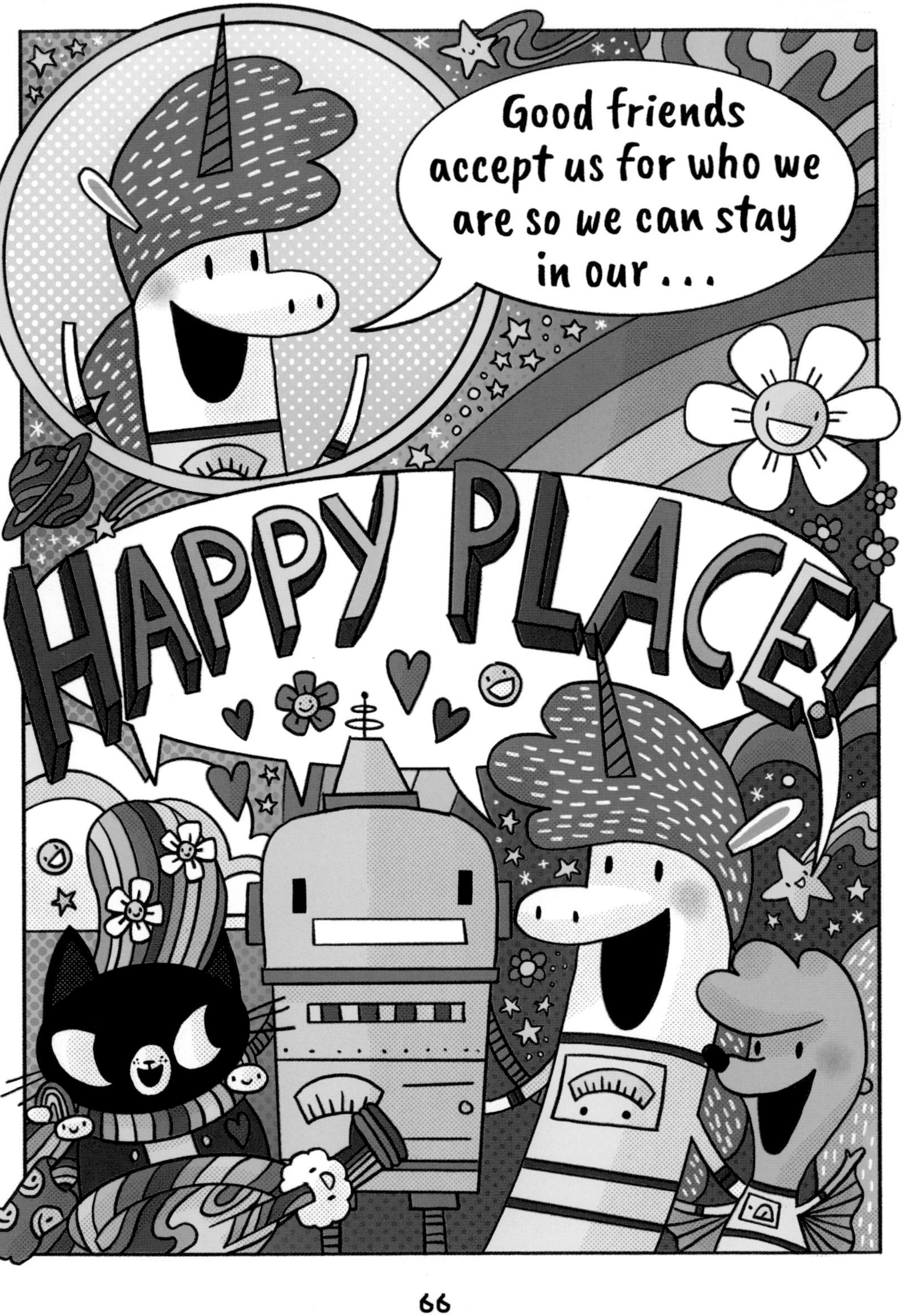
Good friends accept us for who we are so we can stay in our . . .
HAPPY PLACE!

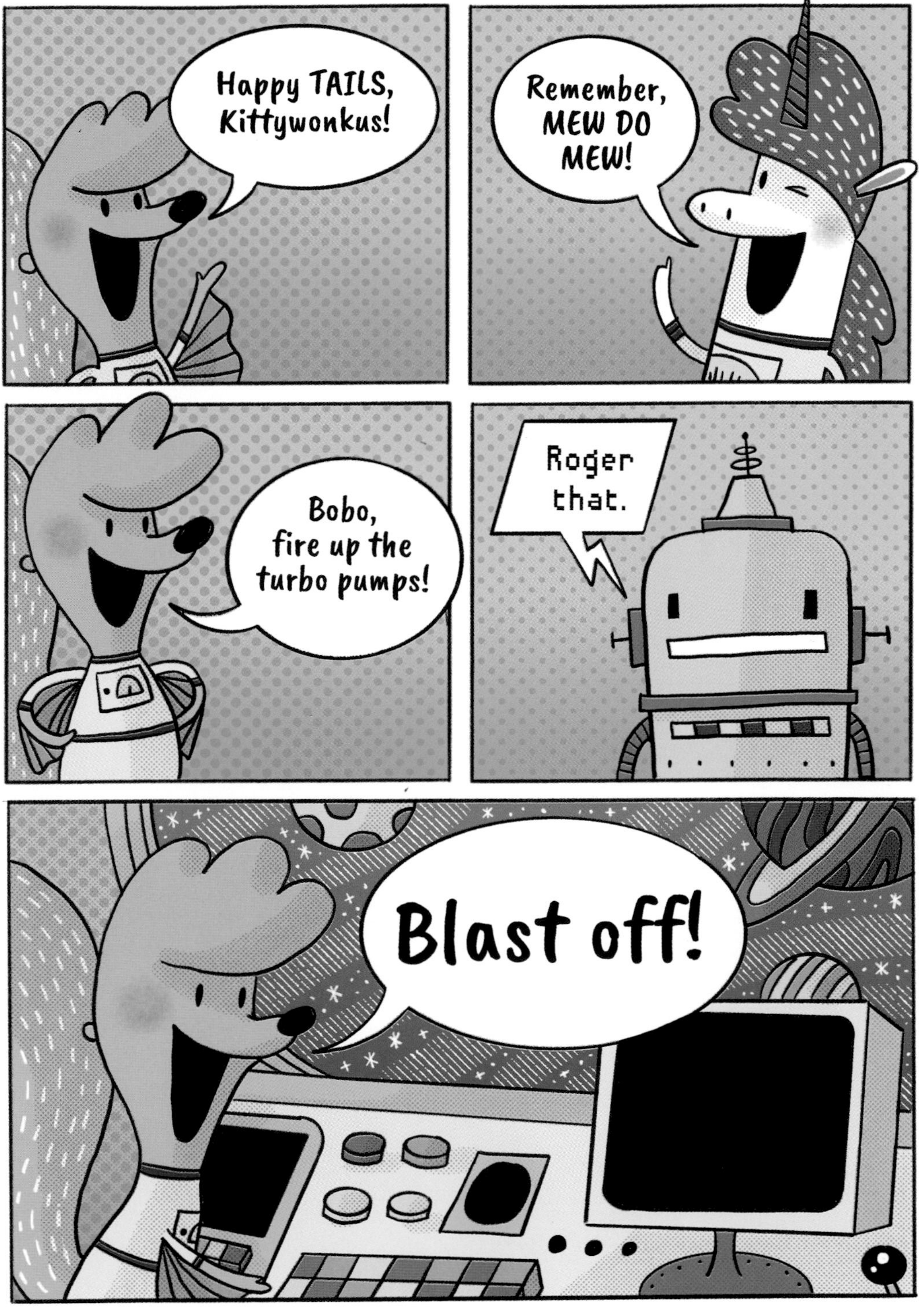
Happy TAILS, Kittywonkus!
Remember, MEW DO MEW!
Bobo, fire up the turbo pumps!
Roger that.
Blast off!

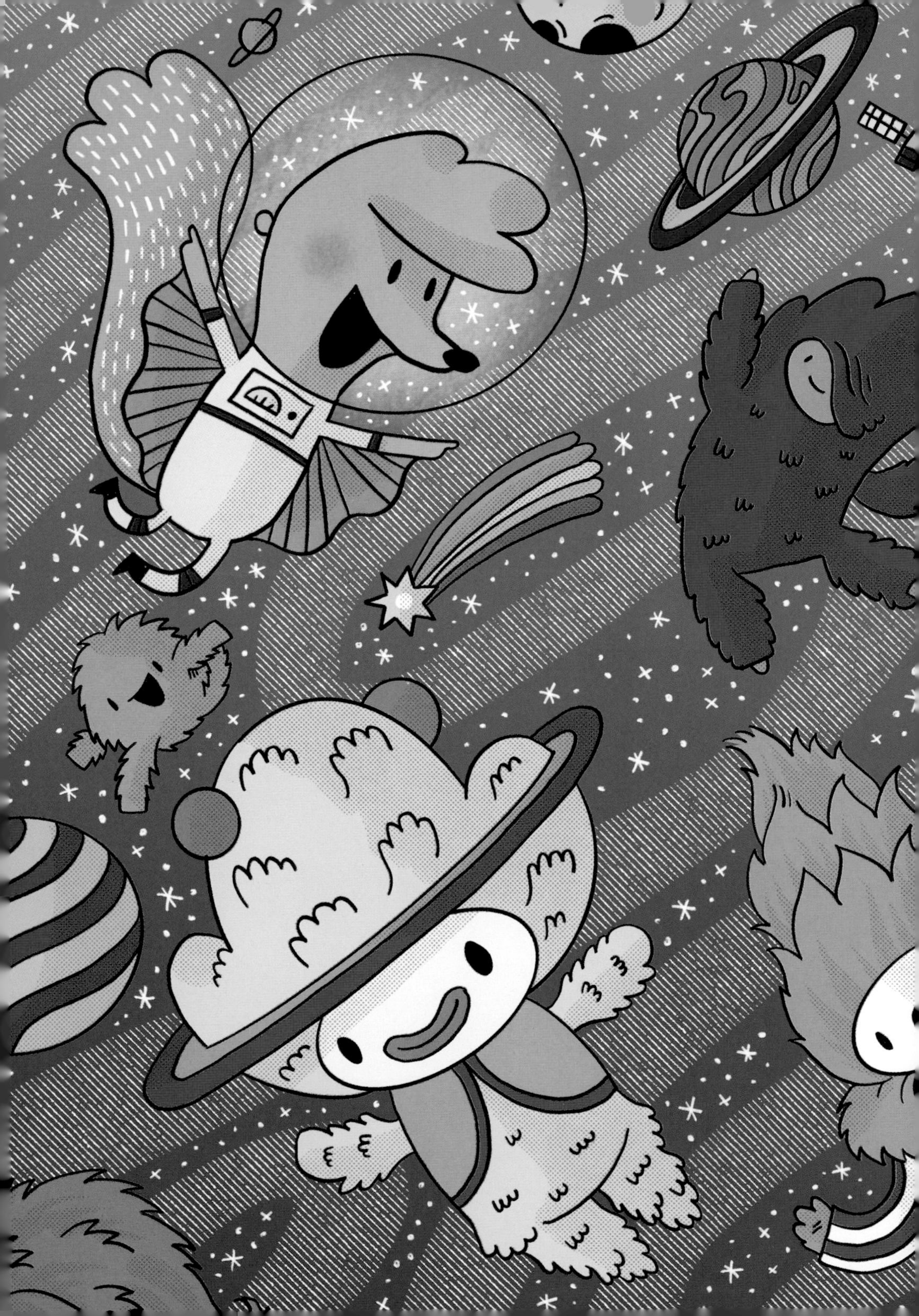

CHAPTER THREE
STAR STRUCK!

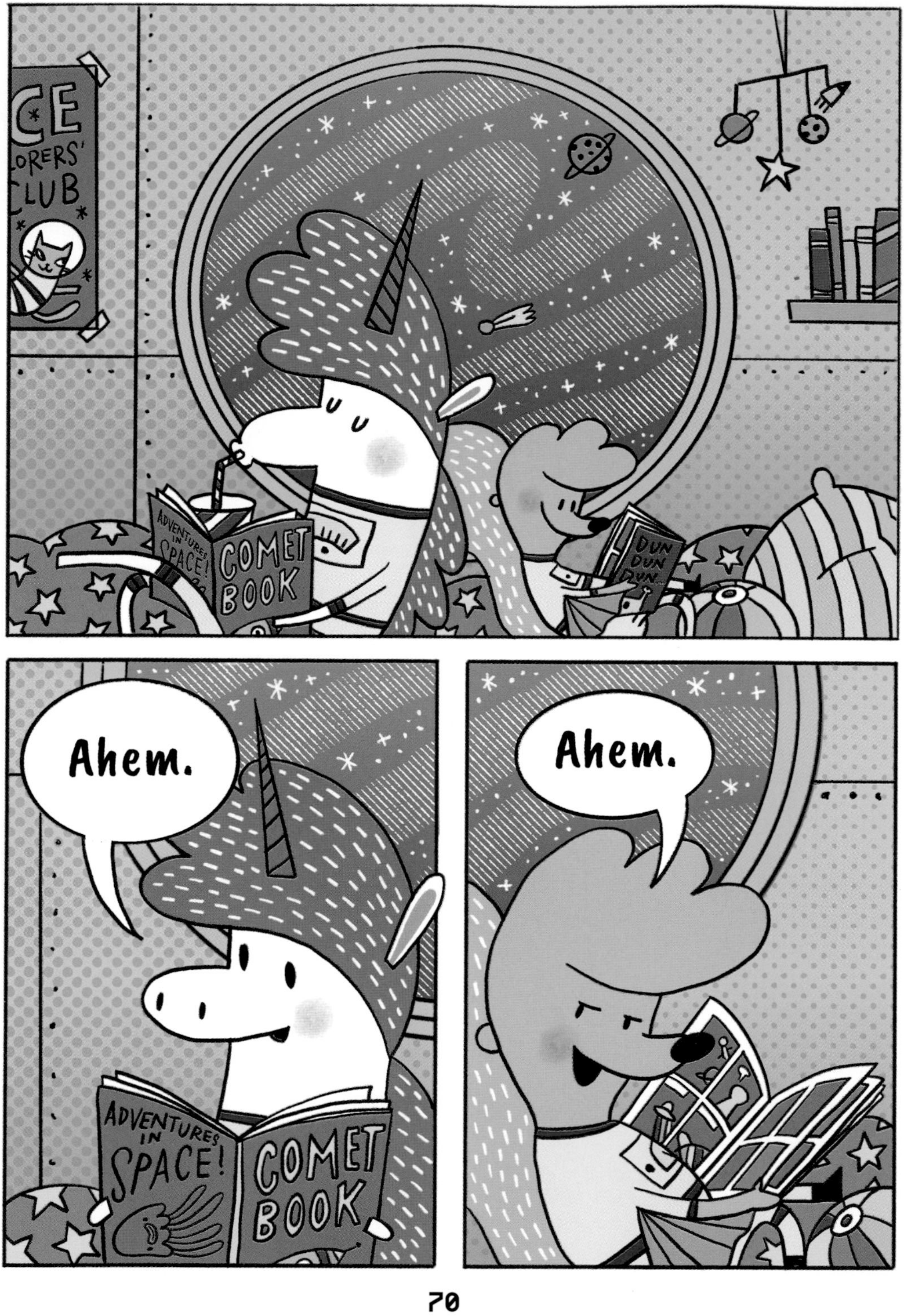

CE
LORERS'
CLUB
ADVENTURES IN SPACE!
COMET BOOK
DUN DUN DUN...
Ahem.
ADVENTURES IN SPACE!
COMET BOOK
Ahem.

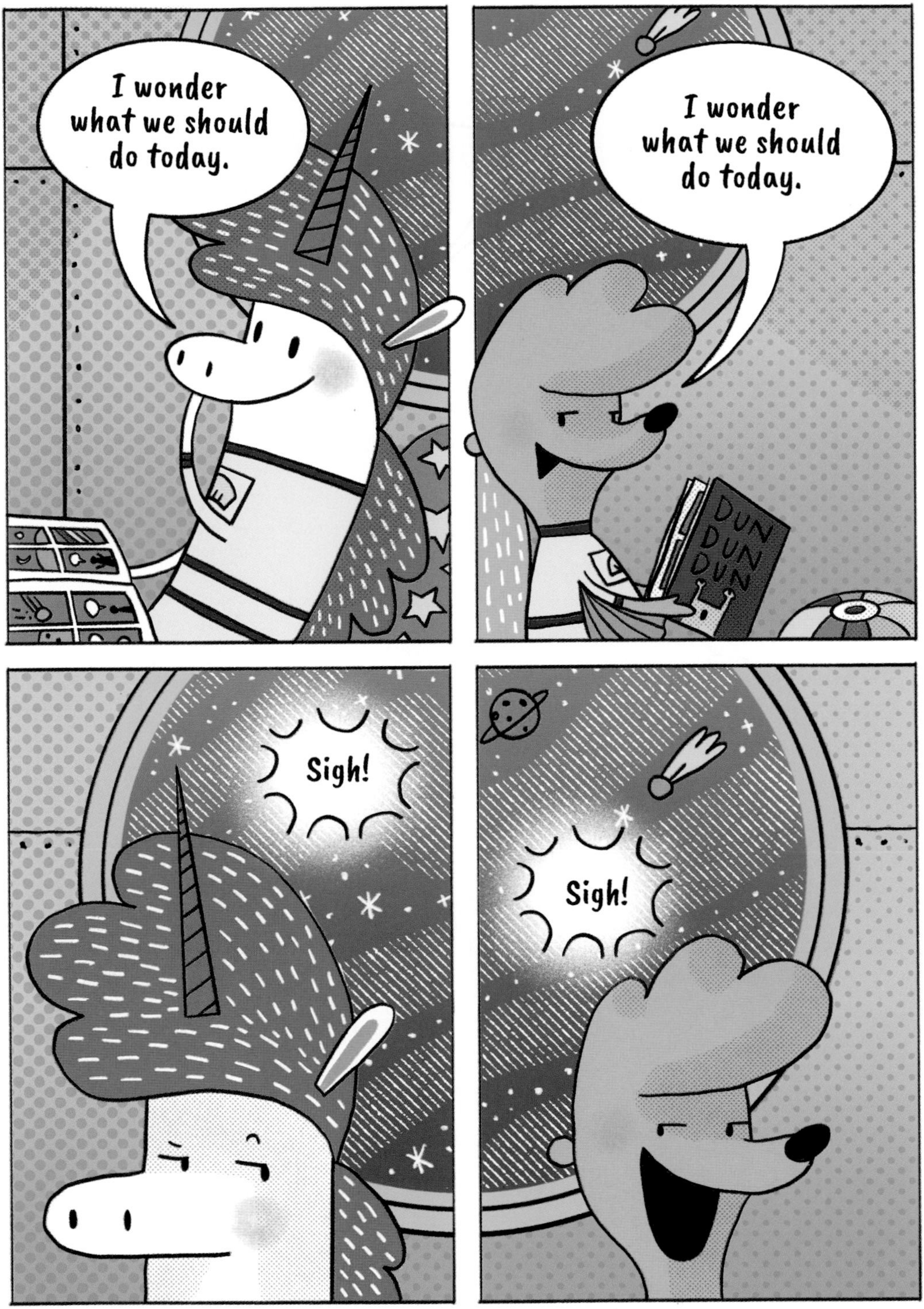
I wonder what we should do today.
I wonder what we should do today.
DUN DUN DUN
Sigh!
Sigh!

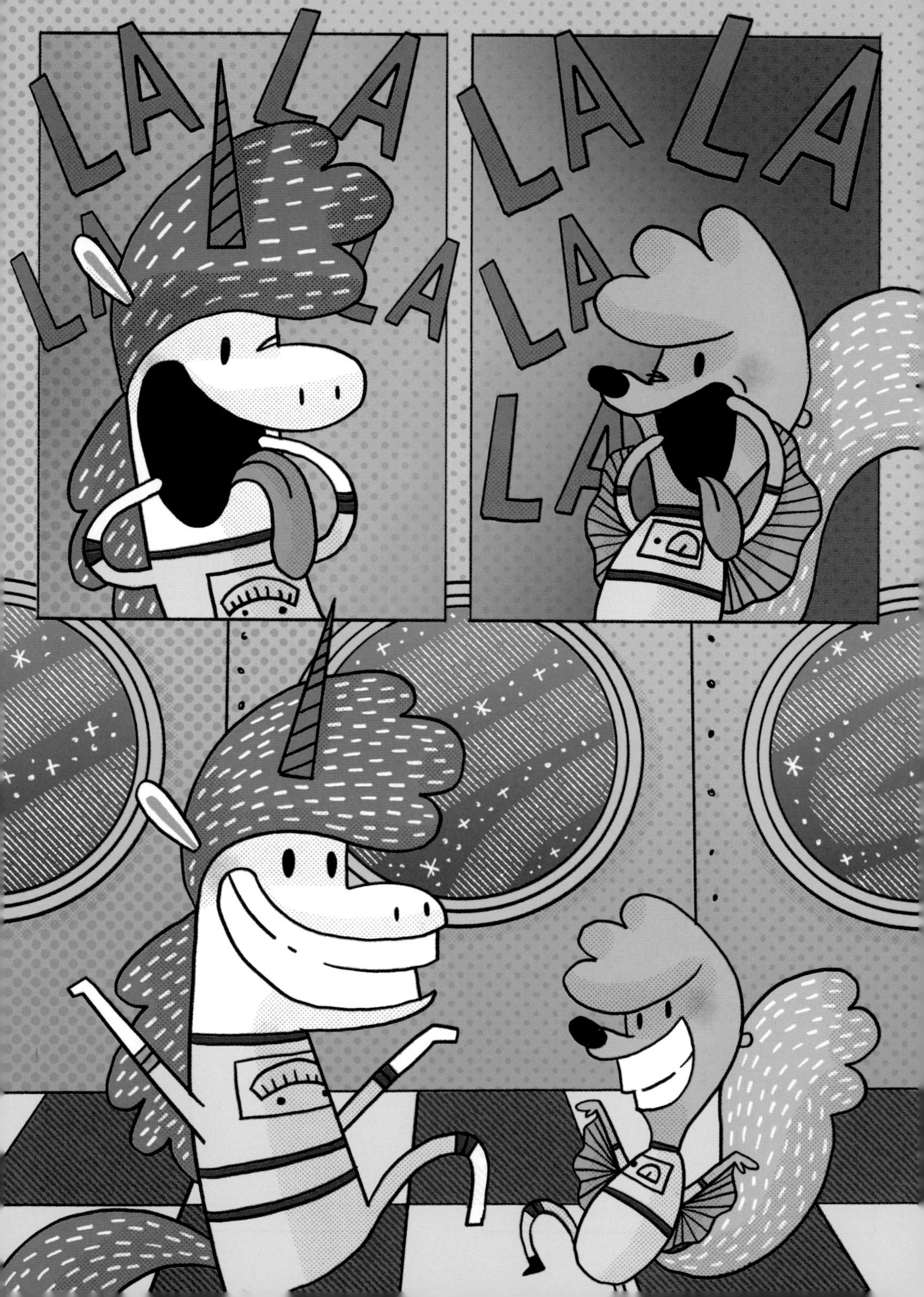
LA LA
LA LA
LA LA
LA
LA

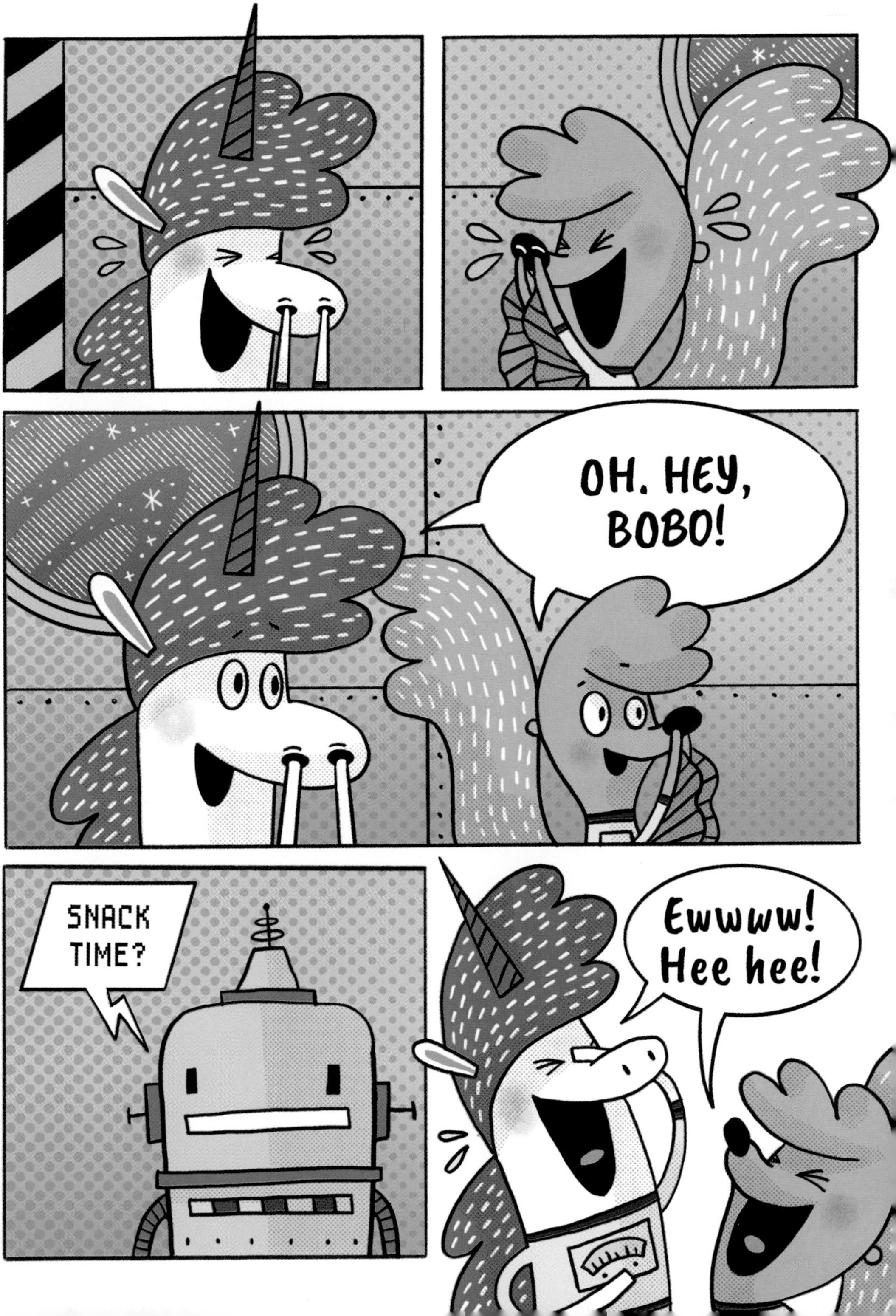

OH. HEY, BOBO!
SNACK TIME?
Ewwww! Hee hee!

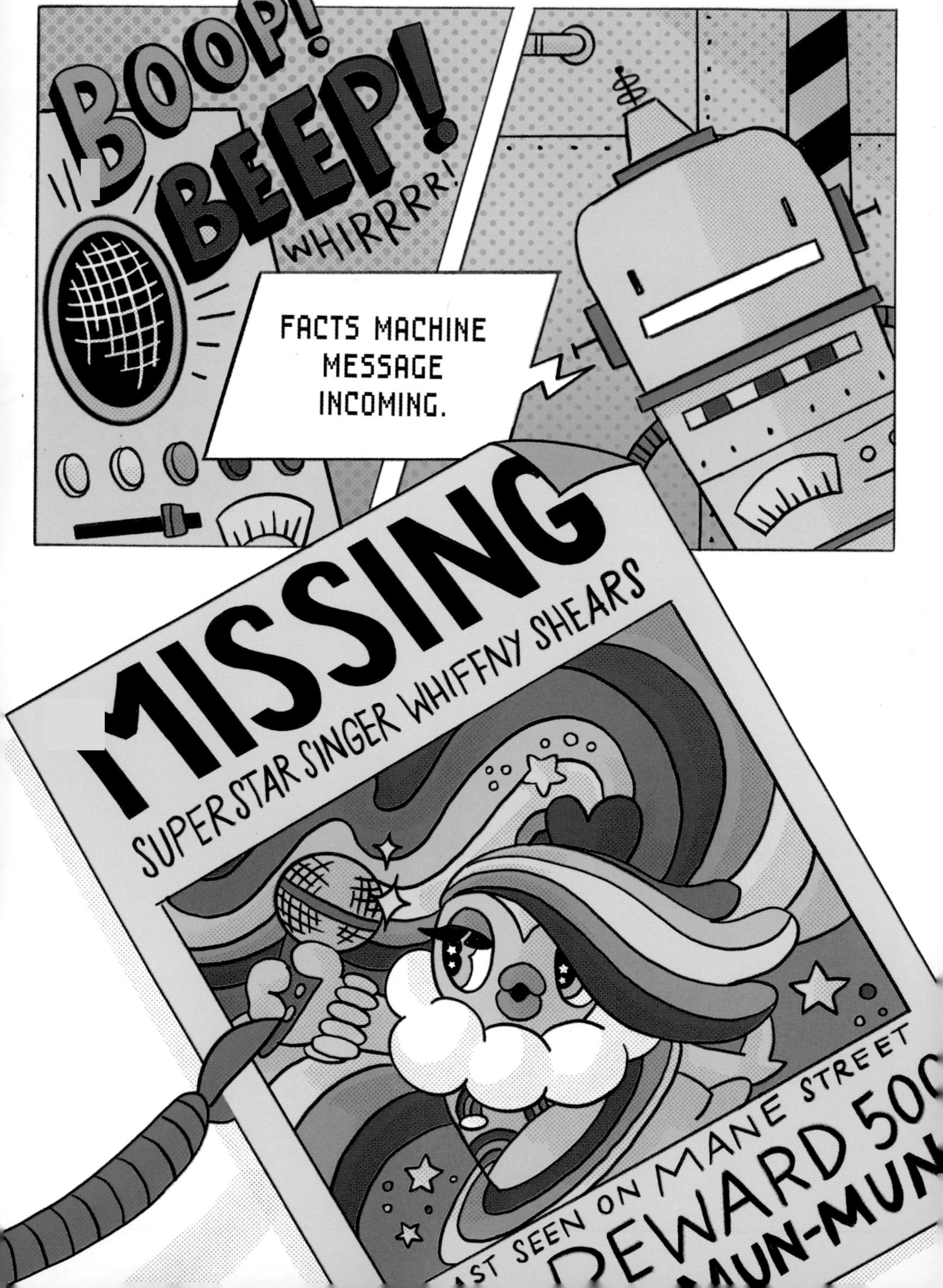
BOOP!
BEEP!
WHIRRRR!
FACTS MACHINE MESSAGE INCOMING.
MISSING
SUPERSTAR SINGER WHIFFNY SHEARS
AST SEEN ON MANE STREET

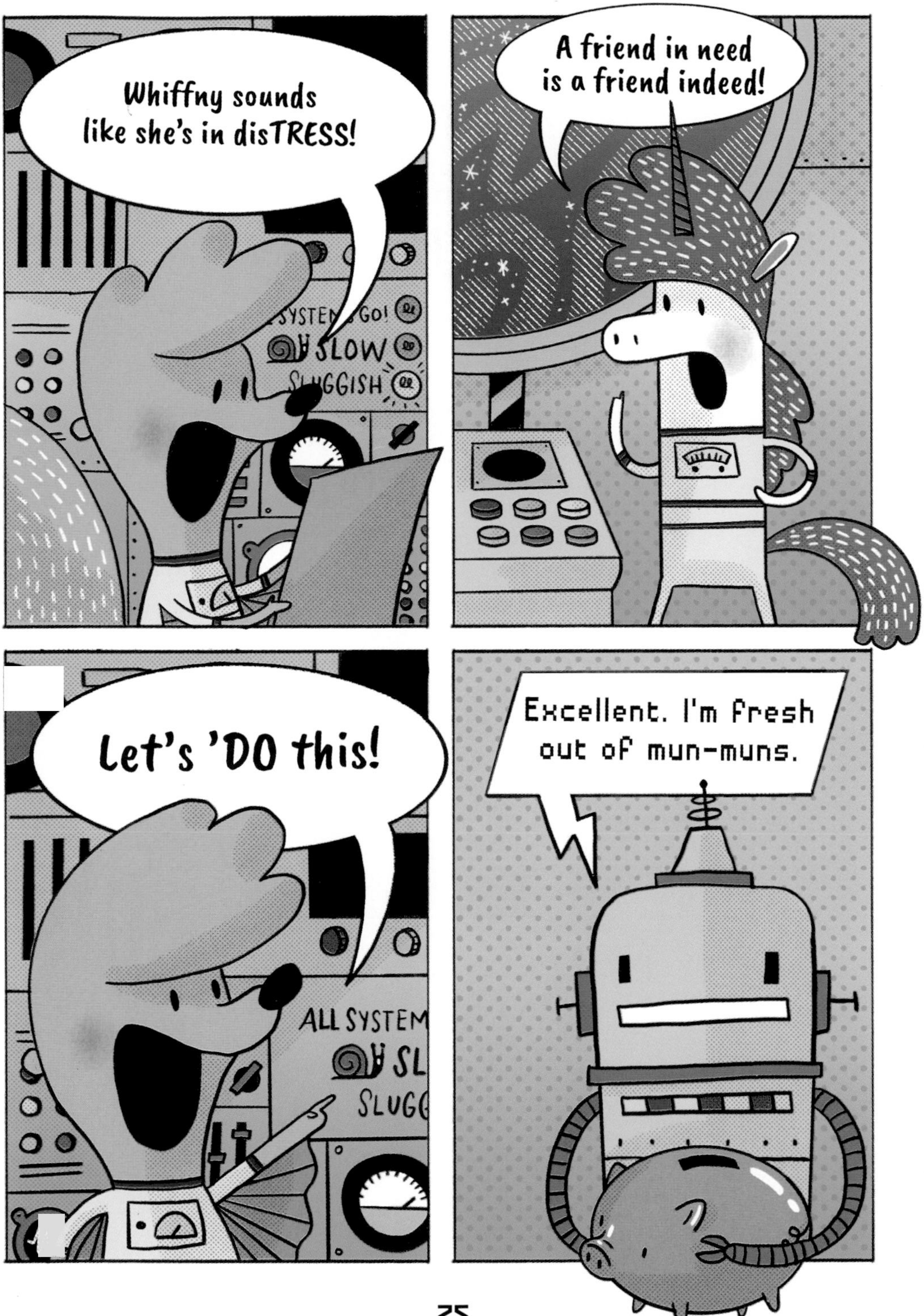
Whiffny sounds like she's in disTRESS!
SLOW
A friend in need is a friend indeed!
Let's 'DO this!
Excellent. I'm fresh out of mun-muns.

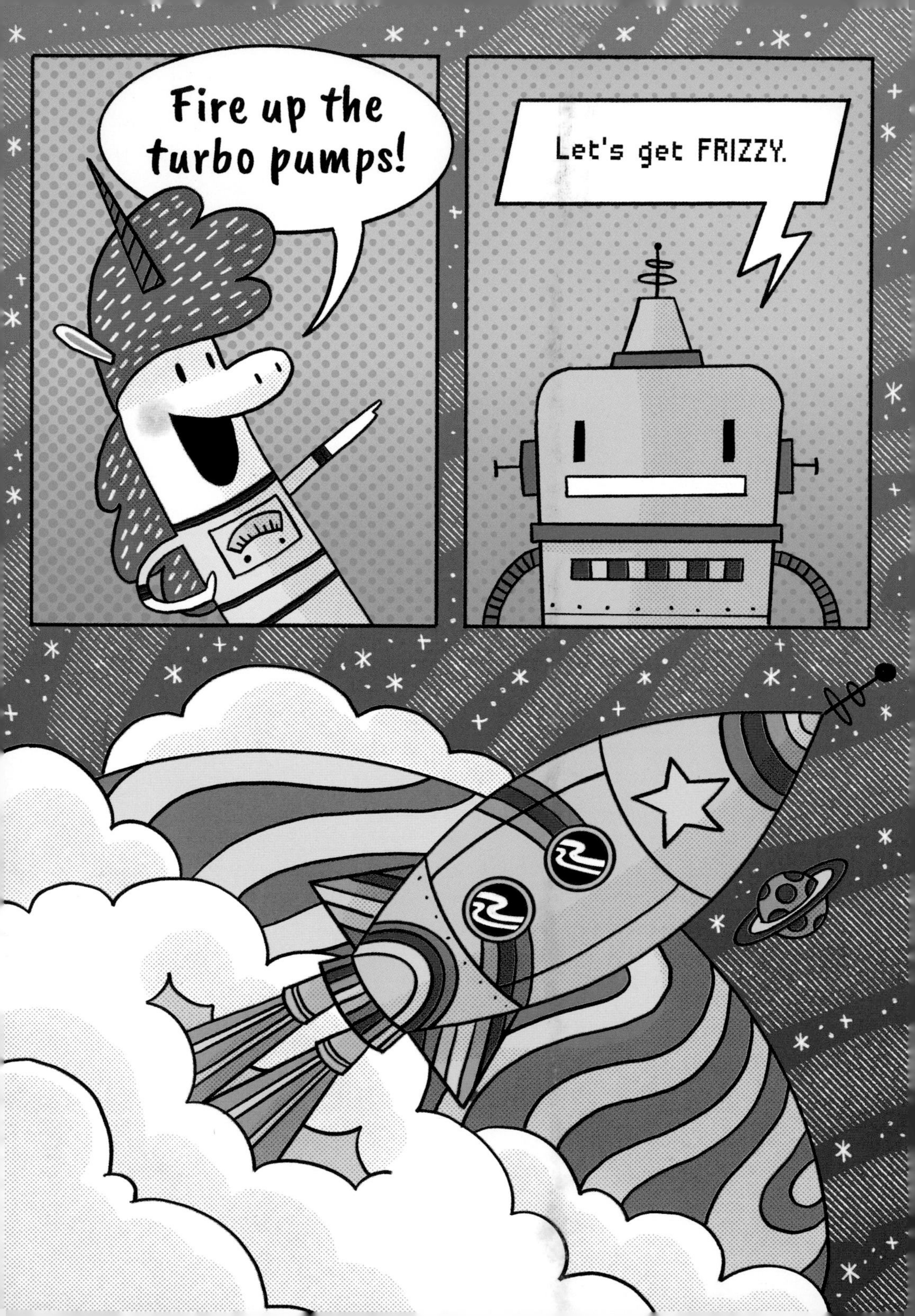
Fire up the turbo pumps!
Let's get FRIZZY.

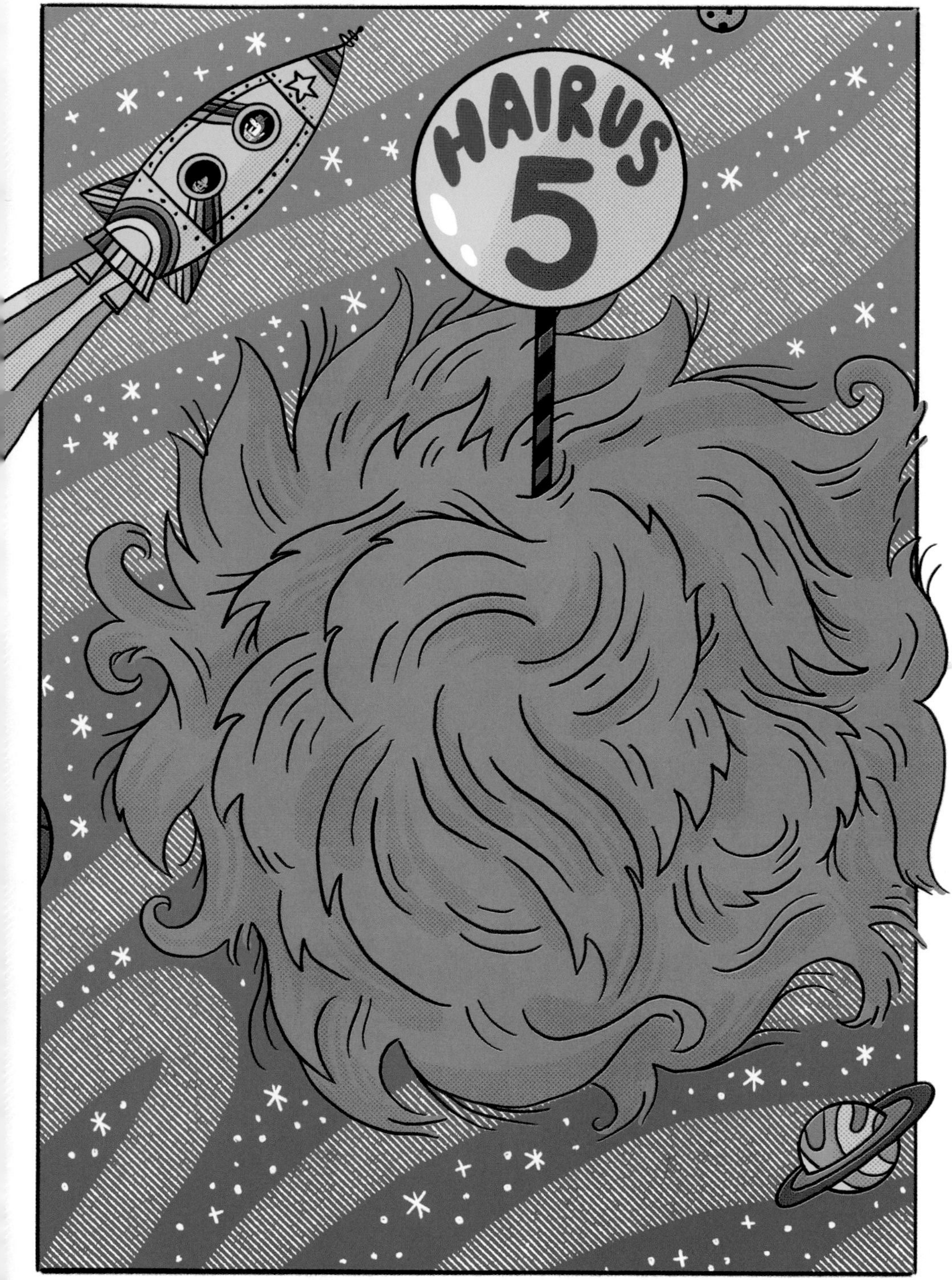
HAIRUS
5

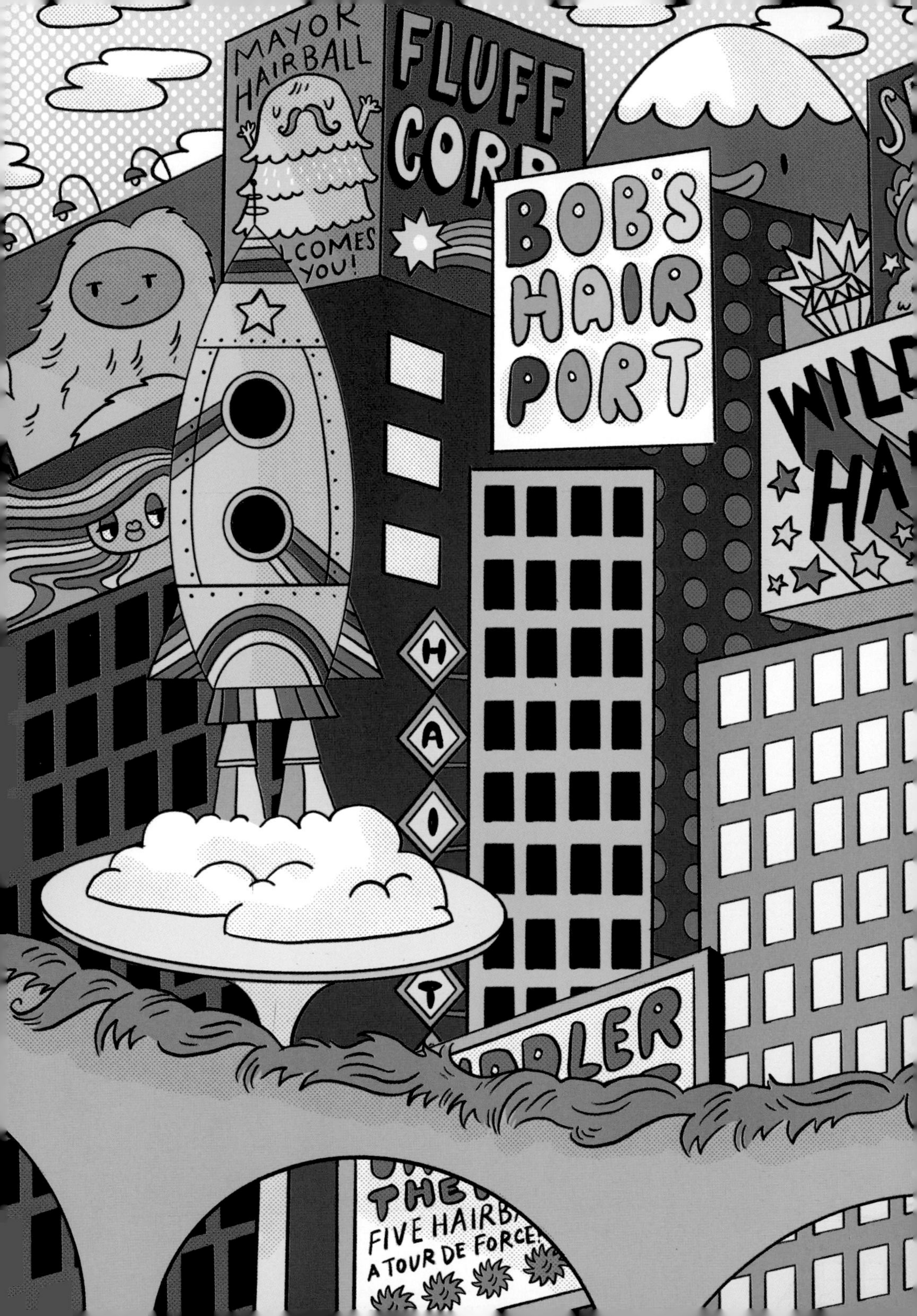
MAYOR HAIRBALL
LCOMES YOU!
FLUFF COR
BOB'S HAIR PORT
WIL
HA
H
A
I
T
DDLER
THE
FIVE HAIRB
A TOUR DE FORCE!

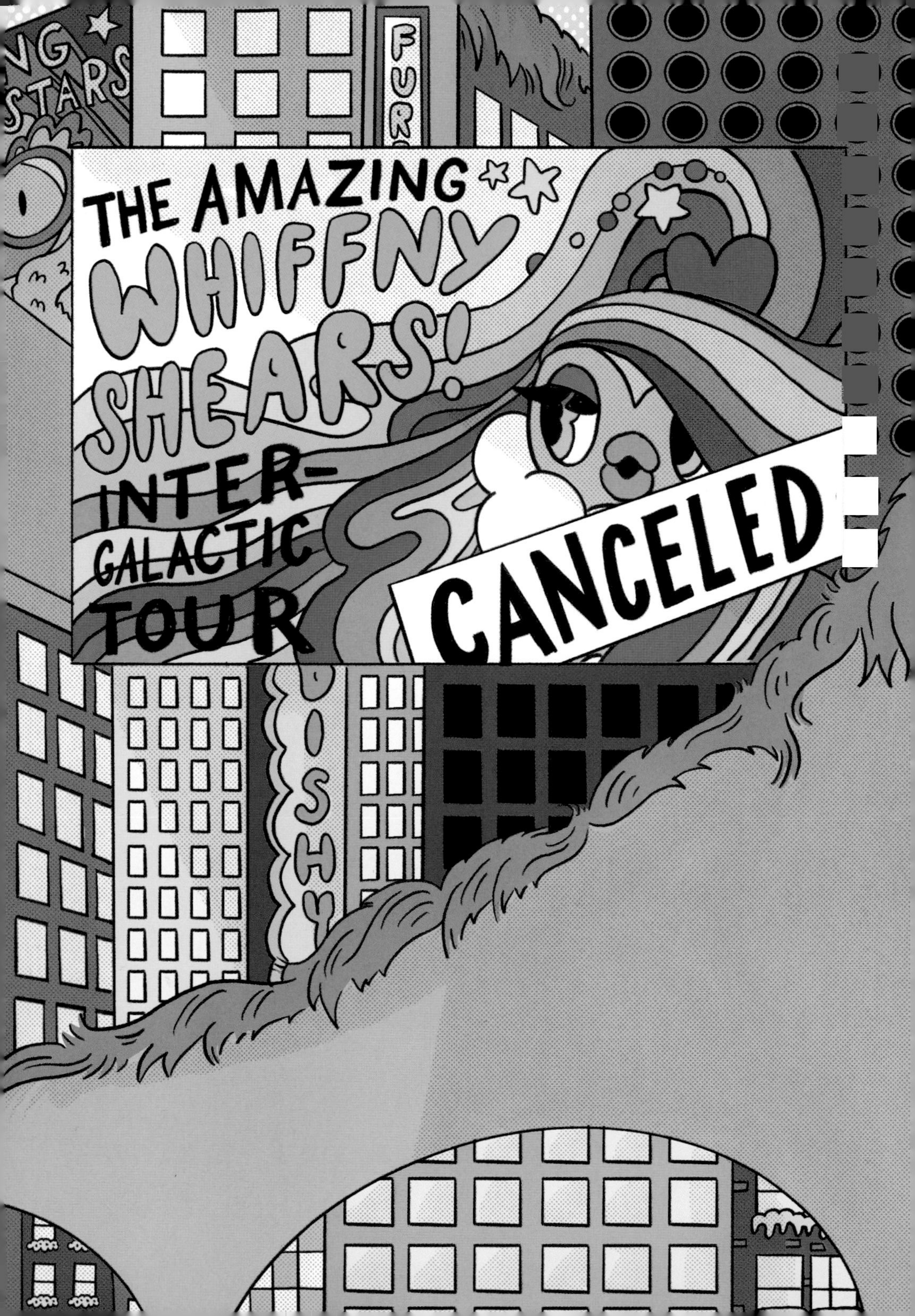
THE AMAZING WHIFFNY SHEARS!
INTER-GALACTIC TOUR
CANCELED

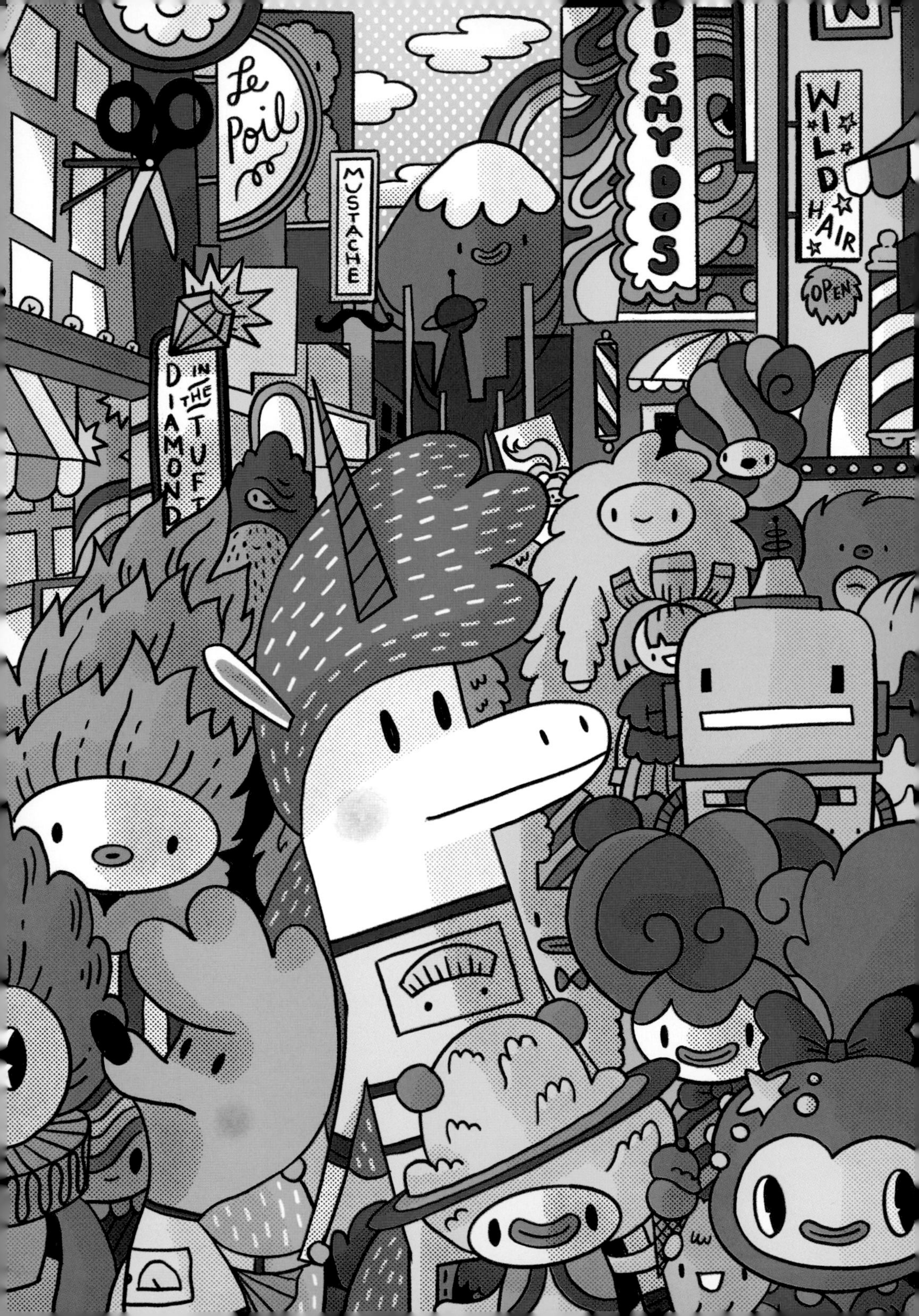

Le Poil
MUSTACHE
DISHY DOS
WILD HAIR
OPEN
DIAMOND IN THE TUFT

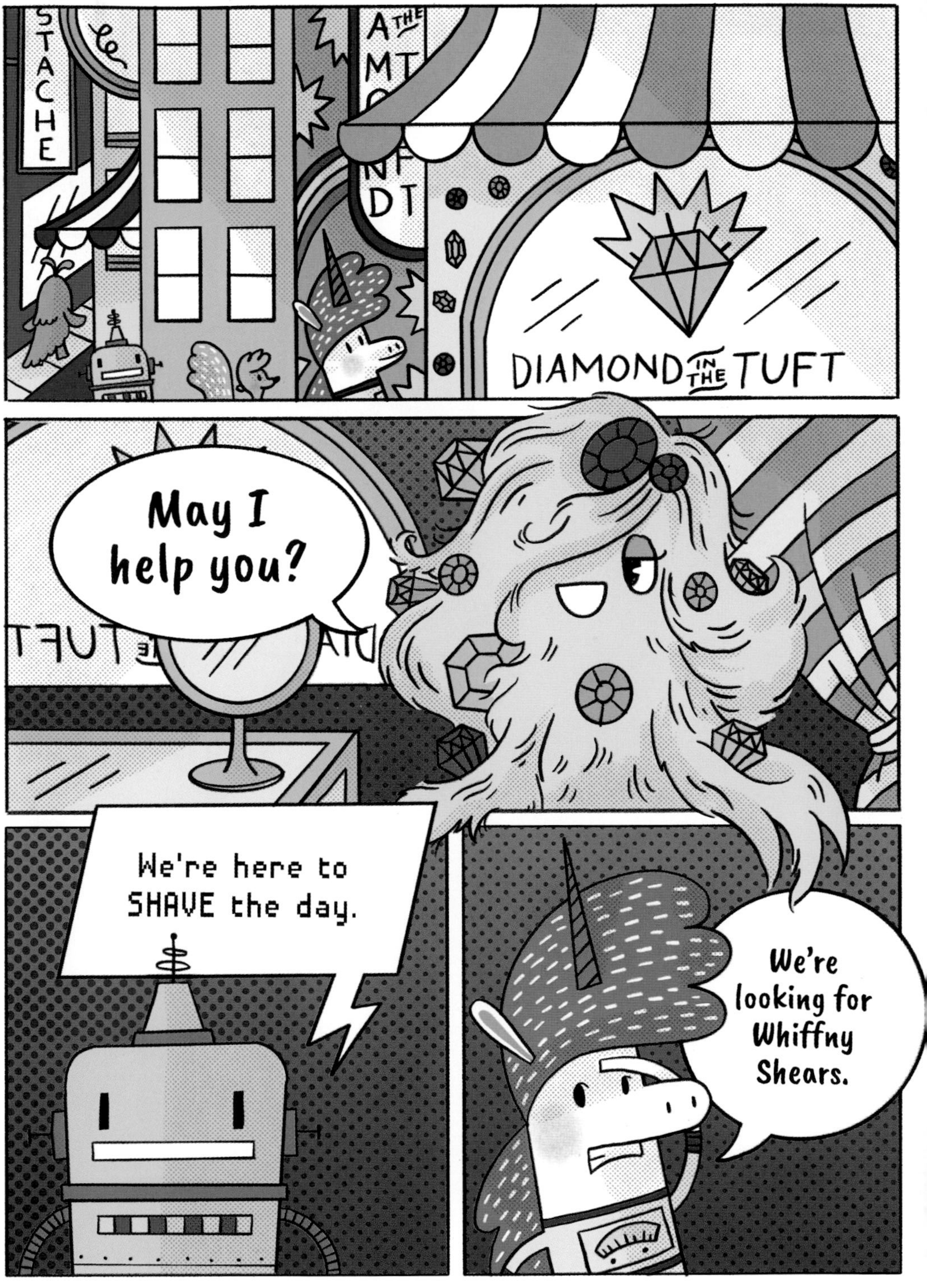
STACHE
DIAMOND IN THE TUFT
May I help you?
We're here to SHAVE the day.
We're looking for Whiffny Shears.

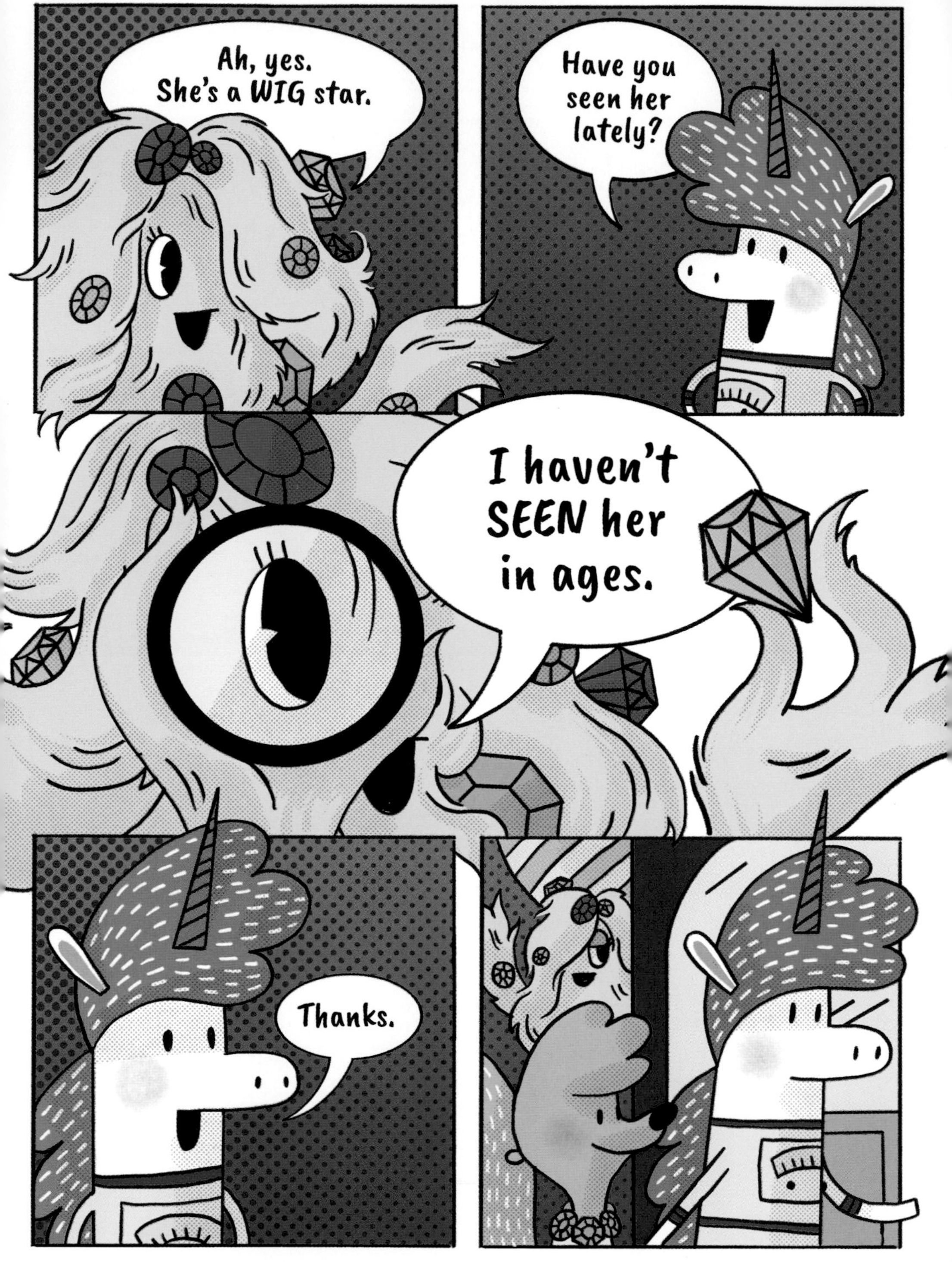
Ah, yes. She's a WIG star.
Have you seen her lately?
I haven't SEEN her in ages.
Thanks.

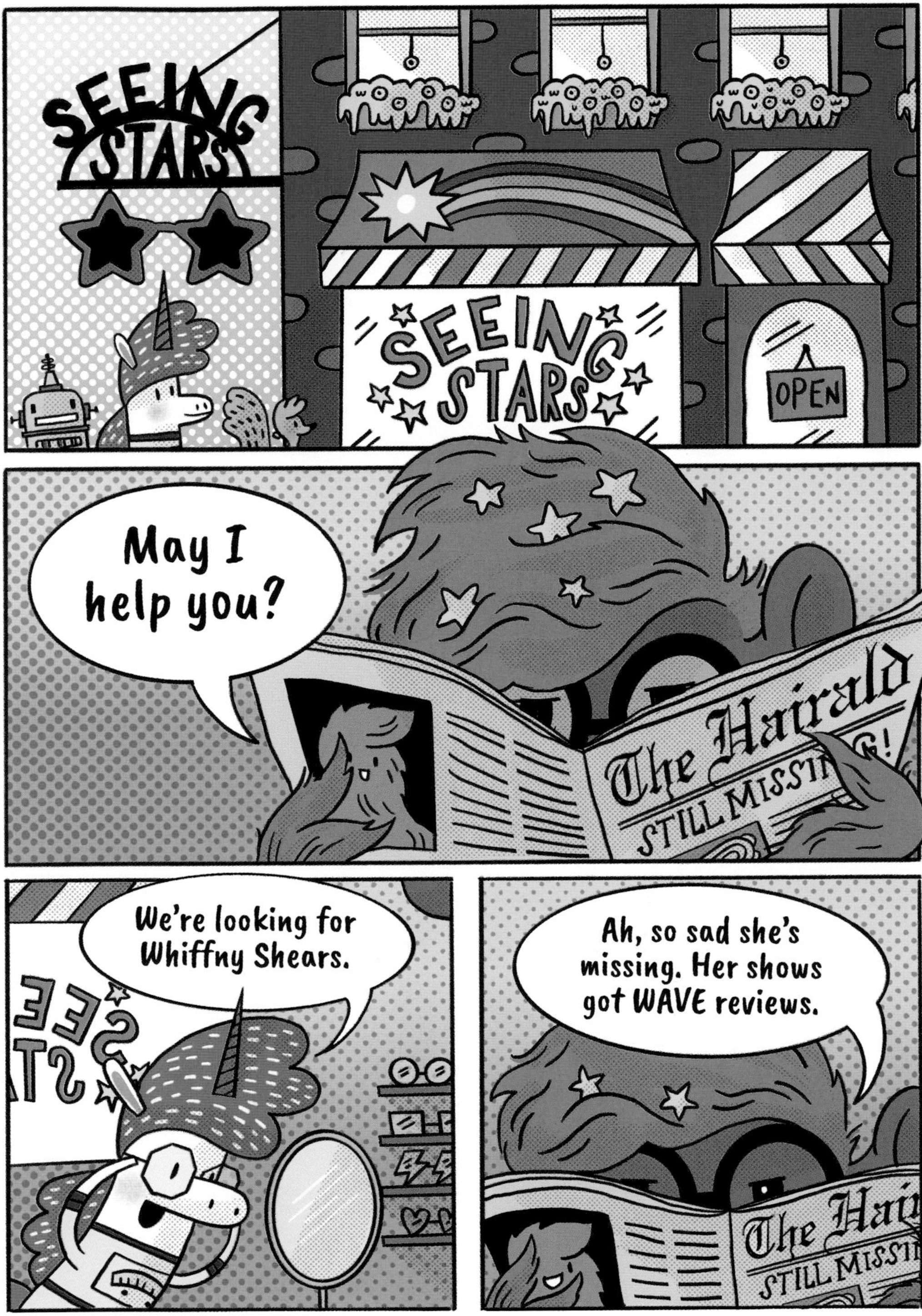
SEEING STARS
SEEING STARS
OPEN
May I help you?
The Hairald
STILL MISSING!
We're looking for Whiffny Shears.
Ah, so sad she's missing. Her shows got WAVE reviews.

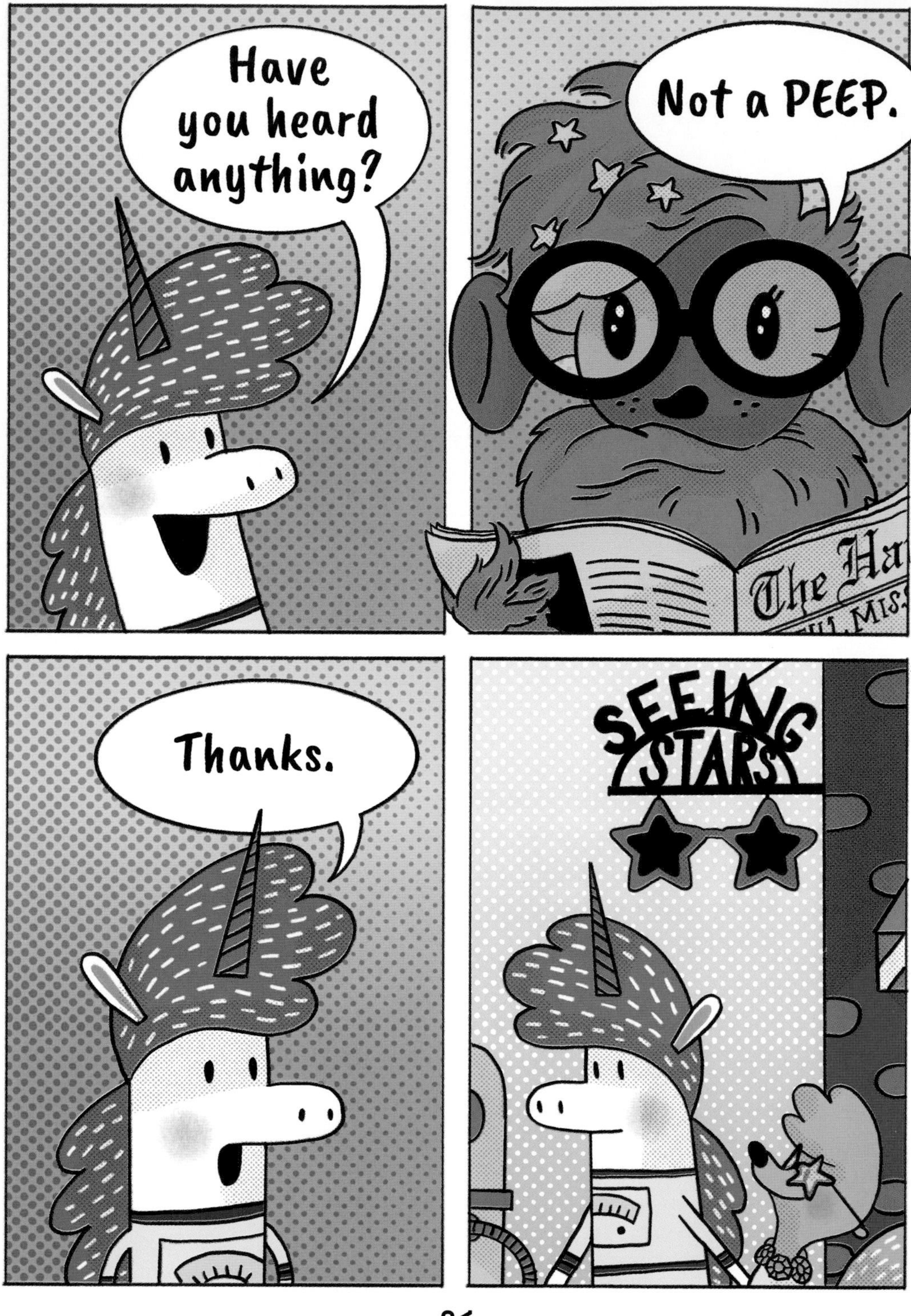
Have you heard anything?
Not a PEEP.
The Ha
Thanks.
SEEING STARS

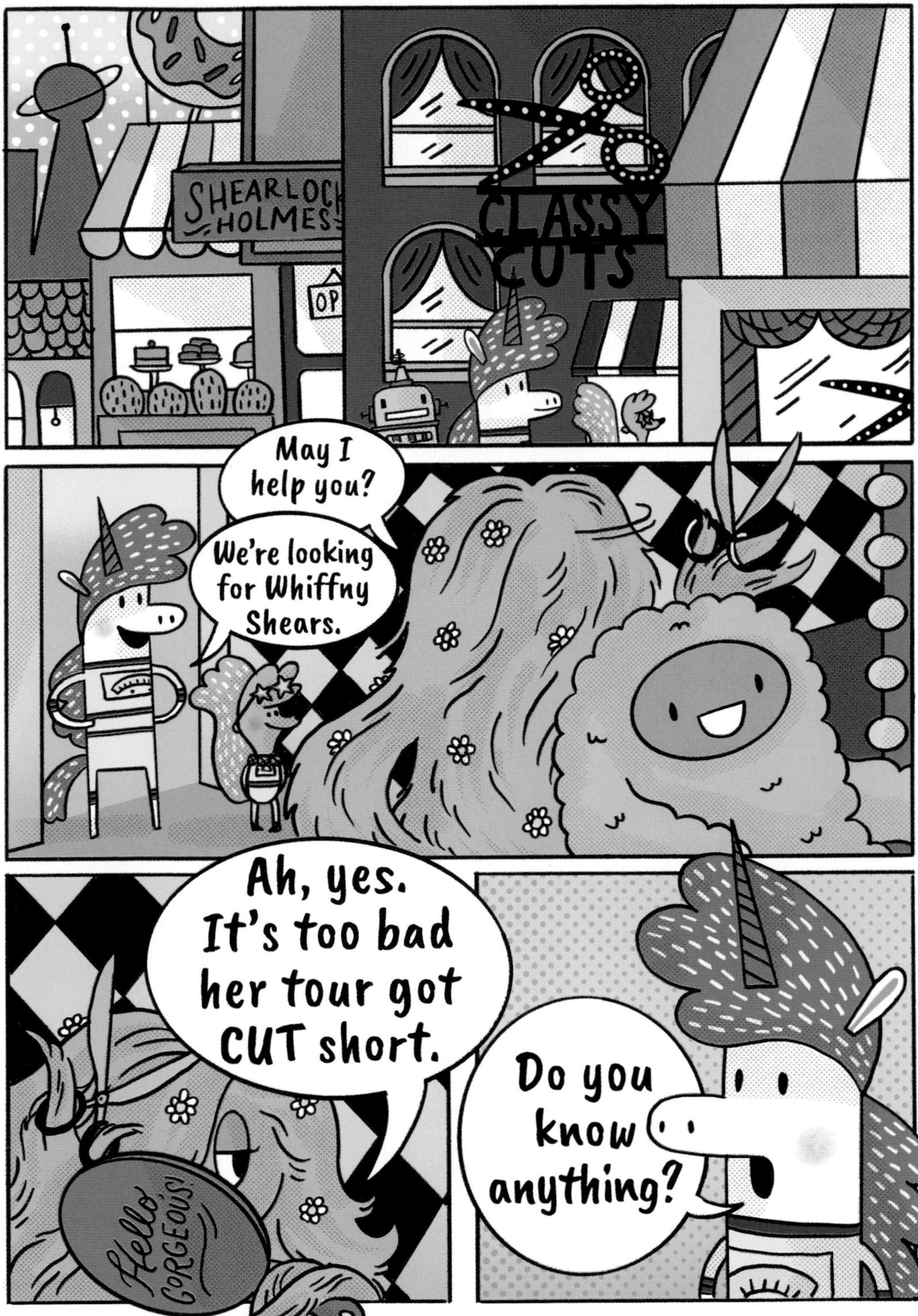
SHEARLOCK HOLMES
OP
CLASSY CUTS
May I help you?
We're looking for Whiffny Shears.
Ah, yes. It's too bad her tour got CUT short.
Hello, GORGEOUS!
Do you know anything?

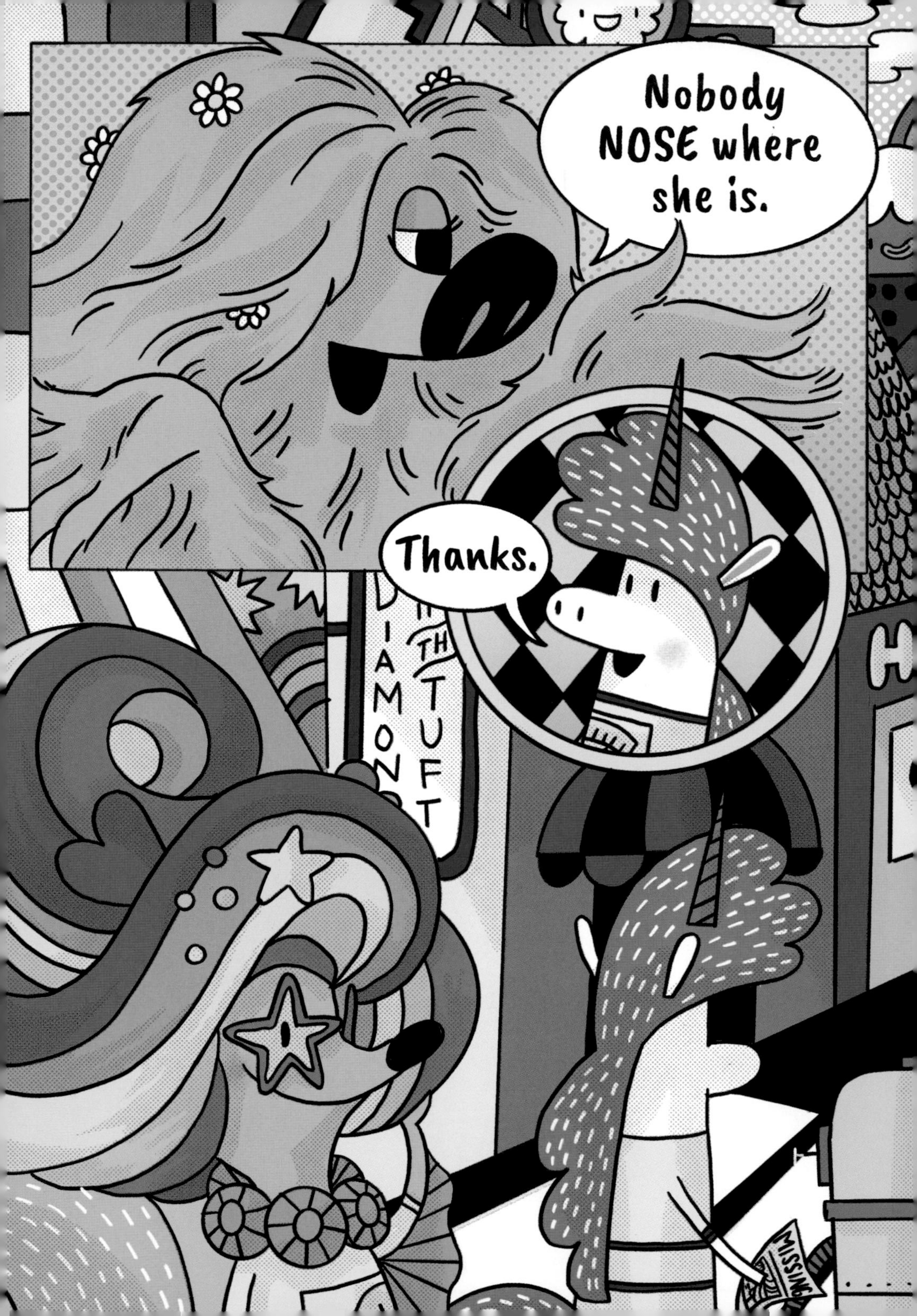
Nobody NOSE where she is.
Thanks.
MISSING

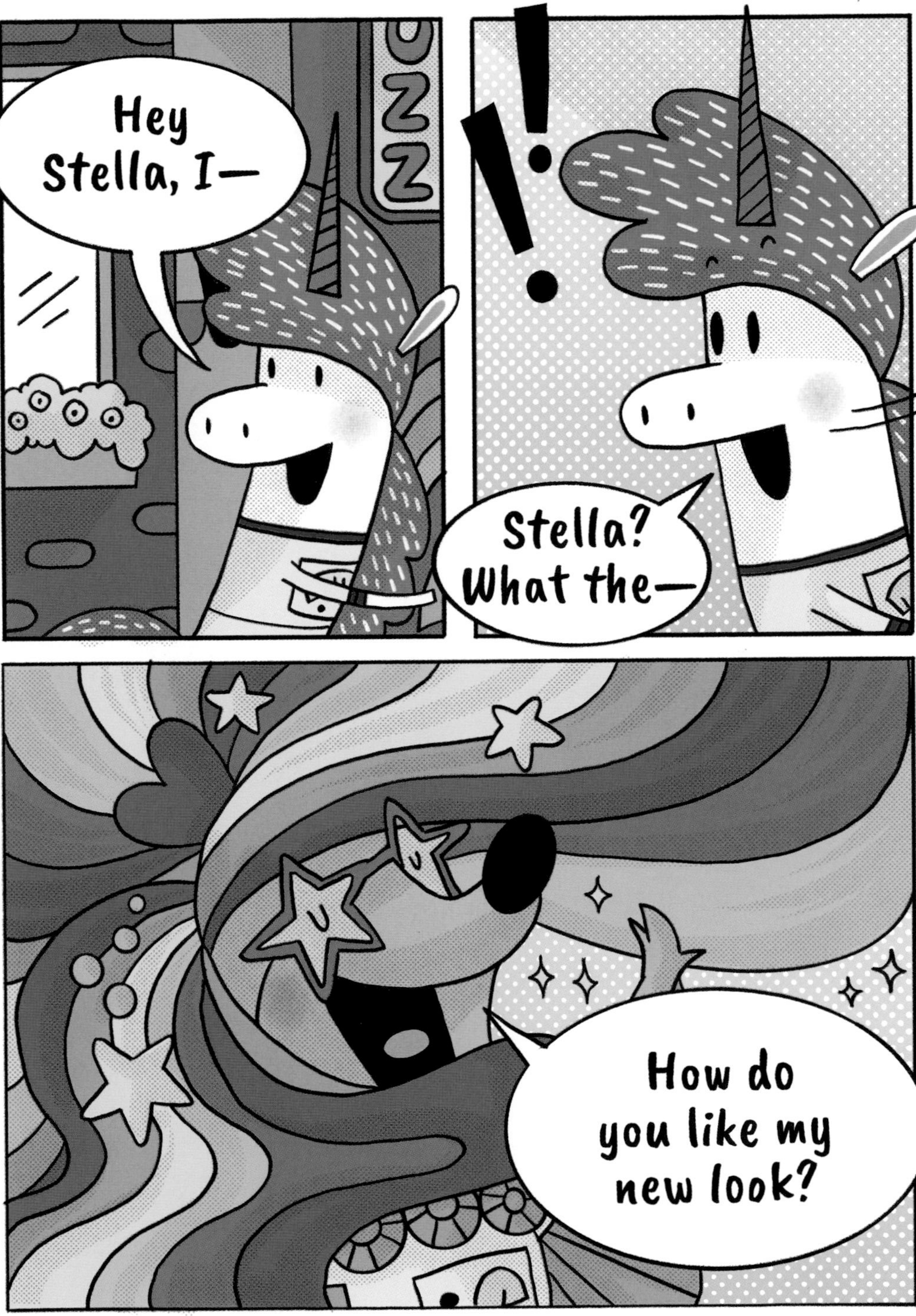
Hey Stella, I—
ZZ
!!
Stella? What the—
How do you like my new look?

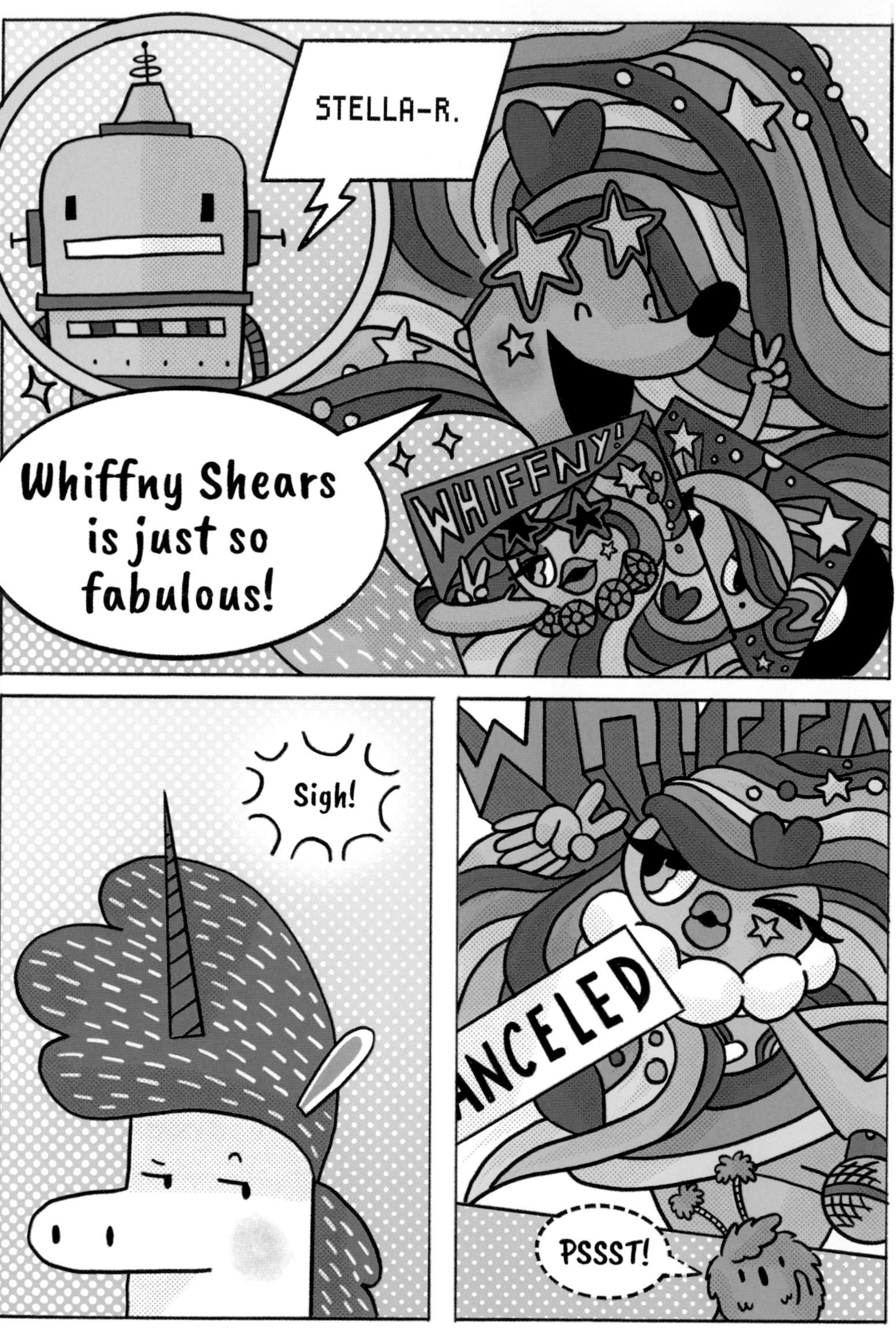
STELLA-R.
Whiffny Shears is just so fabulous!
WHIFFNY!
WHIFFNY
Sigh!
ANCELED
PSSST!

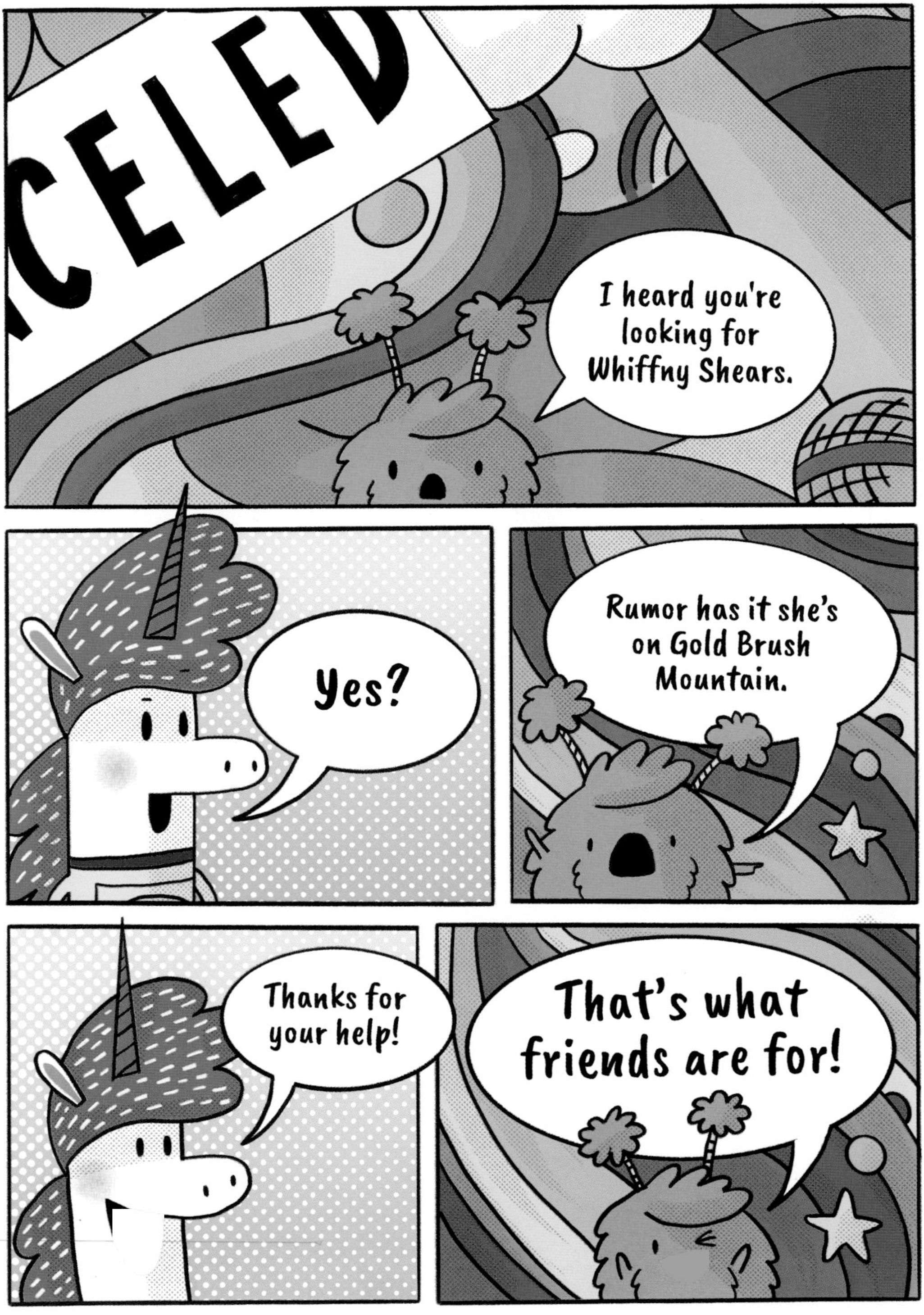
CELED
I heard you're looking for Whiffny Shears.
Yes?
Rumor has it she's on Gold Brush Mountain.
Thanks for your help!
That's what friends are for!

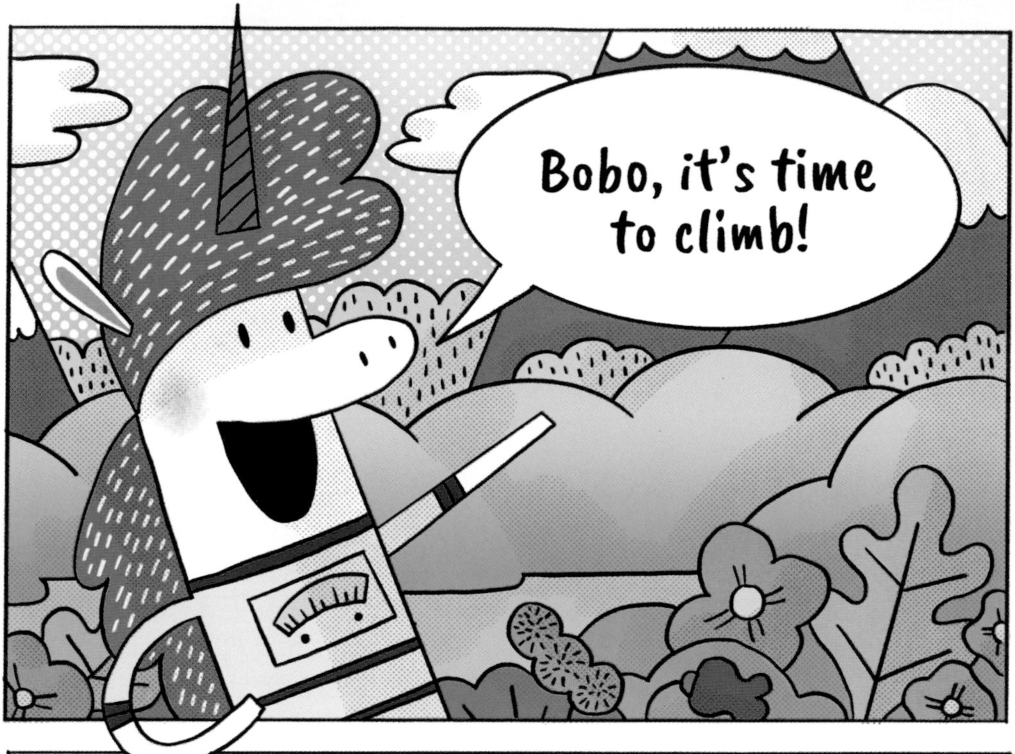
Bobo, it's time to climb!

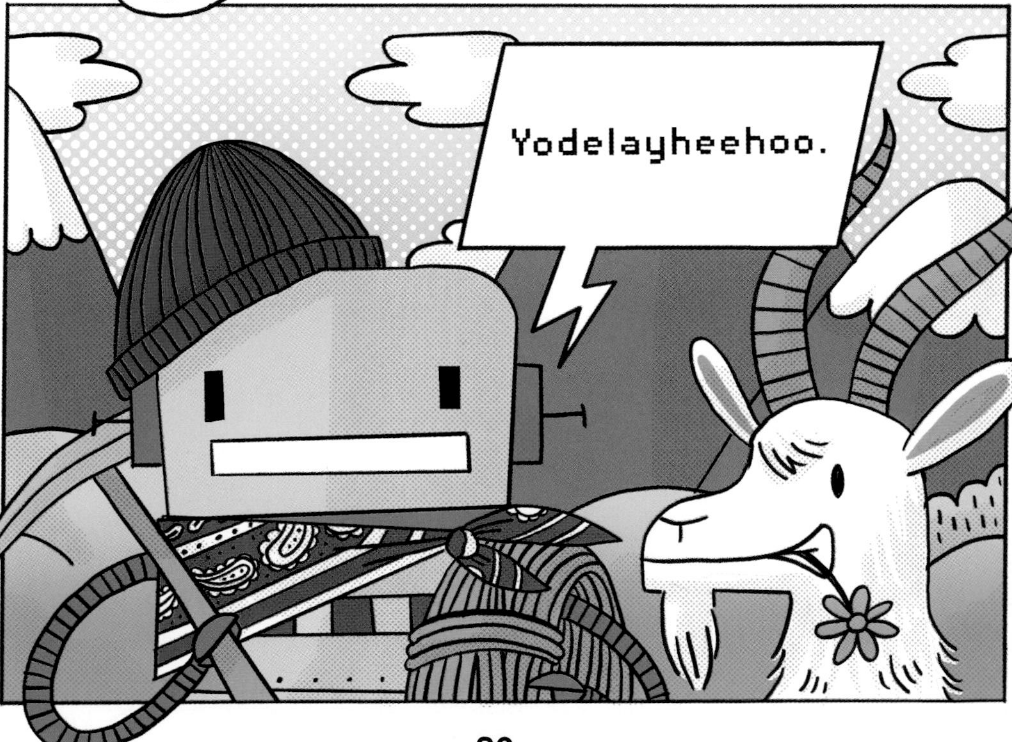
Yodelayheehoo.

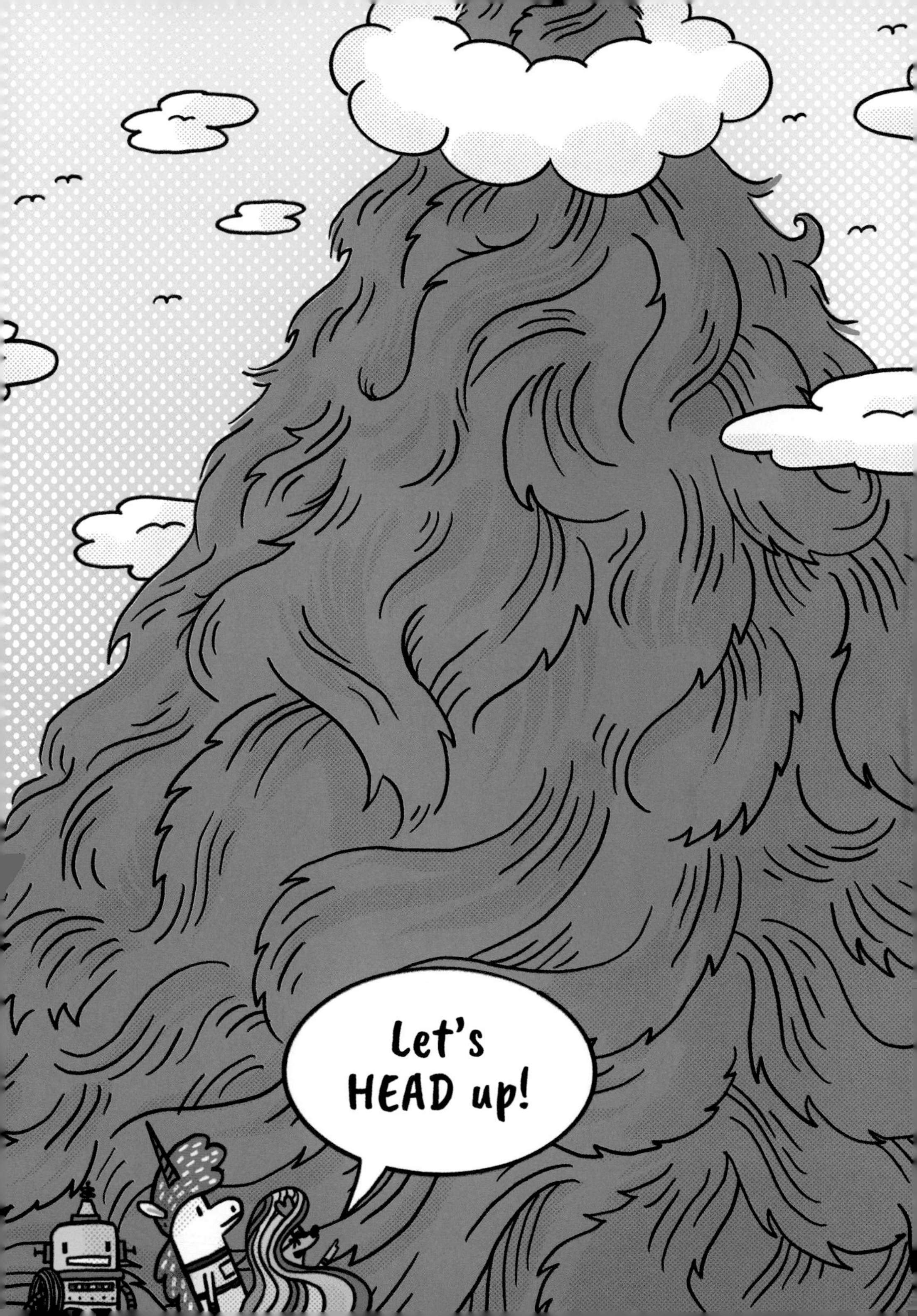
Let's HEAD up!

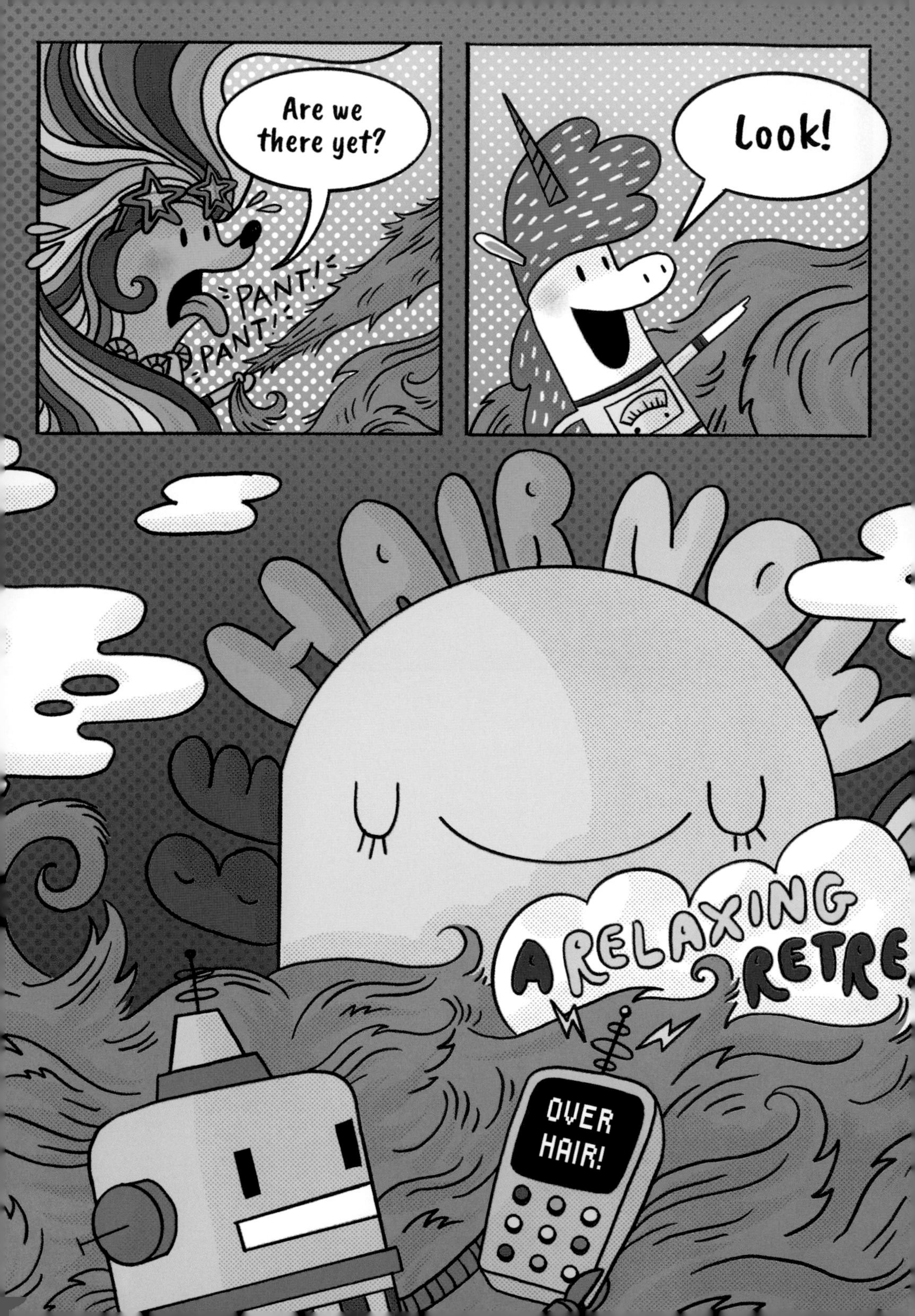

Are we there yet?
PANT! PANT!
Look!
A RELAXING RETRE
OVER HAIR!

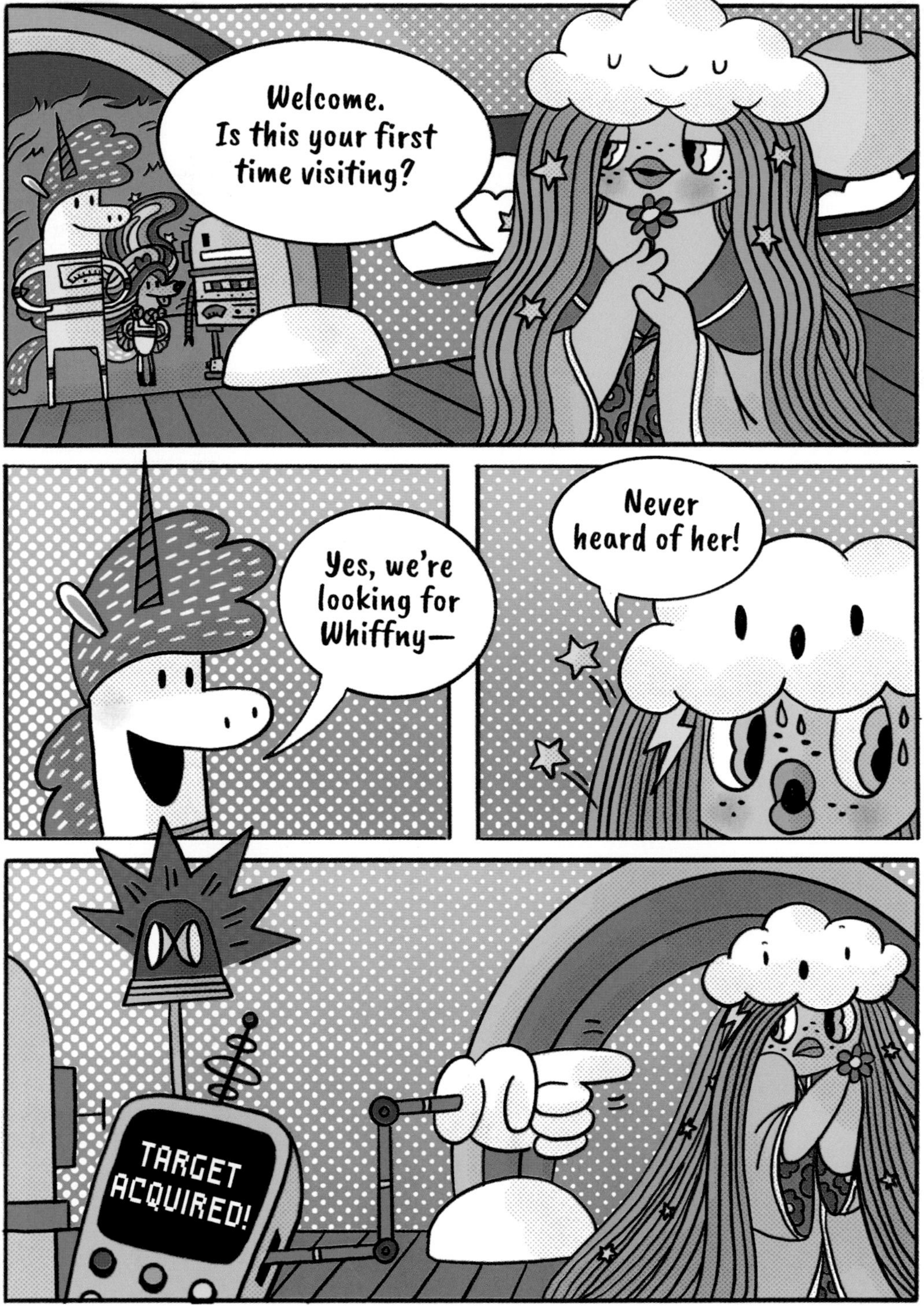
Welcome.
Is this your first time visiting?
Yes, we're looking for Whiffny—
Never heard of her!
TARGET ACQUIRED!

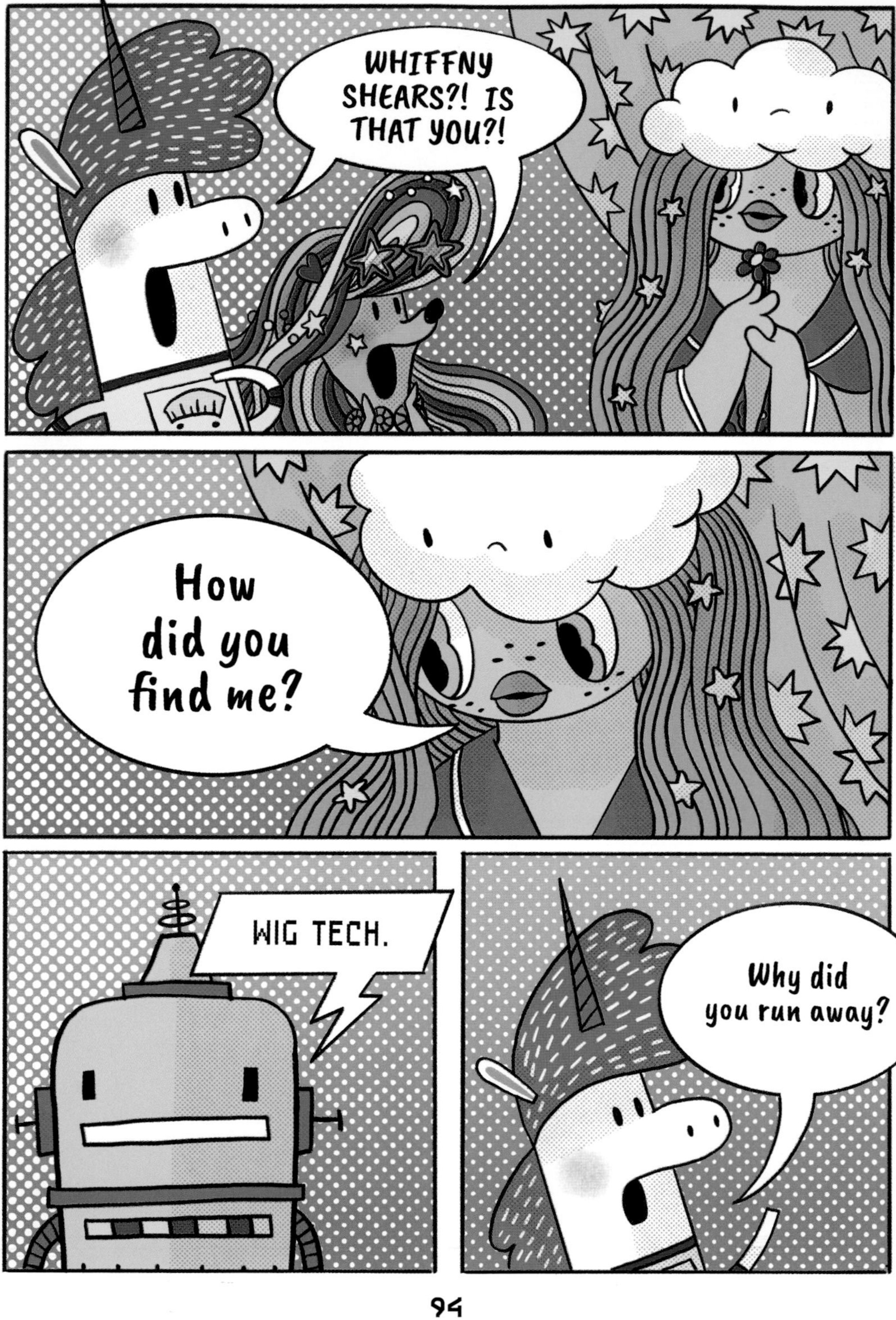
WHIFFNY SHEARS?! IS THAT YOU?!
How did you find me?
WIG TECH.
Why did you run away?

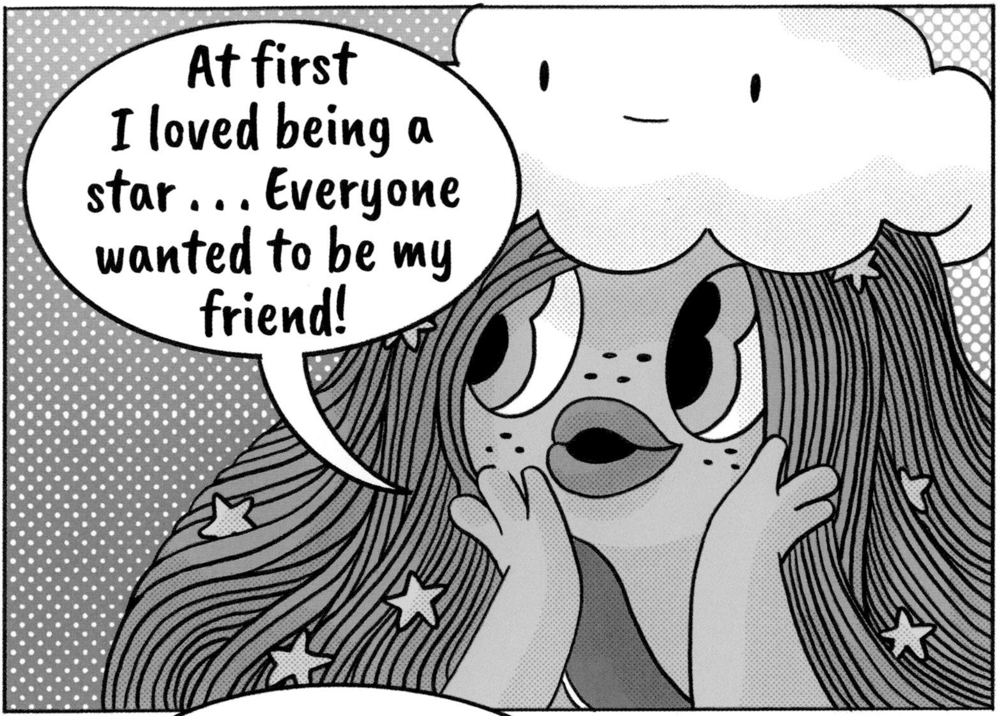
At first I loved being a star . . . Everyone wanted to be my friend!
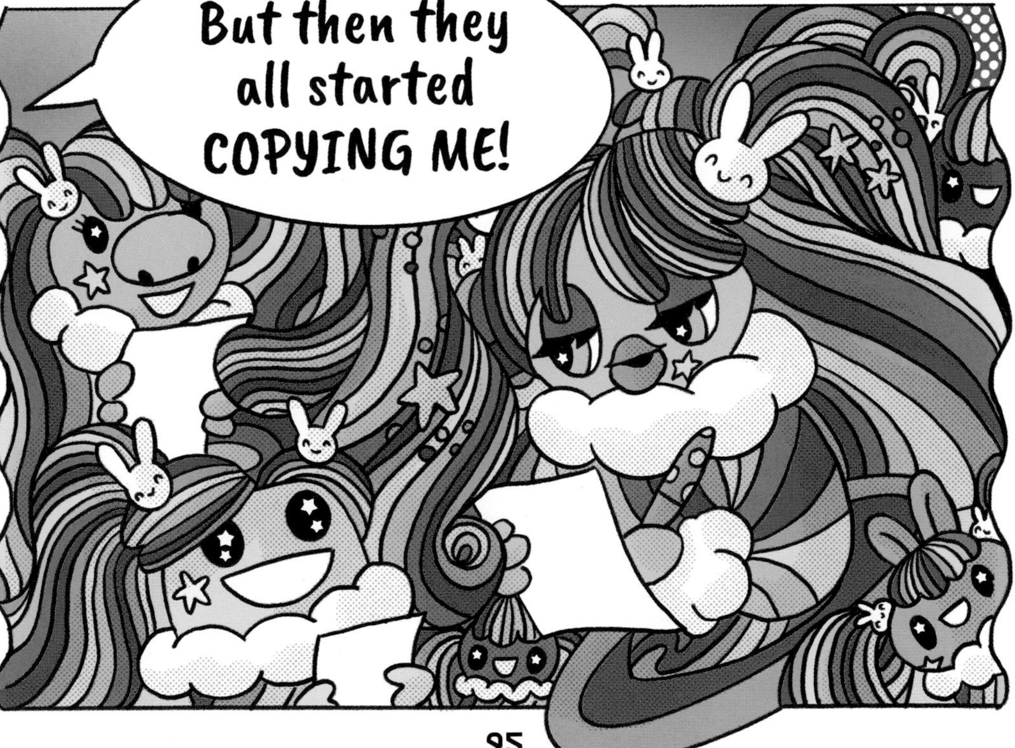
But then they all started COPYING ME!

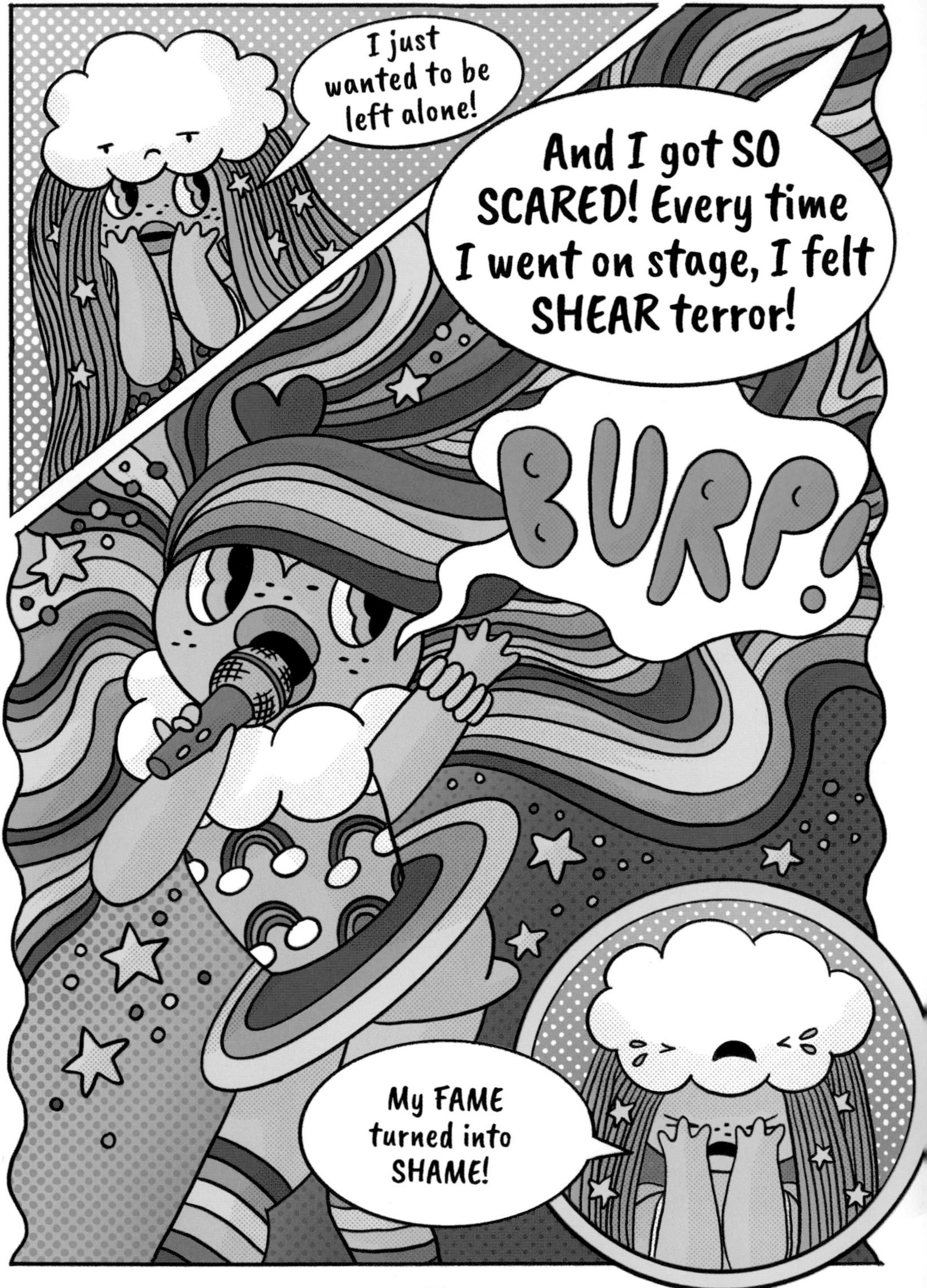
I just wanted to be left alone!
And I got SO SCARED! Every time I went on stage, I felt SHEAR terror!
BURP!
My FAME turned into SHAME!

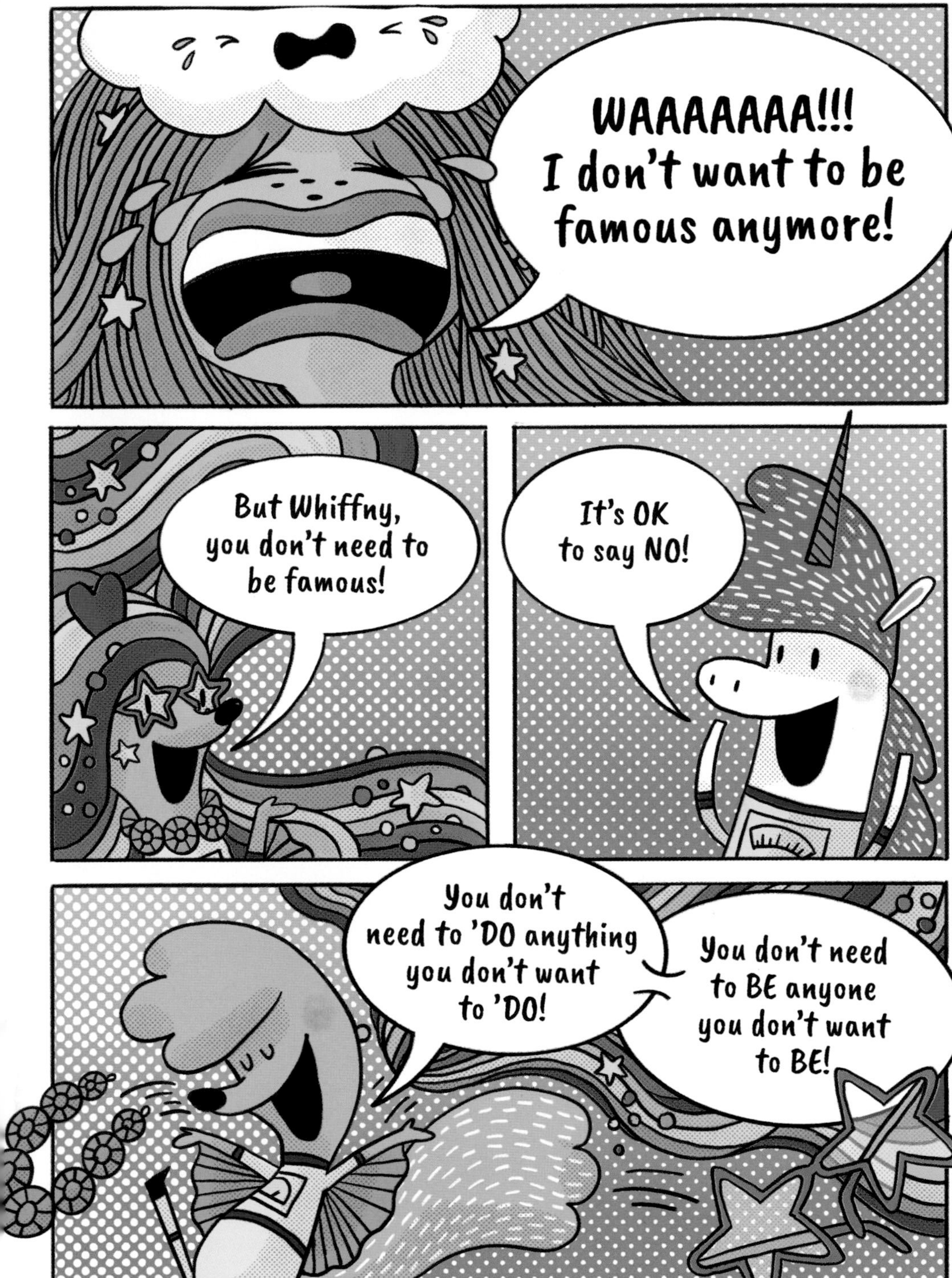
WAAAAAAA!!! I don't want to be famous anymore!
But Whiffny, you don't need to be famous!
It's OK to say NO!
You don't need to 'DO anything you don't want to 'DO!
You don't need to BE anyone you don't want to BE!

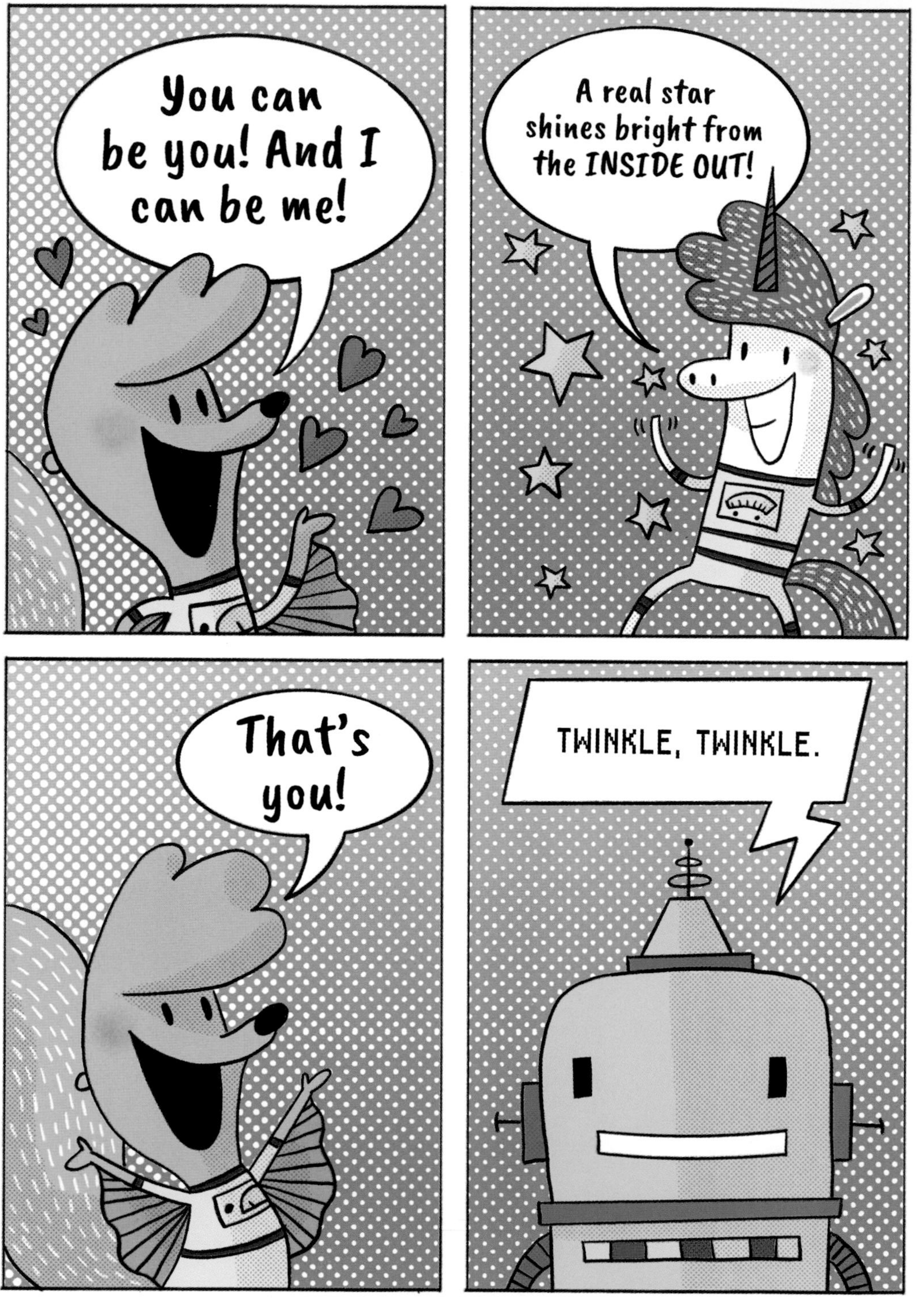
You can be you! And I can be me!
A real star shines bright from the INSIDE OUT!
That's you!
TWINKLE, TWINKLE.

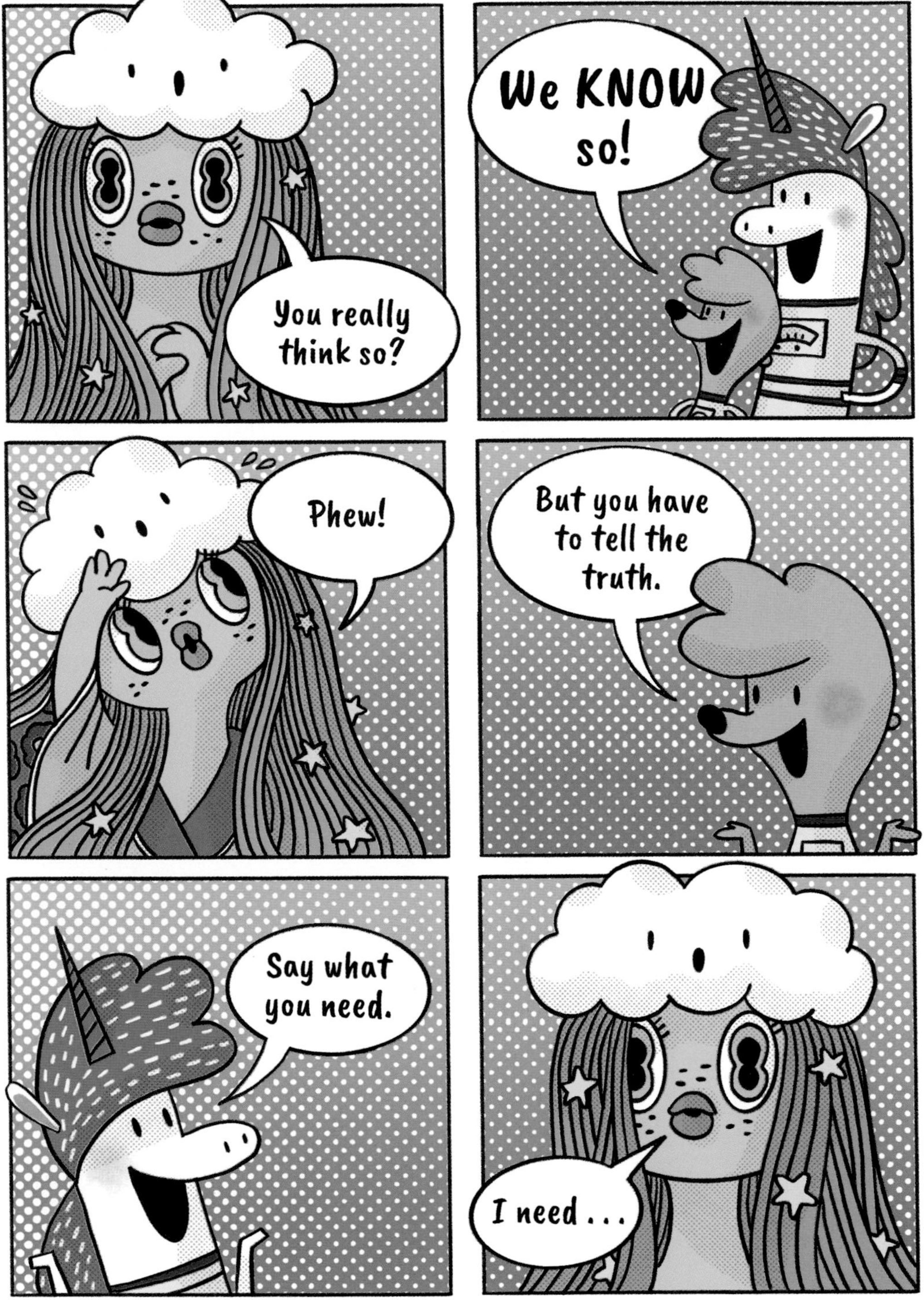
You really think so?
We KNOW so!
Phew!
But you have to tell the truth.
Say what you need.
I need . . .

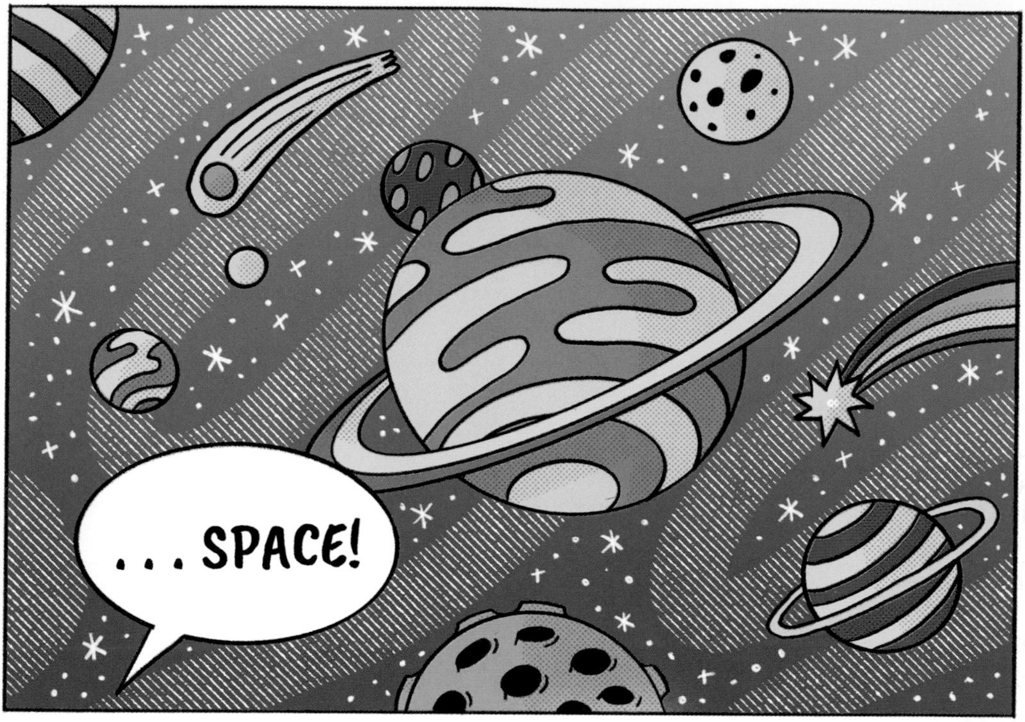
...SPACE!
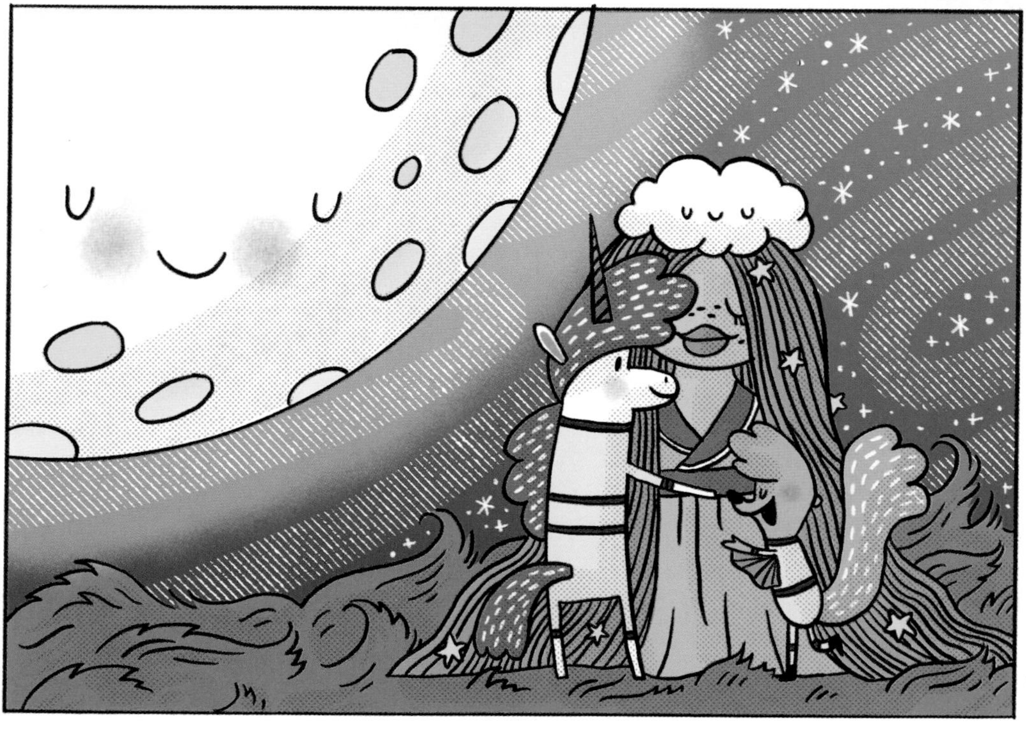

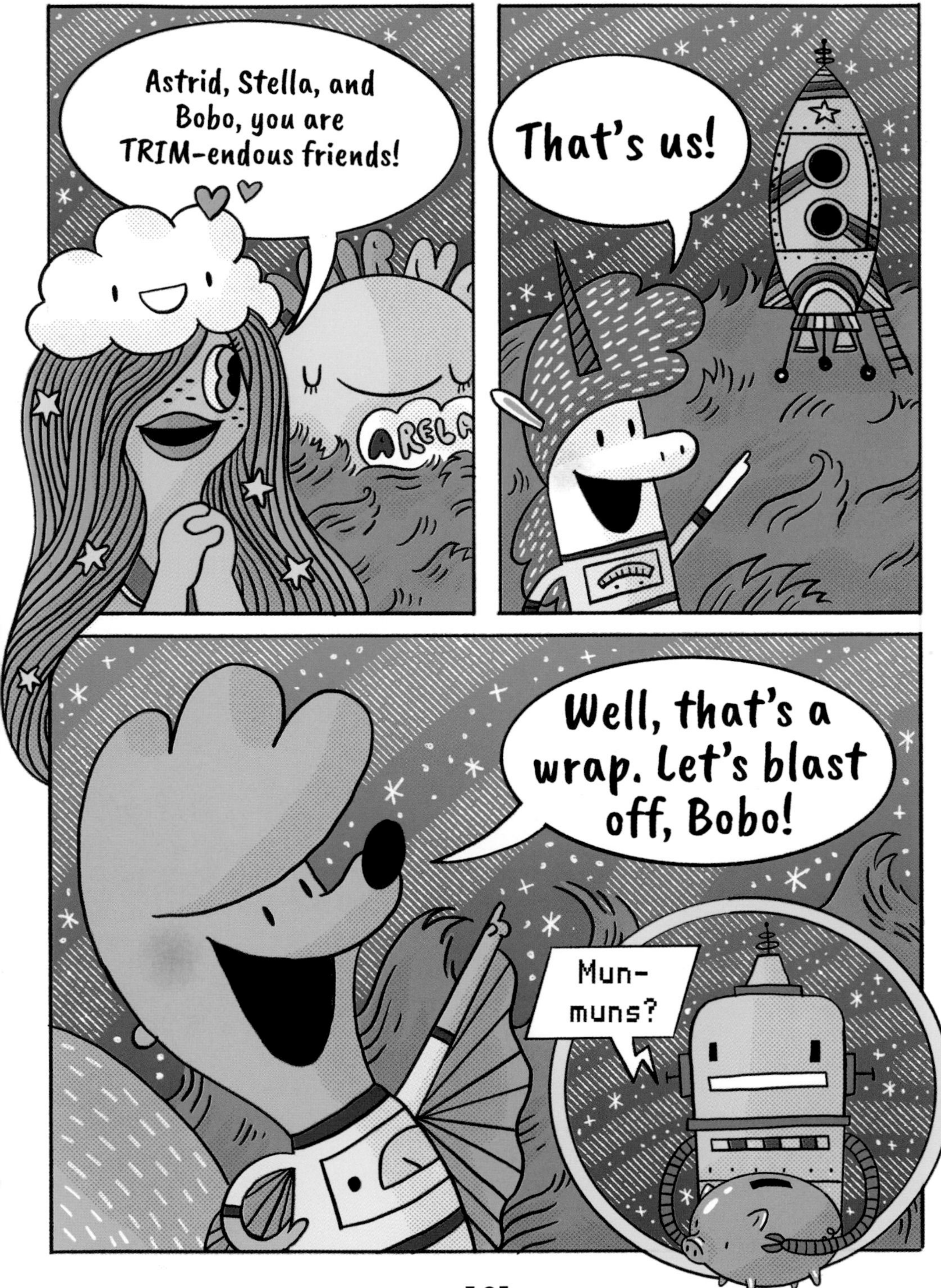
Astrid, Stella, and Bobo, you are TRIM-endous friends!
That's us!
Well, that's a wrap. Let's blast off, Bobo!
Mun-muns?

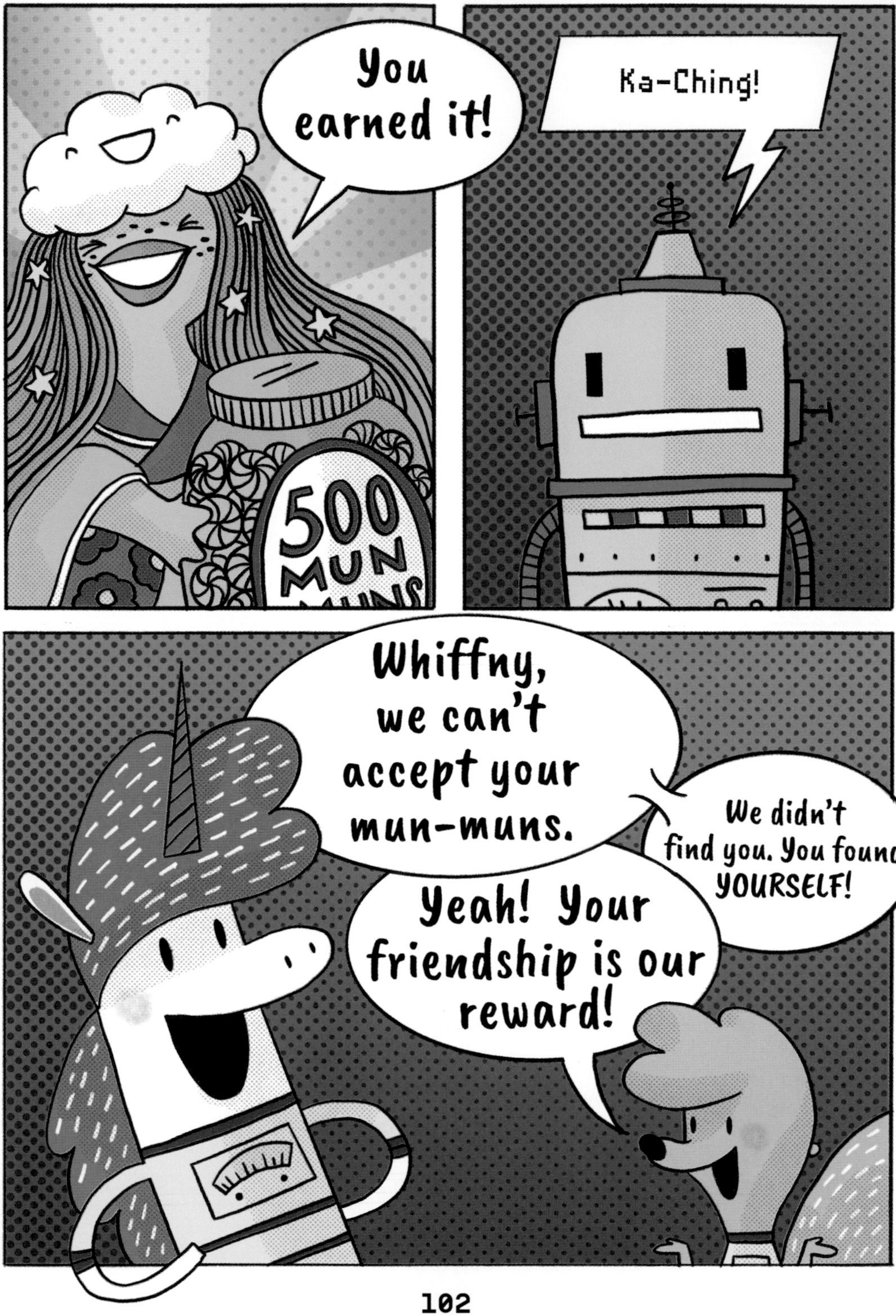
You earned it!
500 MUN MUNS
Ka-Ching!
Whiffny, we can't accept your mun-muns.
We didn't find you. You found YOURSELF!
Yeah! Your friendship is our reward!

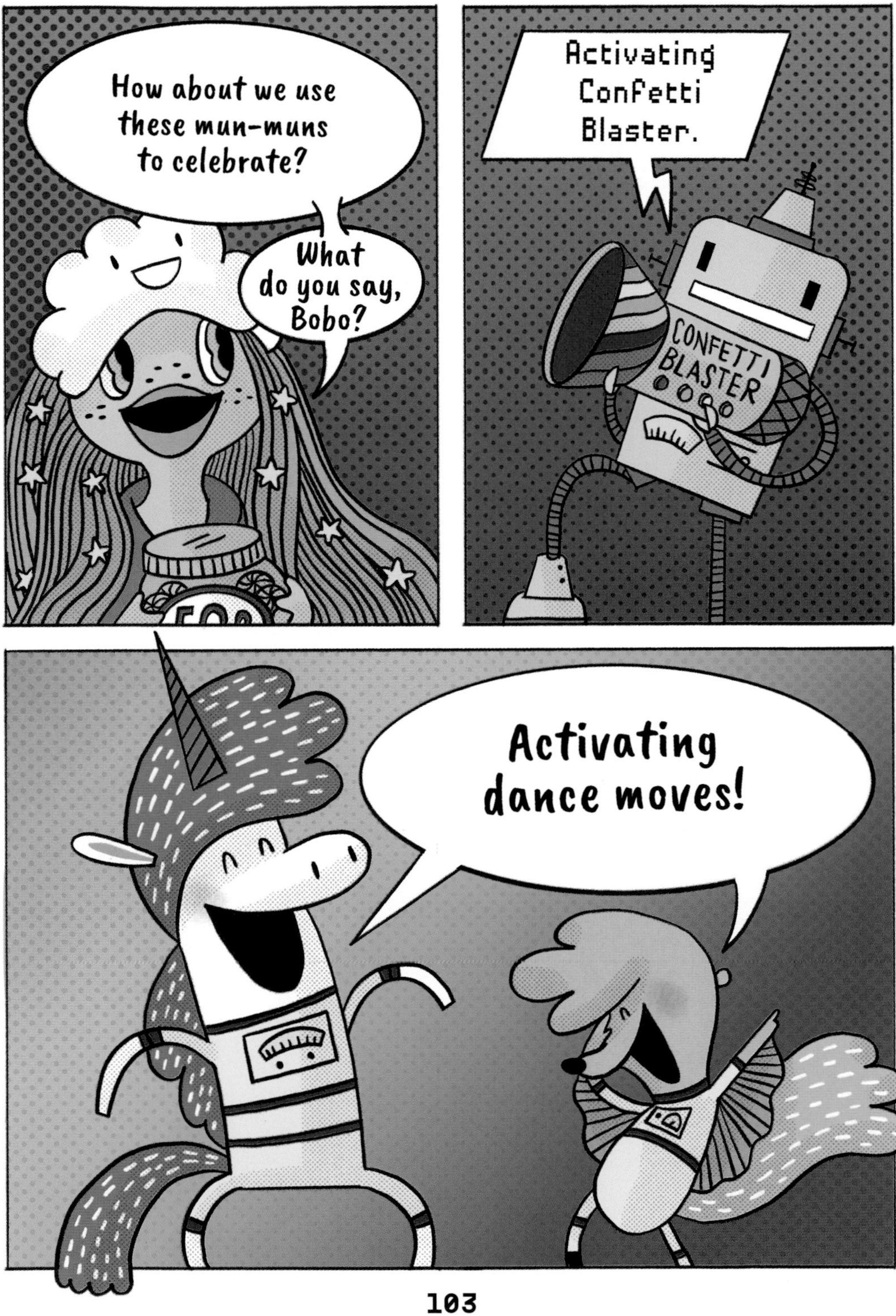
How about we use these mun-muns to celebrate?
What do you say, Bobo?
Activating Confetti Blaster.
CONFETTI BLASTER
Activating dance moves!

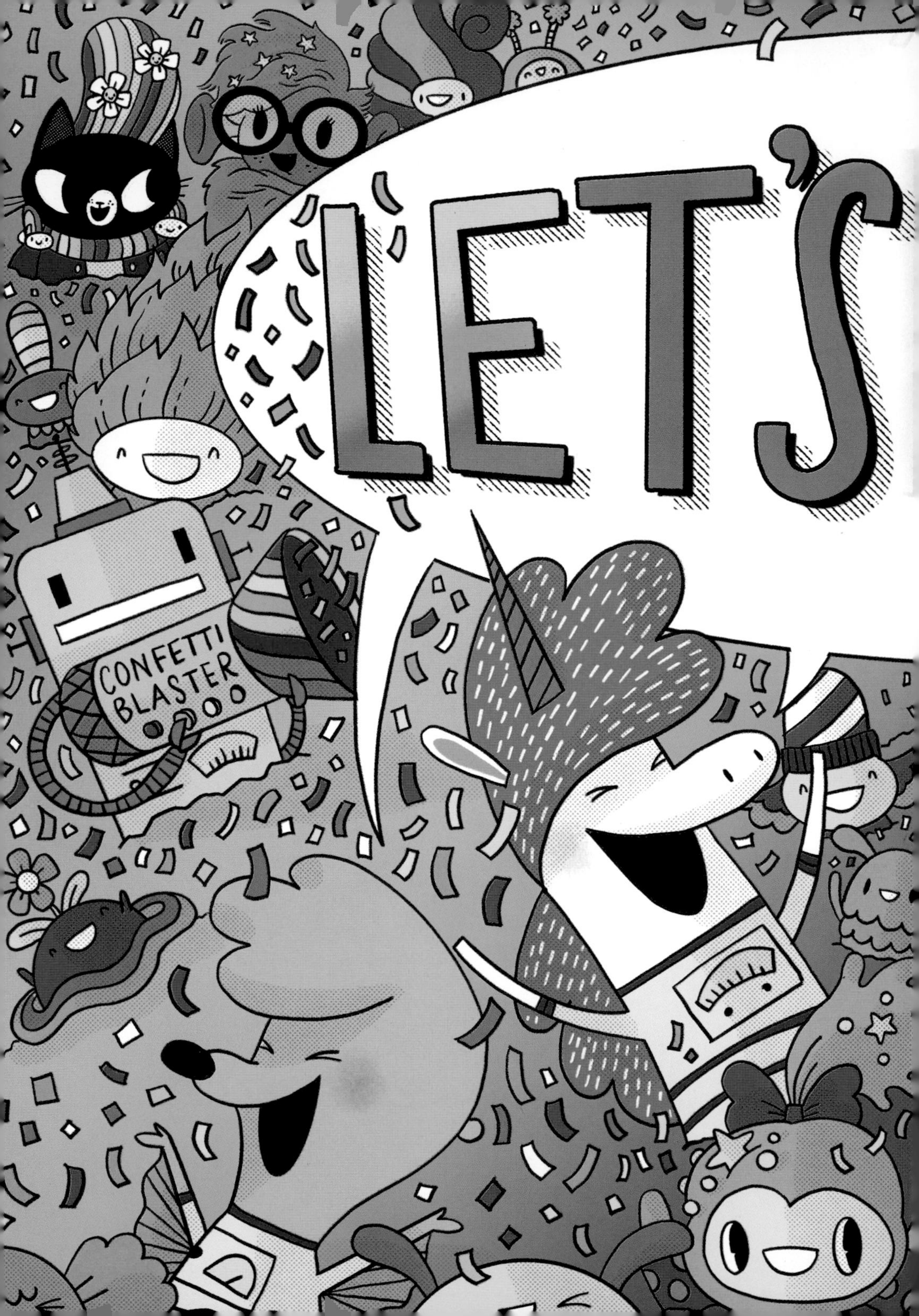
LET'S
CONFETTI BLASTER 3000

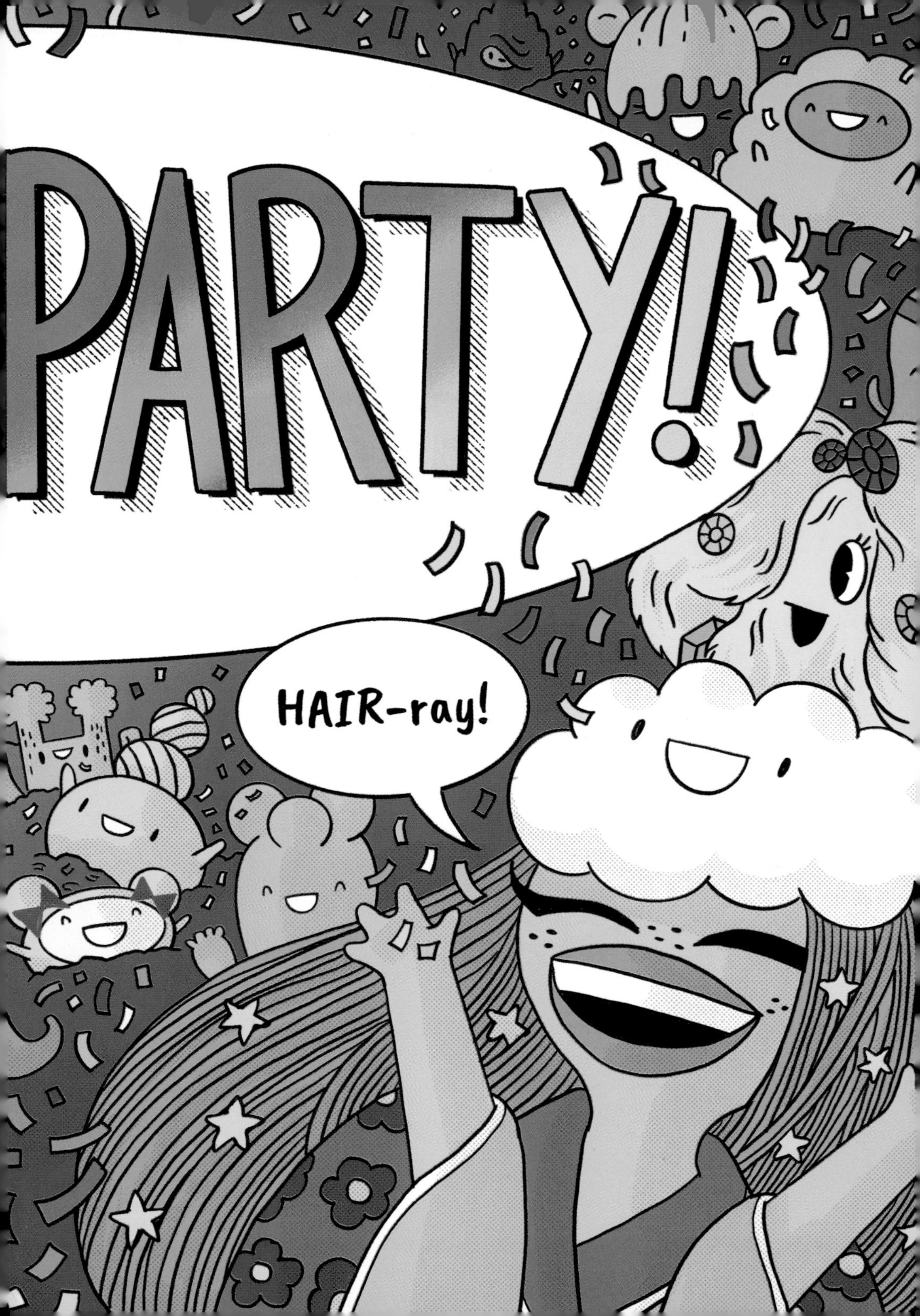
PARTY!
HAIR-ray!

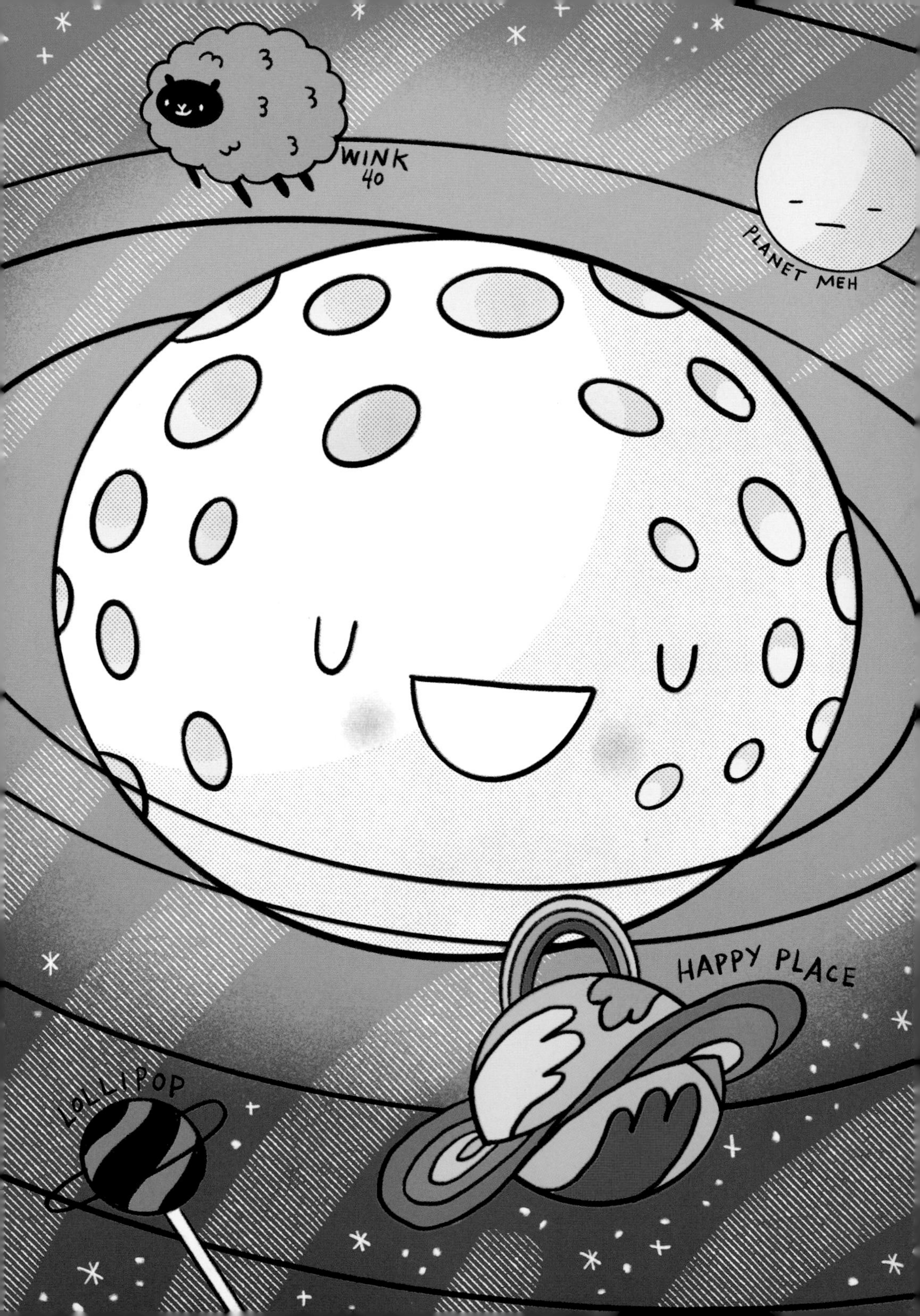
WINK 40
PLANET MEH
HAPPY PLACE
LOLLIPOP

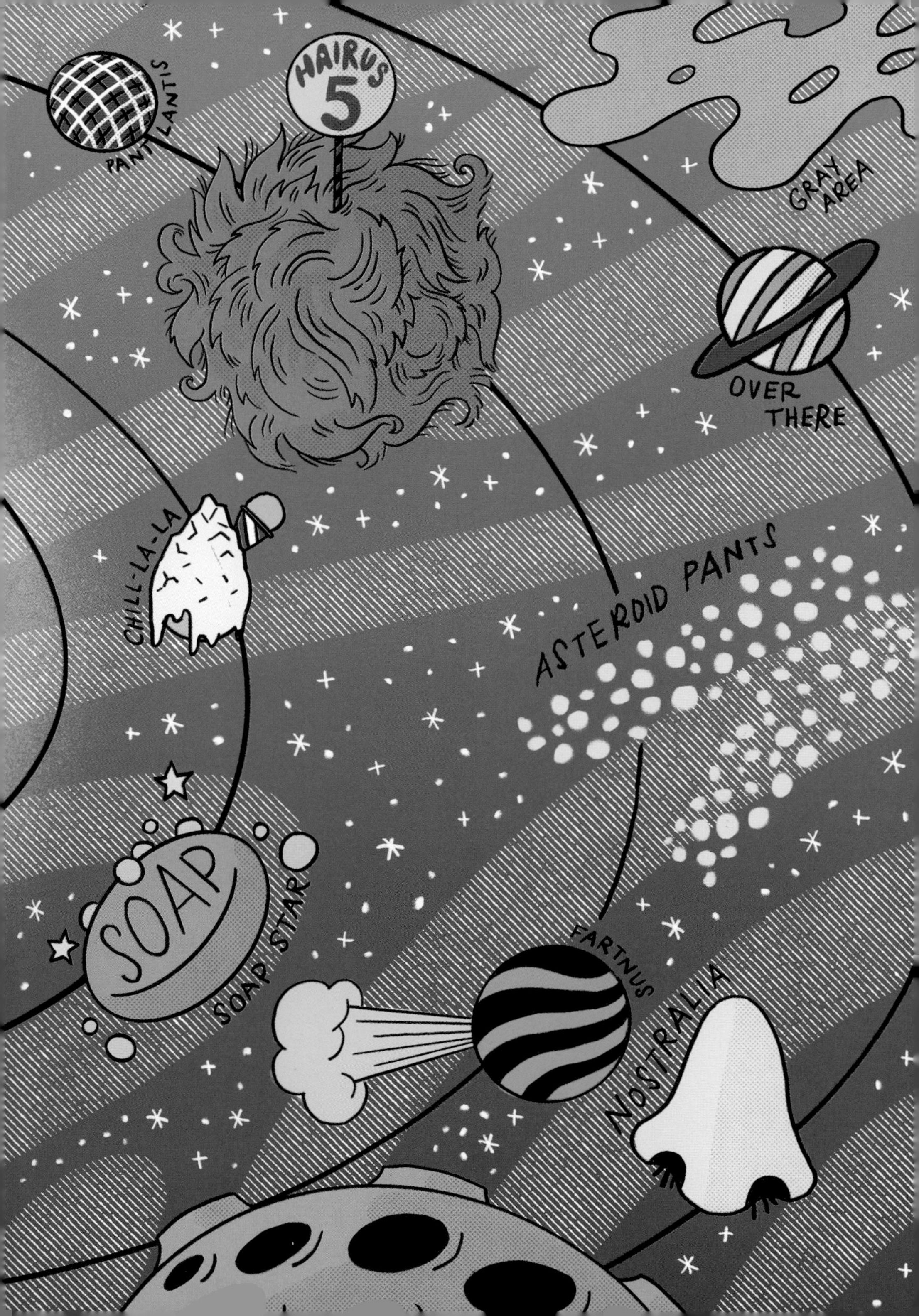
PANT LANTIS
HAIRUS 5
GRAY AREA
OVER THERE
CHILL-LA-LA
ASTEROID PANTS
SOAP
SOAP STAR
FARTNUS
NOSTRALIA

TO AMY, A MOST STELLAR FRIEND
–S.M.

TO ADRIANE, COMICAL COPILOT AND FEARLESS WRANGLER OF ALIEN LIFEFORMS
–E.M.

PUBLISHER'S NOTE: This is a work of fiction. Names, characters, places, and incidents are either the product of the author's imagination or used fictitiously, and any resemblance to actual persons, living or dead, business establishments, events, or locales is entirely coincidental.

The illustrations in this book were created using an iPad and digital tools.

Library of Congress Cataloging Number 2022942358
ISBN 978-1-4197-5702-0

Text and illustrations © 2023 Hello Lucky, LLC
Book design by Heather Kelly

Printed and bound in China
10 9 8 7 6 5 4 3 2 1

Amulet Books are available at special discounts when purchased in quantity for premiums and promotions as well as fundraising or educational use. Special editions can also be created to specification. For details, contact specialsales@abramsbooks.com or the address below

Amulet Books® is a registered trademark of Harry N. Abrams, Inc.

ABRAMS The Art of Books
195 Broadway, New York, NY 10007
abramsbooks.com